THE

DANGER

with

DIAMONDS

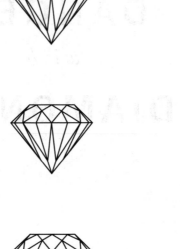

Some secrets are worth keeping. Others are not.

THE

DANGER

with

DIAMONDS

A Falcon Point Suspense

TRACI HUNTER ABRAMSON · SIAN ANN BESSEY

Covenant Communications, Inc.

Cover image: *Man* by Robert A. Boyd, www.robertaboyd.com

Cover design copyright © 2022 by Covenant Communications, Inc.

Published by Covenant Communications, Inc.
American Fork, Utah

Library of Congress Cataloging-in-Publication Data

Names: Abramson, Traci Hunter; Bessey, Sian Ann, author.
Title: The danger with diamonds / Traci Hunter Abramson and Sian Ann Bessey.
Description: American Fork, Utah : Covenant Communications Inc., [2022] | Series: Falcon Point Suspense ; Book 1
Identifiers: LCCN 2022940541 | ISBN 978-1-52442-120-5
LC record available at https://lccn.loc.gov/2022940541

Printed in Mexico
First Printing: October 2022

30 29 28 27 26 25 24 23 22   10 9 8 7 6 5 4 3 2 1

PRAISE FOR
THE FALCON POINT SERIES

PRAISE FOR *THE DANGER WITH DIAMONDS*

"In *The Danger with Diamonds* by Traci Hunter Abramson and Sian Ann Bessey, CIA agent Cole Bridger goes to Budapest to find his coworker, agent Trevor Rogers, who was kidnapped. Cole receives help from Jasmine as well as Cas, known only as Ghost to the intelligence operatives she helps, and they report to Gwendolyn. Cole's cousin Lars receives jewelry that once belonged to their great-grandmother. With help from his friend Marit, they photograph and inventory all the jewelry. Isabelle, a bank employee, secures the valuable jewelry in the bank vault. Upon returning to the vault, Cole and Isabelle are held up at gunpoint for the valuable jewels. It is up to Cole and his team to investigate and find out who the mastermind is behind the heist, even though he may put himself and his family in danger.

"*The Danger with Diamonds* is a thrilling novel filled with suspense and intrigue. The characters are interesting and easy to relate to, although the relationships between Cole, Lars, Isabelle, and Marit become rather complicated—another challenge for the team to solve. I especially enjoyed the camaraderie between Cole and Lars. The story has many twists and turns with a few surprises along the way. The scenes and locations are well described, including Cole's and Isabelle's homes and the interior of the bank. Traci Hunter Abramson and Sian Ann Bessey are fantastic authors, and their stories keep the reader enthralled from beginning to end. All-round, a great novel highly recommended to all adults."

—Readers' Favorite five-star review

PRAISE FOR *HEIRS OF FALCON POINT*
(2021 FINALIST FOREWORD INDIES)

"With historical elements, suspense, action, a dash of romance, and inspiration, this tale will appeal to many readers. It's well-paced, full of twists and turns, and populated by colorful, realistic, well-drawn characters. The Lang family and their descendants are exemplary in their love of history and family, and their story is absorbing and poignant."

—Inkwell Inspirations

"Riveting, suspenseful, and full of lots of unexpected turns! This is a strongly written story reminiscent of the von Trapp family fleeing Austria from the Third Reich, with countless twists and turns before dropping the reader into the present day, where descendants try to unravel the myths and mysteries. It is captivating from the very first page and holds readers attention until the end. The book is creative and historically accurate."

—*InD'Tale* Magazine

"Be sure to take your heart medication when reading *Heirs of Falcon Point,* because the suspense and surprises are sure to raise your heart rate. Four award-winning authors have come together to create a multifaceted book: thriller, mystery, multiple romances, and a settling of scores for ancient crimes—and some really determined villains, to boot. For those of us who love historical fiction, this book is particularly satisfying in that it creates historical scenes brought forward to the present day to tell the rest of the story. I highly recommend it."

—Jerry Borrowman, author of the 'Til the Boys Come Home World War I and World War II fiction series, as well as award-winning historical biography and nonfiction.

"As one might expect from this crew of writers, the characters are portrayed in a strikingly realistic manner, their dialogue is believable, and it's easy to feel they are real people whom we know and care about. The various writers' familiarity and expertise concerning Europe, law enforcement, World War II, and modern international relations all play a part in providing a realistic setting and background for the story. It moves at a comfortable pace and gives the reader a satisfying ending. This novel will appeal to a large number of adults and older teens, both male and female, who enjoy well-written action stories, history, and even a touch of romance."

—*Meridian* Magazine

For Paige Edwards and A. L. Sowards,
whose original vision helped bring our characters to life

ACKNOWLEDGMENTS

WE WISH TO EXPRESS APPRECIATION to all our friends and colleagues at Covenant who work tirelessly to make our books the best they can be. In particular, our managing director, Robby Nichols; our editor, Samantha Millburn; our publicist, Amy Parker; and the graphic designers behind this incredible cover, Margaret Weber and Christina Marcano.

Thanks also to Anna Clawson for her help with all things Vienna; to Scott and Lara Abramson for their beta-reading skills; and to the CIA Publication Review Board for their continued support and their help in making our deadlines.

And finally, but most importantly, we want to thank the many readers who loved *Heirs of Falcon Point* and begged us to continue that story. We hope you enjoy reading *The Danger with Diamonds* as much as we enjoyed writing it.

ACKNOWLEDGMENTS

CHAPTER 1

FROM THE DRIVER'S SEAT OF the surveillance van, CIA agent Cole Bridger lowered his binoculars. Three armed guards in the yard and an unknown number of insurgents hiding inside the cottage. Outnumbered.

Under normal circumstances, Cole would have loved to spend a day or two in this outlying suburb of Budapest. With its rows of quaint houses, the village afforded incredible views of the Danube River and easy access to the Pest side of the city. According to the latest intelligence reports, it was also the current location of Trevor Rogers, the CIA agent who had disappeared from Bratislava two nights ago.

Cole had followed one electronic breadcrumb after another in search of possible suspects and the location of his missing coworker, whom he had never actually met. But even though the trail of surveillance videos and GPS signals had led him here from his home base in Vienna, Cole had yet to uncover why Rogers had been kidnapped and who was behind it.

Cole had staked out the house since early this morning, opting to wait for backup before attempting a rescue. As much as he wanted to take action, if his training as a CIA operative hadn't taught him prudence, his upbringing had. He was the fifth generation of Langs and Bridgers to work in intelligence. As a product of his heritage, he had learned to work smart, and part of working smart was making sure someone always had your back.

Of course, when Cole had requested backup, he had expected his superiors to send a SEAL team in to help him break his man out. Instead, he'd ended up with Jasmine, a fifty-eight-year-old grandmother who hadn't worked in the field in years, and Cas Edgemont, a twenty-five-year-old dead woman.

Cas had faked her death years ago and was now known only as Ghost to the intelligence operatives she helped. Had it not been for a breach in her cover last spring, Cole would be as clueless about her identity as the rest of her limited circle of associates.

In the early-morning light, another guard came into view and circled the A-frame structure with its fenced yard.

Cole slid out of his seat and ducked into the back of the surveillance van. On one side, a long desk held two workstations, complete with computers and monitoring screens. Jasmine and Cas were currently reviewing the area to gain a clearer understanding of their opposition.

"Just saw a fourth guard checking the perimeter," Cole said.

"We saw that too." Cas motioned to where heat signatures illuminated her screen.

Though Cole was usually the first to see overwhelming odds as a challenge, he wasn't crazy about risking the safety of the two women he was with. "Maybe we should wait for more backup before we go in."

Jasmine swiveled in her seat and glared, her dark skin forming a crease at her brow. Pride and indignation competed with her Southern drawl. "You think we can't handle this?"

"Jazz, when was the last time you fired a weapon?" Cole asked.

"It's like riding a bicycle." To prove her point, she pulled the gun from the holster at her ample waist, released the magazine, checked her ammo, and reloaded. "Besides, we have Ghost here. She does this kind of thing for a living."

"Ghost helps agents sneak out of hostile countries," Cole said. "We're talking about taking on who knows how many armed men."

"And we're just a couple of women?" Jasmine asked.

A couple of sassy, overconfident Southern women. Cole didn't care who he was working with. It could be his seventy-nine-year-old grandfather for all he cared, but the sass unsettled him. That type of attitude could translate into an arrogance that could easily get someone killed.

Cas motioned to her screen again. "I'm only showing three heat spots inside the house."

"Assuming one of those is Rogers, that's only six against three," Jazz said.

"And we have the element of surprise," Cas added. "That evens the odds."

Cas had a point. If they could each eliminate one of the guards and breach the house before the people inside knew they were there, they might have a chance of recovering their agent and surviving the day.

Resigned to moving forward with the personnel he'd been given, Cole said, "You win, but if we're going to do this, we need a plan to neutralize everyone in there."

"We'll get our man out alive," Cas promised.

"That's our first objective, but that's not all I want. We need to know who these men are and what they're up to."

Jasmine turned her laptop toward Cole. "Here's what I have in mind."

Lars Hendriks drew his phone out of his pocket and glanced at the screen. No new texts. And still no sign of Marit. He scanned the crowded plaza again. It was the first week of the Stephansplatz Christmas market, and despite the chilly November temperatures, the tourists were out in droves. The smell of roasted almonds and gingerbread wafted in the air, making Lars wish he'd arrived early enough to sample them before his appointment at the bank. Perhaps he could do that with Marit afterward. If she ever arrived.

Above his head, the cathedral clock chimed the eleven o'clock hour. He frowned. When he'd spoken to Marit on the phone last night, she'd just wrapped up a photo shoot at Schönbrunn Palace and had seemed excited to join him this afternoon. It had been weeks since they'd seen each other, and he'd purposely timed his visit to Vienna to coincide with her modeling job here.

Shifting the strap of his large camera bag more securely onto his shoulder, he stepped to the left as someone exited the building behind him. He didn't want to go in without Marit, but Lars was pretty sure Cole's grandfather had pulled some strings to schedule him a secure room at the bank for the entire afternoon. That level of service was not easily come by, and Lars guessed he'd need every hour he'd been given to complete the job ahead.

Reluctantly, he turned to climb the shallow steps leading to the bank's heavy doors.

"Lars! Wait!"

He swung around, immediately spotting Marit's willowy figure, long blonde hair, and bright-red beanie. She broke free of the Chinese tourists in front of the nearby entrance to the U-bahn train station and ran toward him.

"I'm so sorry." She was out of breath. "The train was full, so I had to wait for the next one, and then all the tourists at this stop were blocking the exit—" She came to a halt before him, a smile lighting her face. "It's good to see you."

"It's even better to see you." Lars grinned and drew her in for a hug. "I'm glad you made it."

They exchanged three soft kisses on each other's cheeks. The simple Dutch greeting meant nothing, Lars knew that, but the touch of her lips lingered on his skin when she pulled away.

He took another step toward the bank doors and raised an eyebrow. "Want to see some long-lost jewelry?"

"Of course." Her brown eyes sparkled, and he caught the hint of humor dancing there. "Why else would I be here?"

"I asked for that, didn't I?"

She laughed, moving to stand beside him. "One hundred percent."

Isabelle waited near the bank entrance, her eyes scanning the various customers coming and going. Her training as an undercover CIA operative had taught her to look beyond the basics; it allowed her to recognize both threats and opportunities. That same training also afforded her the ability to shelve her emotions to protect her from unwanted distractions. Too bad she couldn't bury her current emotions permanently.

Her jaw clenched. Five months ago, she would have been excited to spend time with Cole in the hope of continuing their budding romance. Now she looked forward to giving him a piece of her mind.

A woman walked through the door, a toddler on her hip. A little wave of envy mixed with the hurt she felt over Cole. Despite a top-notch education and an enviable career, going home to an empty apartment every night left a lot to be desired.

The woman continued past her, and Isabelle turned her attention to the others in the lobby. A man in his twenties with an ill-fitting suit jacket and worn dress shoes stood beside the information desk. Probably applying for the open teller position. By the main counter, a woman waited her turn, a tan line visible on her finger where a wedding ring would typically be worn. Newly divorced? Or dating someone who wasn't her husband? Isabelle studied the woman's expression of determination mixed with a don't-mess-with-me glare. Definitely divorced.

Gerhart Wimmer, one of the senior vice presidents, passed through security and walked toward her. "*Guten morgen*, Isabelle. What are you doing down here?"

"I'm waiting for a client."

"Very good." He took a step toward the elevator before he turned back. "How soon are you going to have your quarterly reports ready?"

"I should have my portion done by this afternoon." Little did he know she would analyze those same quarterly reports to ensure no funds were filtering through this bank that could be used against the United States.

He gave a nod of approval and continued toward the elevators. Like the others she worked with, Gerhart didn't have a clue that she was more interested in moving up the ranks to increase her access to information than she was about padding her paycheck.

Though she loved the world of finance, her grandfather's work in the intelligence community had planted the seed of patriotism that had bloomed into a desire to do her part to keep her country safe. It was Glenn Bridger, one of her grandfather's dear friends, who had put her in her current situation. When he had contacted her to ask a favor, she had agreed as much to have an opportunity to see Cole again as to help out her longtime family friend.

Isabelle had been present when Cole and two of his cousins had joined forces to find a treasure that had been hidden since the early days of World War II. She had thought her association with the family would continue through her relationship with Cole. She hadn't expected him to jump at the first field assignment that had come his way. Three dates and one kiss goodnight and the blossoming romance had wilted.

Would Cole even accompany his cousin today? Or would he continue to ignore her the way he had for the past six months?

A tall, blond man walked in, followed by a stunning woman with long blonde hair and warm, brown eyes. The man looked around the room. Though he was taller than Cole and his face more angular, the blue eyes were unmistakable. No doubt this man was Lars Hendricks, Cole's cousin. And though Lars wasn't alone, once again, Cole wasn't anywhere to be found.

Lars acknowledged the security guard standing near the bank doors with a polite nod and guided Marit into the vast lobby. Muted voices filled the cavernous room, echoing off the stone pillars and vaulted ceiling above. Across from the main doors, a row of tellers worked behind a high, marble-topped counter, their attention alternating between their customers and their computer screens.

"What do we do now?" Marit asked softly.

"Mr. Hendriks?" An attractive young woman approached them. Her long auburn hair was pulled up into a complicated bun, and she wore a navy-colored business suit. "Welcome to Bankhaus Steiner."

"Thank you," Lars replied in German. How did this woman know him?

His perplexity must have shown because the woman smiled. "It's eleven o'clock, you are carrying a camera bag, and your resemblance to your sister,

Tess, is unmistakable." She extended her hand. "Isabelle Roberts. Mr. Bridger told me to expect you."

Isabelle Roberts. It was the name Cole's grandfather had sent him. His contact at the Viennese bank. Lars had been mildly surprised that someone with so un-German a name would be in a position of such authority. He was twice as surprised now that he'd met her. She couldn't be any older than he was.

"Nice to meet you," he said, shaking her hand before turning to introduce Marit. "This is my friend Marit Jansen."

The two women exchanged a handshake and smiles.

"How do you know Tess?" Marit asked.

"We met at Falcon Point."

"You were the banker who helped locate the Lang family money," Lars said, the pieces of the puzzle coming together in rapid succession. No wonder Cole and his grandfather had chosen to move the valuables from the estate to this particular bank.

"Yes." She gestured toward the door of a lift at their left, and they started toward it. "Have you visited Falcon Point yet?"

Lars noted the swift change of subject. Maybe she didn't want to speak of tracing funds in the middle of the bank lobby.

"I was there yesterday," Lars said, the memory of finally meeting his English cousin, Anna, and of touring the remarkable house with her still fresh on his mind. "It's amazing."

"I agree." Isabelle swiped her ID in front of the lift and waited for the door to open. "I saw it in early summer, so I can only imagine how beautiful it looks now that there's snow on the ground. Did you go too, Marit?"

"No. I've heard a lot about Falcon Point, but I haven't been there."

"Yet," Lars added. Marit had spent weeks recovering from injuries sustained during the deadly battle over his family's legacy. Not only did she deserve to see Falcon Point, but she was also the one person he most wished to share it with. "I'm going to take her there as soon as her work schedule allows."

Marit's eyes widened and Lars inwardly winced. He'd hoped that Marit's recent modeling job would finish early enough for her to go to Falcon Point with him this week, but when she'd told him she wouldn't be free to meet him until today, he'd held off on issuing the invitation. Now it sounded more like a summons.

"Something to look forward to, then," Isabelle said, filling the momentary silence as they stepped into the lift together.

"Yes. Definitely." Marit had recovered her poise. "And I'm excited to see the jewelry today."

Isabelle smiled. "You'll be the envy of jewelers around the world."

With a ping, the door opened, and she led them down a narrow hall. They passed several closed doors. Most of them had name plaques posted on the wall beside them. Lars assumed they were offices. When they reached the last door on the left, Isabelle stopped and swiped her ID again.

"This is our small conference room," she said. "It's yours for the rest of the day." She pushed open the door and stepped aside so Lars and Marit could enter. "Security delivered the safe-deposit boxes half an hour ago."

Lars looked around the small, windowless room. A large painting of the Vienna opera house hung on one wall. In the corner, a computer monitor sat on a rolling cart, an assortment of cables bundled tidily on the shelf beneath. Dominating the room, however, was a highly polished wooden table surrounded by eight chairs. And currently lying on the table were three solid metal boxes.

"I have the bank keys," Isabelle said, holding up a sturdy key ring with several keys of differing sizes hanging from it. "Do you have yours?"

"Yes." Lars withdrew the keys from his pocket.

Cole had sent the safe-deposit box keys to Lars's apartment in Amsterdam by special courier when he'd learned that the American Embassy was sending him out of town this weekend. The cousins had kept in fairly regular contact since their first meeting almost six months ago, so Lars knew that Cole's work often took him away from Vienna. He'd been disappointed to learn that he wouldn't see him on this trip.

Isabelle crossed the short distance to the table and waited for Lars and Marit to join her. "Whenever you're ready," she said.

Lars stepped forward. As Coster Diamonds' lead photographer, he worked with precious gems almost every day. But he'd been in the hospital when Tess, Anna, and Cole had uncovered the treasure at Falcon Point, so this was his first time seeing the jewelry that had once belonged to his great-grandmother. He took a deep breath, attempting to shake off the unexpected emotions coursing through him. No matter that he was in an unfamiliar bank, faced with three sterile metal boxes; this moment suddenly felt intensely personal.

As though she understood his hesitancy, Marit moved closer. "It's okay, Lars." She spoke in Dutch, her voice low. "You've waited months to feel this connection with your past."

He reached for her hand, squeezing it tightly before releasing it and inserting a key into the closest box. Beside him, Isabelle slid her key into place.

"On the count of three," she said.

CHAPTER 2

COLE SLID HIS PISTOL INTO his shoulder holster and tucked his Taser into the pocket of his overcoat. He had driven the van around the corner so it was no longer visible from the house of interest, and even though the sun shone brightly overhead, the rescue plan was already in motion.

"I must be crazy to have agreed to this," he muttered under his breath. With his dark clothes and Cas and Jasmine's dark skin, a night raid made the most sense. But no, his coworkers had decided on a rescue in broad daylight. Jasmine and Cas were being literal when they'd decided to capitalize on the element of surprise.

"This is the most direct way to get inside without endangering our agent," Cas said. "No one will suspect Jasmine isn't a Wolt driver."

Wolt, the Uber Eats of Hungary. "I'd feel better if they'd actually ordered food instead of us pretending we have the wrong house."

"You'd feel better if you were the one making first contact," Cas countered.

She was right. If he spoke Hungarian, he might have been able to win the argument about who should make the food delivery, but Jasmine was the only one of the three who possessed that particular skill.

"Trust Jasmine to do the job," Cas said. "If these guys saw you coming, they'd probably shoot you before you opened your mouth."

"You think I look threatening?"

"I think a young guy is exactly the type of person they would expect to show up to try to rescue our agent."

Cas was right, but Cole didn't have to like it.

Jasmine's voice came over Cole's communication device disguised as a wireless earbud. "On my way. ETA ten minutes."

"Let's move." Cole tugged a beanie over his short blond hair and climbed into the front of the van. He pushed open the door and, together with Cas, made his way toward the house nearest them.

Two fenced backyards separated them from their objective, and they had eight minutes to cross them. After a quick check to make sure no one was watching, Cole reached over the top of the gate leading to the backyard and unlatched it. A dog barked, but the sound was muffled. Praying the animal was inside, Cole darted behind the nearest tree. Cas closed the gate and followed.

They hurried along the trees that bordered the property until they reached the far fence.

Cas gripped the chain link and climbed over. Cole waited for her to reach the next yard before he followed suit. A door opened, and the barking grew louder. Cole quickly pulled himself to the top of the next fence and dropped down beside Cas.

They moved behind the thick trunk of an oak tree as the dog from the first yard, an annoying little schnauzer, rushed to the chain link and barked in earnest.

Great. All he needed was for an animal to draw attention to them when they were already fighting an uphill battle.

Cas reached into her pocket and threw something over the fence. The dog went to investigate and came up chewing.

"What was that?" Cole whispered.

"A dog treat." Cas nodded toward the other side of the yard where a cinder-block wall separated them from the location where their agent was being held. "When we go over, I'll take the far side of the house."

Cole started to object to Cas taking the more dangerous position but stopped himself. With her petite build, she was more likely to slip through the shadows unnoticed than he was.

Jasmine's Southern accent came through his earpiece. "Three minutes."

Cole did a quick calculation of how long it would take them to scale the wall and get into position. "Slow down."

"I'll go the long way. That'll give you another minute or two."

Cas ducked behind a hedge and weaved past a copse of beech trees. Thirty seconds later, they reached the eight-foot wall. Bare, white branches of a birch tree reached over the wall but wouldn't likely provide much by way of cover.

"Give me a boost," Cas said.

"Take a look before you climb over." Cole laced his fingers together and leaned over to lift Cas. She placed her foot in his hands, and Cole raised her up.

She peeked over the top of the wall and quickly ducked back down. She lowered herself to the ground.

"What did you see?" Cole whispered.

"Two guards, one on either side of the yard," Cas said. "I'm not sure I can get over unnoticed."

"What if we climb into the yard behind them? Is there anywhere we can sneak in?"

"I don't think so. The guards aren't standing still. I think they're patrolling."

"We need a distraction."

Jasmine's voice came over his earpiece. "One distraction coming up."

As much as Cole hated using Jasmine as a diversion, they didn't have a choice.

"Tell us when you get here."

Another minute passed. "I'm here. You have thirty-five seconds before I reach the front door."

Cas checked her watch. "Give me a boost again. I'll drop down behind the tree when she rings the doorbell."

Cole really hated this. "I'll be right behind you." He boosted Cas up again. This time she ducked to stay out of sight until the right moment. Then she signaled with her hand, and he vaulted her upward.

She reached the top of the wall. A man shouted, and Cas dropped out of sight.

Cole rushed a few meters forward before he launched himself into the air and gripped the top of the wall. He peeked over the top and spotted a guard rushing to the corner where Cas had dropped, his gun drawn. Cole muscled himself upward.

The moment he reached the top of the wall, he drew his pistol, aimed, and fired.

The guard fell to the ground, but a man on the far side of the yard lifted his weapon. He fired in the same instant Cole dropped to the ground.

A second shout sounded. Footsteps pounded toward them.

Cole dove behind an evergreen as two more guards burst into the backyard.

"Freeze!" Cole shouted the warning and wasn't surprised when it went unheeded. He squeezed the trigger, and another guard dropped. An instant later, the guard's companion also fell to the ground.

Gun drawn, Cas emerged from the far side of the yard. Using hand signals, they approached the back door.

Cas counted down on her fingers, and Cole grabbed the doorknob. When she gave the signal, he yanked the door open and rushed inside.

In the center of the living room, Jasmine leaned over a man on the ground as she zip-tied his hands behind his back. A few feet away, a second man lay on the floor, his hands already bound.

Jasmine straightened and gave a nod of satisfaction. "Like I said. Just like riding a bike."

"That's the last pair from this group," Lars said.

Marit picked up the pearl earrings lying on the square of black velvet Lars had placed on the conference table and carefully set them back inside the small silk-lined box. The red fabric within had faded to pink. She ran her finger along the box's corner. It was worn smooth. "I think your great-grandmother really loved these earrings," she said.

Lars looked up from the adjustments he was making to his camera. "What makes you say that?"

She shrugged. "It's just a feeling I have."

They'd already photographed over a dozen pieces of jewelry, ranging from a small diamond-encrusted tiara to a large opal ring to a silver filigree brooch. Each of the jewelry boxes inside the first safe-deposit box had housed something as unique as it was beautiful.

"You can tell a lot about a woman from her jewelry," Marit continued. "Even though she owned some stunning pieces, I think her favorites were the ones that were simple and elegant."

Lars was studying her, an odd expression on his face. She looked away, suddenly feeling foolish. Who was she to make a judgment call like that? She didn't even know Lars's great-grandmother's name.

"I think you're right," Lars said. She hazarded a glance at him, and he smiled. "Did you notice that the hinge on the tiara box is stiff—like it wasn't opened very often?"

"Whereas the hinge on this earring box is loose," Marit said.

"Because she wore the pearls often."

Marit returned his smile. "Yeah."

She handed him the small jewelry box, and he put it back into the safe-deposit box. Pushing the one they'd inventoried to one side, he reached for the next one. He and Isabelle had unlocked them all before Isabelle had left, so it was already open.

Lars handed Marit the narrow black box on the top. "I guess this one's next."

Marit flipped the tiny metal catch. The lid lifted easily, and her curiosity piqued. If Lars's theory was correct, his great-grandmother must have liked this piece too. She lifted the silk lining, and her breath caught. Wordlessly, she turned the box so Lars could see its contents.

"Whoa. Is that a pink diamond?"

"It sure looks like one," Marit said.

Lars picked up the jeweler's loupe lying beside his camera on the table and reached for the box. He withdrew the stunning cushion-cut gem attached to a finely worked gold chain and placed the necklace beneath the light he'd set up for the photos.

"It's virtually flawless," he said, studying the diamond through the loupe. "And it's at least three carats."

"What do you think it's worth?" Marit asked.

Lars looked up and met her eyes. "A lot."

Marit had modeled enough for Coster Diamonds to know that Lars was not exaggerating.

"Define 'a lot.'"

He took a deep breath. "A couple of years ago, a four-carat pink diamond went up for auction in London. It sold for over a million euro."

Over a million euro. What would it be like to have that kind of money?

Gun in hand, Cole climbed the stairs. Two open doors down the hall to his right. An open and a closed door to his left.

He checked the first two bedrooms. Clear. A bathroom came next, also empty. Cole approached the closed door, a bolt attached to the outside of it. His hand flexed and tightened on the grip of his pistol. He slid the bolt and yanked the door open.

Inside, a man lay on a bed, his hands bound to the headboard, his mouth gagged with a strip of cloth. His light-brown hair was matted with blood on one side, a one-inch scab visible along his hairline. Despite the two-day stubble on the man's face, Cole quickly identified him as Trevor Rogers.

"Time to get you out of here." Cole holstered his gun. He removed the gag and went to work on untying Rogers's hands. "Can you walk?"

"I think so," he said, his voice hoarse. He cleared his throat. "Who are you?"

"The agency sent me. We need to get you out of here before the cops show up."

"What about collecting intel? These guys are hired muscle. They're working for someone."

"My friends are already sweeping the house." Cole squatted and put his arm around Rogers's waist. He helped him stand. One wobbly step followed another.

Cole and Rogers reached the stairs as Cas emerged from one of the empty bedrooms with a stack of papers in one hand and a small cloth bag in another.

"Find anything?" Cole asked.

"We'll talk in the van," Cas said. "The police are on their way. We have less than two minutes."

Rogers grabbed hold of the railing and used the extra support to increase his speed. When they reached the bottom, Cas put her arm around him from the other side to help him to the door.

Sirens wailed in the distance.

The three of them hurried outside, Cole and Cas matching their strides to Rogers's.

The surveillance van pulled around the corner, Jasmine at the wheel, and stopped in front of the house.

Cole and Cas helped their injured charge into the back. As soon as they were all inside, Cole pulled the door closed. "Go!"

Instantly, the van went into motion. Cole helped Rogers into a seat before taking the one behind him.

Cas claimed her spot by one of the surveillance laptops and was already typing something.

"How did you end up with those guys?" Cole asked as the van made a quick turn.

"I was tracking stolen weapons when I stumbled on a meeting between the criminals here and someone else at the docks in Bratislava." Rogers rubbed his hand over his opposite wrist where rope burns were visible. "Where am I, anyway? And how did the three of you take out ten men?"

"Budapest," Cole said. "And what do you mean ten men? We only encountered six."

"When they dragged me into the house the first night, I got a good look at the men in the living room. I counted the guys who brought me here; there were ten of them."

"The others were long gone by the time we got here," Cole said as uneasiness settled inside him. They'd been lucky they hadn't faced extra guns, but where were the other men? And why had they left?

One turn followed another as the sirens grew louder and then faded.

"Looks like we're in the clear," Cas said before asking Rogers, "How did they identify you as intel?"

"I'm not sure. Someone grabbed me from behind, and the next thing I knew, I was in the back of a car with my hands and feet tied up."

"What else do you know?"

"Not much, except they weren't locals."

"Where are they from?"

"They were speaking Ukrainian, but for all I know, they could have been mercenaries. Like I said, they looked like hired hands to me."

"That would explain these." Cas pulled the small velvet bag from her pocket and handed it to Cole.

Cole opened the drawstring and peered inside. Loose jewels. He fished one out, the pink gem fracturing the light that spilled into the back of the van.

"What kind of stone is that?" Rogers asked.

"It's a pink diamond," Cas said.

"How do you know?" Rogers asked.

"Let's just say I spent a lot of time in my childhood around jewelry stores."

"If these people are using precious stones as payment, I don't know how we're going to track down the men behind my kidnapping," Rogers said.

"If there's a way to trace these jewels, I know someone who might be able to help us." Cole turned the stone in his hand. "Hey, Jazz. I need you to drop me off at the train station."

"What for?" she called back to him.

"I want to secure these diamonds," Cole said, addressing the immediate issue before adding, "And I have a cousin I need to see."

CHAPTER 3

COLE RETRIEVED HIS ELECTRONIC TICKET on his phone and glanced at the go-bag on the floor in front of him as Jasmine pulled in front of the train station. Keeping his bag with him would help him blend in among the travelers on the train, but it would hinder him once he reached Vienna.

As though reading his thoughts, Jasmine pointed to it. "I'll take it to my place. You'll show up at some point and need a change of clothes."

She was right. Jasmine's longtime friendship with his family made her among his first options anytime he needed support. "Thanks, Jazz."

"Call me as soon as you know anything."

"You know I will." Cole stepped out of the van with nothing but the clothes on his back, his pistol concealed beneath his jacket, a fake passport, and an untold fortune in diamonds.

He walked into the station and breathed in the scent of sugar and cinnamon mingled with the underlying odor of creosote, steel brake dust, and humanity. He passed the cart where the traditional Hungarian *kürtőskalács*, or chimney cakes, were sold. His mouth watered.

A quick check of the time on his cell phone confirmed he had time for a detour, so he circled back to the cart and ordered his selection by holding up one finger and pointing. After he counted out the correct currency, he traded bills for his cake.

He broke a piece off and popped it into his mouth, savoring cinnamon and sugar combined with the light texture of the pastry. Cole supposed he should feel guilty for eating dessert instead of a meal, but his mother had given up on scolding him for such things years ago.

Crossing through the open space by the entrance, he stopped by the large display board that hung from the ceiling. He read the listing of outgoing trains, but his train wasn't among them yet. Forty-five more minutes until he would leave. He was here too early.

He took another bite of his cake and glanced around the station. Benches lined the wall, all of them occupied with at least one person. A few people lingered along the far wall near the tracks.

Find a place to sit and wait, or find a corner to hide?

Not a fan of being out in the open, especially in a place where people-watching was a common pastime, Cole headed for an alcove where the restrooms were located.

Footsteps approached, and Cole glanced over his shoulder. He'd barely caught a glimpse of a man behind him when the telltale sensation of a gun barrel pressed into his back.

The man spoke in a low voice, his words English but with a European accent. "Keep going."

Cole kept going.

The possibility of the man pulling the trigger once he entered the restroom was all too real, so Cole asked, "What do you want?"

"Open the door."

The door opened before Cole had a chance to reach for it. Two men walked out, followed by a third. The man behind Cole simply shifted his body and held his position so his weapon wouldn't be visible to those passing them by.

Cole moved through the still-open door. He visualized the moment when he could dart to the side and face his potential assailant. That plan fizzled when a boy of around six approached the doorway with his father.

As soon as the two exited, the lock on the door clicked, and the gunman said, "Hand them over. Slowly."

A robbery? If all the man wanted was his money, he could live with that. Cole's eyes swept over the now-empty restroom before he reached for his wallet. He pulled it from his front pocket and held it up above his shoulder.

"Not your wallet." The gun pressed more firmly into Cole's back. "The diamonds."

The diamonds? How did the man know about those? And how did he even know Cole had them? Or for that matter, where Cole would be?

This changed things. Cooperating was no longer an option, at least not as an end result. With his gun not a viable defense, Cole resigned himself to using the one thing he didn't want to lose. He dropped his wallet to the floor. Then he shifted his weight and retrieved the diamonds from his jacket pocket. Raising his hand slowly, he brought the cloth bag into the gunman's view.

The moment the man reached for the gems, Cole sprang into action. He tossed the bag of diamonds to the center of the restroom, pivoted on one foot, and struck out with his hand, deflecting the gun as a bullet puffed through the silencer and impacted the wall to his right.

Cole grabbed the man's wrist with both hands, pitting his strength against his opponent's. He managed to angle the weapon upward as another shot fired, this time into the ceiling.

Plaster dust rained down on them, and Cole threw all his weight forward. The man stumbled back, his body slamming against the door. He grunted in pain and lifted his knee in an attempt to disable Cole. Cole evaded. Both hands tightened on the man's wrist, and he slammed his attacker's hand against the door twice before the gun fell free.

Cole eased back enough to kick the weapon. It skittered across the tile.

He stepped back to give himself the distance he needed to draw his own weapon, but his foot landed on his wallet, and his ankle turned. He tried to regain his balance, but the other man rushed him. A hand flew at Cole's gun hand, knocking the weapon free. It fell to the floor, and Cole dropped down beside it.

The man leaned down and grabbed for Cole's gun. With his weapon two meters in front of him and his opponent's only a half meter to his side, Cole reached for the closest option.

Cole lifted the other man's gun as his opponent aimed Cole's weapon at him. With no option but to kill or be killed, Cole squeezed the trigger.

Lars rolled his shoulders and glanced at the clock. The bank would be closing in an hour, and he still had a half dozen more pieces of jewelry to photograph and itemize on the spreadsheet he'd created for this inventory.

"Do you think we can finish before Isabelle comes to kick us out?" he asked.

"Yes," Marit said. "If we hurry." She opened the next box and withdrew a rose-gold rope necklace. Without asking for directions, she laid it across the velvet fabric on the table and adjusted the chain slightly so it draped just right.

"It's like you've done this before or something," he teased.

She laughed. "Once or twice."

Lars shifted the small spotlight so it reflected the gold's sparkle, and then he picked up his camera. He'd invited Marit to join him at the bank primarily because he'd wanted to spend time with her and because he knew she would

appreciate the jewelry as much as he did. Her familiarity with the art of photography had been an unexpected bonus.

He took a photo, changed his angle, and took another.

Marit waited until the camera clicks stopped. "Good?" she asked.

He nodded. "What's the next one?"

She handed him a ring box. The original satin sheen was gone, and the metal
layer beneath the outer covering could be seen on one of the corners where the
fabric had rubbed away.

"It looks like this might be another of your great-grandmother's favorites,"
Marit said.

He lifted the lid. It moved easily, falling back to reveal a plain gold band on
a miniature velvet cushion.

"I think it's her wedding ring," he said.

Marit moved closer. "Look how thin it is on this one side." Her finger traced
the narrow circumference of the ring. "She must have worn it all the time."

"Simple and elegant," Lars said, echoing Marit's earlier assessment of his
great-grandmother's taste. He'd been more touched than he cared to admit
that Marit's thoughts had been on the jewelry's original owner and not on its
monetary value.

"Yes." She gave a wistful smile. "I wonder what she looked like. Do you
have any pictures of her?"

"No. But there's a painting of her and my great-grandfather in the hall at
Falcon Point."

She looked at him, and he got the feeling she was weighing her words
carefully. "Do you really plan to take me there?"

"I'd love to. Would you like to go?"

"Very much." She hadn't even hesitated.

He'd finally officially asked her, and she'd said yes. Hope rose in his chest. "If
we were to visit sometime in the next few months, maybe we could go skiing."

Her smile lit up her face, and Lars swallowed against his dry throat. Marit
was a beautiful model. Her incredible smile was one of the reasons big-name
companies hired her. He could not read too much into it. They were good
friends, but as much as he'd daydreamed about their relationship developing
into something more, it had yet to happen.

A knock sounded. Marit started, and they both turned to face the door.
It opened, and Isabelle stepped in.

"Sorry to interrupt, but I thought I should give you a heads-up. The bank
will be closing in forty-five minutes, which means security will be here soon

to take the safe-deposit boxes back to the vault." She took in the open jewelry boxes on the table. "Are you almost done?"

"Yes." Lars set his great-grandmother's wedding ring on the velvet. "We're down to the last few pieces."

He took half a dozen photos of the wedding ring before handing it to Marit. She set it beside the box containing the rose-gold necklace in the safe-deposit box and handed him the next one.

"Anything I can do to help?" Isabelle asked.

"Stall the security guard if he comes early," Lars suggested.

She laughed. "I can probably buy you two minutes, but that's about it. If Leon's ready to go home for dinner, there's no stopping him."

"I don't blame him." Lars had skipped lunch, and since Marit had taken the train to join him, she probably had too. Dinner—especially if it was with her—sounded like a really good idea.

He took a moment to admire the emerald earrings in their container before placing them on the velvet cloth.

"Those are beautiful," Isabelle said.

"We haven't found anything that isn't," Marit said. "The whole collection is amazing."

Isabelle nodded. "I guessed as much. I think Tess felt the same way about the paintings she discovered at the estate." She smiled at Lars. "Your ancestors obviously had exceptional taste."

"Yeah. About that." Now that he'd taken a moment to think about it, there was no way the security guard could be hungrier than he was.

"About what?" Isabelle said.

"Taste." He glanced at Marit and grinned. "Is there anywhere around here that you would recommend a couple of Dutch visitors go for dinner, especially if those same visitors missed out on lunch?"

Isabelle laughed. "What kind of food are you looking for?"

"Anything nearby that tastes good."

"Lars isn't quite as discerning as his great-grandparents," Marit said, but he caught the humor dancing in her brown eyes. "He'd probably be okay with McDonalds."

"Hey, when you're desperate, a lukewarm hamburger can really hit the spot."

Marit shuddered, and Isabelle's lips twitched. "What would you like, Marit?"

"Something typically Austrian or Viennese," she said. "I'd love to try something we don't have in the Netherlands."

"Well, the Stephansplatz Christmas market is closer than McDonalds," Isabelle said. "I haven't visited it yet this year, but they usually have fantastic traditional food."

Memories of the warm gingerbread smell that had reached him on the bank's front steps this morning assailed him, and Lars's stomach growled. He looked at Marit and raised a questioning eyebrow. She smiled and nodded.

"Sold," Lars said, turning back to Isabelle. "You had me at 'closer than McDonalds.'"

CHAPTER 4

COLE HATED LEAVING MESSES FOR others to clean up, but he'd had little choice after his altercation in Budapest. He'd hidden the body of his now-dead assailant in the last stall in the restroom and used wet paper towels to clean the blood off the floor.

He'd then sent a message to Cas and Jasmine to request that one of them alert the police to the problem . . . after he was safely away from Budapest.

The moment the train pulled to a stop in Vienna, he exited. No police hovered nearby, waiting for him, but he'd yet to hear from Cas or Jasmine.

His phone buzzed, and he checked the message. Jasmine's text was simple and succinct. *Clear.*

ID? Cole texted back.

Gaspar Ervin. Hired gun.

Typical. Cole texted his thanks and left the station. As he strode past a sandwich shop, a sushi place, and a Starbucks, his stomach grumbled in protest over the lack of real food today. The *kürtőskalác* he'd grabbed in Budapest didn't count, especially since he'd eaten only two bites of it.

Pushing past his hunger, he continued toward the bank. Isabelle's bank. He really should make some time to see her again while he was back in Vienna. He'd enjoyed her company the few times they had gone out, not to mention she was brilliant, witty, and resourceful.

Cole shook the image of Isabelle and her gorgeous green eyes from his thoughts. Spending time with her would have to wait. For now, he needed to find Lars, and he needed to secure the gems currently tucked in his inside jacket pocket.

He debated briefly going to his apartment first, especially since Lars was staying at his place while he was in town, but he couldn't shake the sense of urgency he'd experienced after finding the diamonds in Budapest. If Cole's guess was right, Lars would still be at the bank inventorying the Falcon Point jewels.

Cole didn't have a clue how much the stones Cas had found were worth, but he would guess it was pushing close to fifty thousand dollars. Maybe more.

Someone bumped into him, and Cole checked to make sure his wallet was still in his front pocket. He turned a corner and approached the bank. A security guard stood inside. Whether the man would notice the nearly imperceptible bulge of Cole's gun remained to be seen.

In an effort to appear nonthreatening, Cole approached the guard and asked in German, "Can you tell me where I can find Lars Hendriks? He's using one of the conference rooms today."

"Someone at the information desk can direct you." The guard motioned to his right.

"*Danke*." Cole followed his directions.

A woman in her thirties greeted him. "May I help you?"

"Yes. I'm looking for Lars Hendriks."

"I'm sorry." The woman shook her head. "We don't have anyone here by that name."

"He's a customer."

"I'm sorry. I can't give out client information."

"What about Isabelle Roberts?" Cole asked.

"The bank closes in fifteen minutes. Is she expecting you?"

"No."

"Your name?"

Cole debated briefly. The only ID he had on him was for his alias, which Isabelle didn't know. "Tell her Glenn Bridger sent me."

She picked up the phone off the counter and dialed. After relaying the information, she hung up. "Ms. Roberts's assistant will inform her you are waiting. She should be down momentarily."

"Thank you." Cole stepped aside, deliberately turning so the slight bulge under his jacket would not be in the guard's line of sight.

After a couple of minutes, Isabelle emerged from an elevator, her deep-auburn hair pulled back in a sleek bun.

She spotted him, and something flashed in her eyes before her shield of professionalism locked into place. She extended her hand. "It's good to see you again."

Cole noted the way she avoided using his name. "You too." He fought the urge to hold on to her hand a moment longer than was polite.

"Please, follow me." Isabelle led him into the empty elevator. The moment the doors slid into place, she whirled to face him. "What are you doing here?" she whispered. "And what are you thinking, coming in here armed?"

"Sorry." Cole apologized automatically even though he wasn't sure what he'd done to warrant the wave of hostility flowing off Isabelle. "I came straight here from a job."

"Again, why are you here?"

"I'm looking for Lars. I know he's supposed to be here today."

"I see." Her jaw tightened.

Cole cringed at his mistake. "I wanted to see you too . . ."

"If you wanted to see me, you should have called a few months ago."

Cole opened his mouth, but no words came out. What could he say? He had assumed Isabelle would understand that he was on the move as often as not. And when he was in town, he rarely had time for a social life.

The elevator came to a stop, and the doors slid open. "Lars is in the vault with security. It's this way."

"Isabelle, wait." Cole grabbed her by the elbow before she could distance herself from him.

She glared at him before casting a warning glance at the hand on her arm. Cole released her.

Lars turned the corner, a gorgeous blonde on one side of him and a gray-haired man on the other. Lars said goodbye to the man and turned toward Cole. The moment he spotted him, he quickened his pace. "Cole. I didn't think I was going to see you this trip."

"I came home early." He shrugged. "I hate to break it to you, but you get the couch tonight." Cole's gaze slid to the woman.

"Marit Jansen, my cousin, Cole Bridger."

Marit shook his hand. "Nice to meet you."

"You too."

"We were about to go get some dinner," Lars said. "You should join us. Isabelle, you're welcome to come too."

Even though Cole itched to get to his office to find out what intel Jasmine had gathered from her debriefing with Rogers, he said, "That sounds great."

"I don't want to impose," Isabelle said. "This is a family thing."

"Don't be silly," Marit said. "I'm not family either. Besides, you said yourself you haven't been to the Christmas market yet."

"That's true, but—"

"Let us take you to dinner," Lars interrupted. "It will be our little thank-you for all your help today."

Isabelle glanced at Cole, and he raised an eyebrow. He didn't take her for the kind of woman to avoid someone she was mad at. She must have seen the glint of challenge in his eyes, because she nodded.

"I guess I can spare an hour or two."

"Great," Lars said. "I just need to get my camera bag from the conference room."

Cole followed them into a small room with a conference table and a half dozen chairs. "Before we go, I need a favor."

"What kind of favor?" Lars asked.

Cole reached into his jacket and retrieved the bag of gems. He moved to the table, but before he could tip over the bag, Lars stopped him.

"Wait." Lars retrieved a piece of black velvet from his shoulder bag and spread it in front of them. "Now show me what you have."

Cole gently tipped the bag and let the six stones spill onto the cloth. Diamonds sparkled beneath the overhead light, the pink diamond nestled in the center.

Lars picked up two of the stones and set them on the palm of his hand. "Where did these come from?"

Isabelle closed the door.

"That's what I'm hoping you can tell me." Cole debated how much more to say. As far as Lars knew, Cole worked at the embassy. His cousin had no idea he worked intelligence. Opting for a piece of the truth, he said, "These were recovered from some kidnappers."

"If these were a ransom, whoever was kidnapped must have been part of a very wealthy family."

Lars set the stones back down, drew a small magnifying glass out of his pocket, and picked up the pink diamond.

"How much are these worth?" Cole asked.

Lars didn't answer. He was already focused on the stone. "This is incredible." He held it up to show Marit. "It's hard to be sure without diamond tweezers, but as far as I can tell, the color's almost the same as the one we examined earlier. So's the clarity."

"So these are common?" Cole asked.

"Not at all," Lars said. "They're quite rare."

"What are the odds that we would see two in one day?" Marit asked.

"Not high," Lars said.

THE DANGER WITH DIAMONDS

Cole leaned closer. "Is there a way to trace it?"

"Maybe. If we're lucky." Lars slowly rotated the pink diamond, studying it from every angle through his small magnifying glass. He frowned and exchanged the pink diamond for one of the other stones. Seconds later, his frown disappeared.

"Someone write this down," he said.

Marit reached into her purse and pulled out a small notepad and paper. "Go ahead."

Lars rattled off a string of numbers.

"I'll read them back to you," Marit said.

Lars listened, his attention riveted to the diamond under his magnifying glass. "That's it." He raised his head and offered Marit a smile. "Thanks."

"Want to tell me what that was all about?" Cole asked.

"If a diamond is certified by the GIA or the HRD, a serial number is engraved into the stone. We struck out with the pink diamond, but this one has a number."

Could this be the lead he needed? Cole looked at Isabelle. "I know we've got to clear out of here, but can he check the others real quick?"

She hesitated for only a second. "Work fast, Lars."

Lars checked each stone before setting the pink diamond and the one he'd already identified apart from the others. "There's only one with a serial number," he said. "If these stones all came from the same place, you might be able to trace them using that one or maybe the pink diamond because it's so unusual." He shrugged. "I have a few contacts who should be able to narrow your search for you if I give them the number. It's too late to call tonight, but I can reach out tomorrow."

"That would be great," Cole said. "Thanks."

"Where are you going to store these?" Lars asked. "You don't want to carry a million euros' worth of diamonds around in your pocket."

Cole's eyebrows lifted. "A million?"

"The pink one's worth the most, but they all have excellent clarity. I'd say they'd go for at least a million."

Isabelle stepped forward. "Would you like me to secure them in a safe-deposit box for the night?"

"Yeah. I'd really appreciate it if you can help me take care of that."

Isabelle gave a curt nod. "We'd better hurry, then. The bank is closing."

"And I'm hungry," Lars added.

Cole returned the stones to the bag. "Lead the way."

CHAPTER 5

DUSK WAS TURNING TO DARK. Tiny lights twinkled on every tree in the plaza and above each booth at the Christmas market. St. Stephen's Cathedral was bathed in the glow of multicolored spotlights, and people flitted in and out of the shadows as they milled around the merchants' stalls.

Marit tucked her hands into her jacket pockets, grateful that she'd chosen to wear her beanie this morning. The temperature was dropping rapidly now that the sun was gone.

"Cold?" Lars asked.

"A little."

She'd given him the perfect opening. Today they'd worked together as friends and professionals, but if Lars had any romantic interest in her, this was his cue. He didn't need to offer her his coat. He could simply take her hand or put his arm around her. Withdrawing the hand closest to him from her pocket, she waited.

"Sorry," he said. "It probably would have been smarter to go to a sit-down restaurant." His voice rang with sincerity. But that wasn't the emotion she'd been hoping for.

Drawing on every acting class she'd ever taken, she pushed past her disappointment. "This will be fun. I've always wanted to go to a Christmas market, and to have Cole and Isabelle here to show us around is even better."

"Yeah. I'm glad they came with us."

Needing a distraction from the man not holding her hand, Marit studied the couple walking a few paces ahead of them. She thought she was a pretty good judge of character—she had to be to survive in the cutthroat world of modeling—and instinct told her she could easily become good friends with both Cole and Isabelle.

From their initial introductions, they'd been welcoming and pleasant. Unfortunately, and somewhat curiously, that same warmth wasn't flowing between Cole and Isabelle. Even though the plaza was crowded, the two remained several feet apart, and as far as Marit could tell, they'd barely exchanged more than a few words since they'd left the bank. In fact, if Isabelle's rigid posture was any indication, Cole hadn't said anything right for some time.

As if he felt her gaze, Cole turned and waited for Lars and her to join him.

"This is where most of the food booths are located," he said. "What sounds good to you guys?" He pointed to a booth with a cloud of steam hanging over it. "The *kartoffelpuffer* are over there. They're the best potato pancakes you'll ever eat, and you have a choice of toppings. Next to it, there's bread bowls and soup." He strained to read the handwritten chalk sign. "Looks like it's creamy garlic or goulash tonight. The pulled pork sandwiches are awesome. They're over there." He pointed to his left. "Or you could join that massive line for raclette."

"What's raclette?" Lars asked, eyeing the queue of people that disappeared around the back of the booth.

"It's a melted tangy swiss cheese that's poured on top of an open-face sandwich."

"That sounds good, but I'm too hungry to wait in the line."

Cole grinned. "Same. I'm going for the kartoffelpuffer. Can I get some for anyone else?"

"I'd like soup in a bread bowl," Isabelle said. "How about you, Marit?"

"I'll join you. Hot soup sounds perfect right now."

Cole raised his eyebrows. "Am I the lone man going to the kartoffelpuffer stand?"

"I'll give them a try," Lars said. He tucked some euros into Marit's pocket. "I saw some empty tables by the woodcarver's booth. Let's meet there when we have our food."

"Lars," Marit protested, offering him his money back. "You don't need to pay for my dinner."

He was already moving toward the kartoffelpuffer stand. "No arguments," he called. "Besides, I told Isabelle this one was on me."

He disappeared into the crowd, and with a sigh, Marit put the money back into her pocket.

"Lars seems really nice," Isabelle said. She'd moved to stand beside Marit.

"He is."

Isabelle gave her an inquiring look. "I sense a 'but.'"

They started toward the end of the soup-and-bread-bowl line, and Marit shook her head. "There's no 'but,' really, it's just that . . ."

Isabelle's green eyes twinkled. "Ah, the problem is more of an 'it's just that' than a 'but.'"

Marit smiled. "It sounds silly when you say it like that."

"Not so silly when you're navigating it though."

"No."

"No?" Isabelle said. "That's all you're going to tell me?"

Marit watched the man behind the counter ladle thick, steaming goulash into a bread bowl. It looked so good—and so hot. She shifted her feet, hoping the movement would warm them. What did it matter if she bore her soul to Isabelle? She probably wouldn't see her again after today anyway.

"Lars and I have been friends for a long time," she said. "Going through the accident together when all the stuff with Falcon Point was happening only drew us closer. But then came rehab. My parents insisted that I recuperate at home, far from Amsterdam, and Lars was stuck in a rehab center in the city. We were hours apart and didn't see each other for weeks."

"Did you talk on the phone?"

"Yes. Almost every day." She smiled at the memory. Lars's calls had been the bright spot in her very boring days. His funny stories about life at the rehab center had kept her laughing; his concern for her had warmed her heart. And somewhere along the way, she'd fallen in love. "I recovered from my surgery faster than he did, and my agent was anxious to have me back at work right away. Soon, I was traveling again. I'd miss his calls, and then he'd be at therapy when I tried calling back. Before long, we were going days—sometime weeks—without talking." Marit shrugged, hoping her heartache wasn't too obvious. "My crazy schedule makes it hard to keep in touch."

"Hard but not impossible," Isabelle said firmly. "Especially if you want it badly enough."

Something in Isabelle's voice told Marit this was not just about her and Lars anymore.

They'd reached the counter. Marit placed an order for goulash. She waited for Isabelle to do the same before giving her a sidelong glance.

"So which is it with you and Cole? 'It's just that' or 'but'?"

It was as though a shutter came down across Isabelle's face. "More of an 'it was never meant to be.'"

"Really?" Marit was genuinely surprised. She'd noticed the way Cole looked at Isabelle. "For what it's worth, I don't think that's what Cole's thinking."

"No one—not even Cole—knows what Cole is thinking," Isabelle said.

Marit paid with the money Lars had given her, and the man behind the counter handed them their soup.

"This smells so good," Marit said, wrapping her hands around the warm cardboard container.

"Right?" Isabelle's smile was back. "Let's find a table."

Three kartoffelpuffers later, Lars thought he might live to see another day after all. "It's official," he said. "These are the best potato pancakes I've ever had."

Cole chuckled. "Did you save room for gingerbread?"

"I always have room for gingerbread." Lars turned to Marit. She'd been unusually quiet since they'd sat down. "Would you like some?"

"Can I take it back to the hotel with me?"

"Absolutely. How about you, Isabelle?" he asked.

Isabelle shook her head and rose to her feet. "Thank you, but no. Dinner was wonderful, but I really need to get home. I have some work I need to finish up before bed."

"I'll walk you back." Cole was on his feet too.

"That's not necessary."

"I know you're perfectly capable of walking home alone, Isabelle." Cole did not drop his gaze. "But I was hoping for a chance to talk to you. I need to schedule a time to pick up my bag at the bank."

In the dark, Isabelle's face was impossible to read. "All right. But only as far as the U-bahn station."

Lars sensed Cole's relief, along with his need to not keep Isabelle waiting. He stood. "I'll see you later at your place."

Cole nodded. "Nice to meet you, Marit."

"You too," Marit said. She and Isabelle exchanged a brief hug.

"Enjoy the rest of the market," Isabelle said. "Don't miss the booth with the hand-carved wooden Christmas tree ornaments. It's usually near the back of the cathedral."

"Thanks, Isabelle," Lars said.

"My pleasure." She waved, and moments later, she disappeared into the crowd, with Cole at her heels.

Lars watched them go. "Not sure what the standoff between Cole and Isabelle was all about."

Marit gathered their empty plates and cups. "I think it's got something to do with an 'it's just that' or 'but' issue."

Lars stared at her. "We both speak fluent Dutch, German, and English, but I didn't understand anything you just said."

She dropped the waste into the nearby receptacle. "I know."

Isabelle clenched her jaw as much to keep her teeth from chattering as to prevent her from lacing into Cole in public. She couldn't deny the brief flare of excitement she had experienced when Cole had arrived at the bank. She might have considered forgiving him, after an appropriate apology, and even opening the door to rekindling the romance that had started at Falcon Point, but finding out he hadn't come to see her slammed that door shut and deepened the hurt still simmering from the months of silence.

She shivered.

Cole moved closer and spoke in a low voice. "Are you cold or mad?"

Both, but admitting to her anger would force her to acknowledge the hurt he had caused. She tucked her gloved hands into her coat pockets and adopted a professional tone. "You can access your safe-deposit box at the bank any time during regular business hours."

Cole didn't press for an answer to his question. "I'll talk to my boss to see what she wants me to do with them." Always the CIA operative. He never broke character, not even to acknowledge that they both worked for the same person. "Maybe I can stop by tomorrow and take you to lunch. We can catch up."

Now he was asking her out? Seriously? "We don't need to catch up. We barely know each other."

"That's not true," Cole countered. "I thought we had a good time when we went out before."

"You're right. We did, but that was a long time ago." She turned toward the U-bahn station.

"Yeah, but it's not like I've been in Vienna much over the past few months. I thought you understood how unpredictable my work schedule is."

"I do understand it, but I'm not interested in dating someone who is just as unpredictable." She paused briefly when they reached the ticket booth. "Good night, Cole."

She turned away from him and headed for the platform.

"Wait a minute." He caught up to her and stepped into her path.

The confusion on his face would have been comical if it weren't for the conflicting emotions swirling through her: a secret thrill caused by Cole's persistence competing with the deep fear that she would never find anyone who would make her the center of his world. Beneath it all, anger and pride festered.

"I said you could walk me to the station," Isabelle said as her train approached. "We're here."

"You didn't say which station."

"I can get home by myself."

"I never said you couldn't."

The train whooshed to a stop, and Isabelle walked to the closest door. She pushed the button to open it and climbed aboard, enveloped by the warmth of the train. Maybe her fingers and toes would thaw by the time she reached her stop.

Cole followed.

Isabelle turned. "What are you doing?"

"We aren't done talking." He pressed his hand against the small of her back, sending a delicious tingle shooting through her.

She fisted her hands and willed her body to get in line with her determination. She was not letting Cole back into her life.

"Where do you want to sit?" Cole asked, gently guiding her forward through the sparsely populated train.

Resigned that she couldn't get rid of him, not without making a scene, she chose an empty seat near the back of the compartment.

As soon as Cole settled beside her, she shifted in her seat so she could see him more clearly. "Why are you doing this?"

"Doing what?"

"Escorting me home, asking me to lunch—all of it?" Isabelle asked. "You clearly don't care about me enough to keep in touch, so what's your endgame here?"

"I care about you," Cole said, looking truly shocked. "I wouldn't have asked you out if I didn't."

The man really was clueless. Taking a different approach, Isabelle said, "Let me ask you this: How many times have you seen Lars since the last time you and I went out?"

"I don't know. Five or six." Cole shrugged. "I passed through Amsterdam a few times while he was going through rehab."

"With the way Lars greeted you today, I assume you talked to him on the phone since he expected you would be out of town this week."

"We texted."

"You've kept in touch, then."

"Yeah. He's my cousin. I wanted to get to know him better."

"And that's great," Isabelle said, "but it proves my point. If you wanted to get to know me better, you could have called or texted. You could have let me know if you were going to be in town so we could have met for lunch or even had a conversation on the train like we are now."

Awareness lit his incredible blue eyes. "I'm sorry. You're right."

The minor victory did little to soothe the ache inside her. The train approached her stop, and she stood. "If you ever want to have a real relationship with me or anyone else, you need to know what direction you're going."

She left the train, casting a quick glance over her shoulder to ensure Cole remained seated. A hollowness filled her when she stepped into the cold.

The train pulled away, and she headed toward her apartment. How long would he go the wrong way before he made a course correction? The train was heading away from his apartment. The man really should get better about finding his way home.

CHAPTER 6

COLE'S CONVERSATION WITH ISABELLE REPLAYED on a loop. He went three stops before he realized he was going the wrong direction. Instead of turning back toward his apartment, he headed for his office. Maybe he could use work to distract him from the darts currently piercing his heart.

What was wrong with him? He'd gone out with Isabelle only a few times, so what did it matter if she wasn't interested in him anymore? She was right that he hadn't made much of an effort to stay in touch, but in his defense, their brief dating history had started at the same time his family had more than doubled in size. Isabelle had met two of his newfound cousins when things had come to a head in their search for his ancestral home. She knew how important his family was to him. Didn't she? Maybe she didn't. Beyond a brief conversation after meeting them, Cole couldn't recall talking to Isabelle about his cousins.

In truth, even he didn't fully understand how his love for them had developed so quickly. Then again, relying on each other to survive tended to create bonds that few people would ever experience.

He was closest to Lars, but he checked in on Lars's younger sister, Tess, every few weeks. He'd had even more contact with his British cousin, Anna, who was intimately involved with Falcon Point's remodel. The project couldn't be in better hands.

Cole had made his family a priority, allowing them to compete in importance with his work, and Isabelle resented him for it. He shook that thought away. She didn't resent his relationship with his cousins. She resented that Cole hadn't given her equal billing.

Juggling three new relationships had been hard enough. Maybe it was just as well that Isabelle had turned him down. But that thought brought a dark cloud with it.

He reached his destination and checked his weapon at security before making his way to his office. He passed by several empty desks. It must have been a slow day in Vienna if no one had to stay late today. Just as well. If he didn't have to chat with any of his coworkers, he'd be able to accomplish his task that much faster.

Shedding his coat, he dropped into his chair and booted up his computer. Surely Jazz would have filed her debriefing report by now. He logged in and searched recent reports but didn't find what he was looking for.

Desperate for a distraction, he retrieved his phone and called Jasmine.

Her Southern accent came over the line after the third ring. "Couldn't wait for me to type up my notes, huh?"

"You know me too well." Some of the tension binding his heart eased. "Any IDs on our guys? Or anything new from Rogers?"

"Hold on a second. I'll have to check," Jasmine said. "I got sidetracked by something else."

"Something more important than recovering a kidnapped agent?" Cole's curiosity heightened. "What's going on?"

"First, I had to finish covering up the mess you left us in Budapest."

"Yeah, sorry about that." Cole cringed at the memory but forced himself to put aside the emotions that always came when he had to defend himself in such a way. "Was that all, or did something else happen?"

"Someone set off a bomb in Frankfurt. Six people were killed, including two Americans."

"When did that happen? I didn't hear anything about it."

"This morning, not long after we liberated Rogers," Jasmine said. "It was all over social media."

"I'm not a big social media fan."

"Me neither, but that's where the news hit first." Jasmine paused. "Okay, I have the information on the kidnappers. Three have been identified so far." Another pause. "These guys are bad news. One of them was convicted of murder for hire six years ago, but he escaped during a prison transfer. From the images I was able to pull from the incident, I'd say some of his friends were responsible."

"Any clue who they're working for?"

"No. I put in the request to have headquarters run their financials," Jasmine said. "Hopefully that will give us some idea."

"If they're getting paid in diamonds, we may not find a money trail."

"We'll see. What did you find out about the diamonds?"

"They're worth at least a million euros."

"That much?" Jasmine asked.

"Yeah, I didn't expect that either. The pink one is the most valuable." Cole leaned back in his chair. "There was a serial number on one of the other stones. My cousin is going to reach out to some of his contacts and help me trace it."

"Did you already secure the diamonds at the embassy?"

"No. It was too late by the time I got here. I should be able to get them over there sometime tomorrow afternoon."

"Where are the diamonds now?" Jasmine asked.

"I locked them in a safe-deposit box at a local bank," Cole said.

"Isabelle's bank?"

So much for forgetting about her for the night. "Yes."

"How are things going between you two?" Jasmine asked.

"They're not."

"Why ever not? Are you an idiot?"

"Apparently so," Cole muttered. It was bad enough that Isabelle found him lacking. He didn't need it from Jazz too.

"What did you do?"

"Nothing."

"What didn't you do?" Jasmine asked, getting to the heart of the matter. "When you called last spring and asked me to do a background check on her, you were thrilled when you found out she was agency."

Jasmine was right, but somewhere along the way, his interest in Isabelle had taken a back seat to everything else going on in his life. He had stupidly thought she would be ready and willing to pick things up where they'd left off. He'd even found comfort in knowing he could look forward to seeing her when life settled down a bit.

Though tempted to shut down the interrogation, Cole let himself confide in his longtime friend. "I figured she'd know I was busy on assignment, but she was pretty annoyed I hadn't called her."

"How long had it been?"

"I don't know. I think the last time I saw her was right before I went to Belgium."

"Cole!" Jasmine's voice rose in a sharp verbal slap. "That was over five months ago."

"I know, but between that and the issue in Paris, I haven't had a lot of downtime."

"That doesn't mean you can't send a text to let her know you're thinking about her."

"So you're siding with her on this one," Cole muttered.

"Do you like her?"

What wasn't to like? "Well, yeah, but what's the point now? I asked her out. She said no." Cole tried to convince himself he didn't care that he'd screwed up, but he couldn't quite pull it off.

"She said no because you haven't given her a reason to say yes."

A sliver of hope pierced him. "How do I do that?"

"I don't know, but if I were you, I'd start with roses. Lots of roses."

Flowers. He could do that. "I guess it's worth a try. Thanks, Jazz."

"Don't thank me yet. It's going to take some doing to get out of this doghouse you put yourself in."

"I'm starting to get that."

Jazz's laughter carried over the line. "Honey, you'll figure it out."

He hoped so, because as much as he didn't want to admit it, now that he was faced with the possibility of losing Isabelle completely, he had to acknowledge the truth. He missed having someone to talk to besides his colleagues. He wanted a life outside the office or the next assignment. And even though he'd enjoyed spending time with Lars and Marit, it was Isabelle who had captured his attention tonight. The attraction Cole had experienced when he'd first met her hadn't faded, and as much as he appreciated the friendship they had formed during their first few dates, he wanted more. A lot more.

There were times when Lars hated being Marit's friend. Approaching her five-star hotel with that platonic label still firmly in place was definitely one of them.

Not willing to allow a fantasy to ruin the relationship they currently shared, he'd spent the entire day stepping away when he'd wanted to step toward her, tucking his hands into his pockets when he'd wanted to clasp hers. He was pretty sure that not kissing her good night was going to take him to a whole new level of torture.

A silver Lamborghini pulled up at the hotel entrance. A uniformed valet darted forward to open the car door, and a well-dressed man stepped out. The man circled the vehicle to open the door for the woman sitting in the passenger seat. She exited wearing a shimmery blue dress and the highest heels Lars had ever seen. If the playbill in the woman's hand was any indication, they were returning from the opera.

The man exchanged a few words with the valet and handed over his keys. With one hand on the woman's back, he guided her toward the glass revolving doors. Lars and Marit paused to let them enter the hotel ahead of them. The man muttered his thanks, his eyes lingering on Marit a fraction longer than was normal. Except that it was normal.

Lars stifled a sigh. Marit's beauty was undeniable. But there was so much more to her than that. Did any of the men she associated with in her glamorous world ever look past her appearance to appreciate her innate goodness, her subtle humor, and her genuine kindness? He pressed his hands more firmly into his pockets and waited for her to enter the revolving door. If he wanted his heart to have any chance at survival, he'd have to make their parting in the lobby quick.

"Hey, Marit!" a heavily accented voice called.

Lars stepped out of the revolving door in time to see a tall, dark-haired man cross the sumptuous lobby toward Marit. He wore designer jeans and Italian shoes. His shirt was open wide enough at the collar to display the gold chain around his neck, and in his hand, he carried a glass of wine.

His dark eyes raked over Marit, and Lars swallowed the bile in his throat. "Where have you been, *bella*? I missed you at the pool this afternoon."

"I was out with friends," she said.

The man's gaze flickered to the small bag in her hand that contained the gingerbread man and the small wooden Nativity ornament Lars had bought her. He didn't bother looking at Lars.

"Well, you're back now, so come join me at the bar. I'll buy you a drink."

"Thanks. But not tonight, Marco."

Marco Mancini. Even if the male model's accent had not been clue enough, Lars should have recognized the man's chiseled features from the Giovanni Russo menswear ads plastered all over the walls at the U-bahn stations.

"Come on. Just for a little while," Marco coaxed.

He claimed Marit's hand. She pulled it free and moved back a pace. As though it was an expected part of the game he was playing, Marco grinned.

Something inside Lars snapped. "She said, no thanks." He stepped forward and placed his hand on the small of Marit's back.

"And you are?" Marco's suave mask was still in place, but Lars caught the spark of anger in his dark eyes.

"Lars Hendriks." There was no way he was going to give Marco the satisfaction of hearing him preface his name with the words, *Marit's friend*. He kept his hand on Marit's back, awareness of her pulsing through his fingers even as he met the Italian's irritated look with his own icy glare. If Marit was upset with him for interfering, he'd deal with it afterward. First, he was going to get rid of this idiot. "I'm Marit's boyfriend."

He felt her stiffen, but to her credit, she didn't immediately call him out. Instead, she gave him a wide-eyed look and made the introductions with only a slight hitch to her voice. "Lars, this is Marco Mancini. We work together occasionally."

Marco raised a skeptical eyebrow. "Your boyfriend?"

"That's right." Her tone brooked no argument.

"Why did I not know of this boyfriend?"

"We're coworkers, Marco, not confidants."

"Don't feel bad," Lars said. "She didn't tell me about you either."

Marco's famous jaw tightened. "An unfortunate oversight for us both."

Behind them, the revolving door admitted a small group of people, and loud laughter filled the lobby. Someone called Marco's name.

The tension in the Italian's shoulders eased, and he smirked. "If you'll excuse me, it seems I'm needed elsewhere."

"Sure." As far as Lars was concerned, the cocky Casanova couldn't leave fast enough.

Marco raised his glass to Marit. "*Ciao, bella.*"

Marit waited only until he'd turned around before grabbing Lars's hand and towing him to the other side of the lobby.

"You okay?" Lars hardly dared ask—especially if it meant she let go of his hand in favor of laying into him.

The wide-open space, with its small groupings of elegant chairs and an occasional potted plant, offered virtually no privacy, but it seemed that she was aiming for the grand piano in the far corner.

"I'm sorry, Marit," Lars tried again. Her prolonged silence was a bad sign. She'd never resorted to it before.

"What are you sorry for?" She stopped walking, and he all but ran into her.

"For putting you in an awkward position with your coworkers."

"My coworkers or Marco?"

"Both." He released a defeated sigh. "It's just that when Marco looked at you like that, I couldn't . . ." He trailed off. She was smiling.

"Did you say, 'It's just that'?"

"Yeah." Why was she making this so difficult? He was willing to apologize properly if she'd only let him.

Her smile softened, and she placed her hand on his chest. "I think you'd better kiss me."

Heaven help him. Being this close to her was muddling his brain. "You . . . you want me to kiss you?"

"Marco and my other coworkers are probably watching us."

"Great."

She laughed. It was a warm, joyful sound that brought back memories of their long phone calls when they'd both been recuperating from surgery. For those few short weeks, they'd been the center of each other's lives. But then Marit's agent had pulled her back into her modeling work, and everything had changed.

He raised his hand and brushed a lock of her blonde hair from her face. He'd missed her so much his heart ached. Her brown eyes met his, and he felt his guard slipping. He would kiss her. Just this once. To keep Marco away. He slid his arms around her, drawing her close. Her arms wrapped around his neck, and his pulse quickened. He lowered his head, waiting one excruciatingly long second for any indication that she did not want this. She breathed a gentle sigh, and he closed the distance between them.

At the touch of her lips on his, the protective wall he'd built around his heart crumbled. He pressed her closer, deepening the kiss as months of longing and coming up wanting flooded over him. Marit shifted slightly, and from somewhere far away, he heard the small bag in her hand drop to the floor.

The sound of distant chatter and the ping of a lift arriving were the first things to filter into his conscious thoughts. Slowly, reluctantly, he raised his head. Inches from him, Marit's eyes fluttered open. She appeared as stunned as he felt.

"Why did you stop calling every day?" she whispered.

Why had he? Whatever the reason, it had been a bad one. Digging deep, he brought back the memories of those lonely days. "You were never available."

"But I always returned your calls."

"By then it was late and you were tired. I didn't want calling me back to be something that was always on your list of things to do—something that felt like a chore."

She shook her head. "It was never like that. Not for me."

He swallowed hard. He'd messed up. "I missed talking to you."

"I missed talking to you too." She smiled—a shy smile that sent his heart soaring and gave him the courage to continue.

"Do you think we could start again?" He hesitated. "But this time, I don't want to just be your friend from work."

A spark of humor flared in her eyes. "I don't especially want to be your friend from the hospital either."

He still held her in his arms, and she made no move to escape. "How would you feel about being my girlfriend instead?" he asked.

She appeared to ponder the question. "It would make things a lot less complicated with Marco."

"True."

"And I could hold your hand whenever mine are cold."

"Also true."

"And you might kiss me like that again."

He chuckled. "The truest thing you've said all evening."

She offered him an impish grin. "Then I think I would like it very much."

His smile widened. "What are your plans tomorrow? Can I see you?"

"The production crew is leaving in the morning, but since I don't have another booking for over a week, I thought I might stay a day or two in Vienna to do some sightseeing."

"How about we explore the city together?"

She nodded. "I'd love that."

"Me too." He placed a gentle kiss on her lips before releasing her and stepping away. "I'll call you in the morning."

CHAPTER 7

COLE DIDN'T WAIT UNTIL MORNING to order the flowers. He didn't even wait until he got home. The minute he boarded his train, he pulled out his cell phone and got online to search for local florists.

When he saw the price of flowers, he nearly discounted Jasmine's suggestion. Did a woman really need two dozen roses? But the memory of his two most recent scoldings chased that thought away. He could handle Jazz laying into him for screwing up, but he suspected Isabelle wasn't just mad at him. She was hurt. That alone warranted the exorbitant cost.

By the time Cole arrived at his apartment, Lars was already stretched out on the couch.

Cole was halfway across the dark room when Lars said, "You can turn on the light if you need to."

"I thought you were already asleep." Cole flipped on the overhead light and took in his cousin's expression. "What's with the goofy grin?"

"Nothing." His grin widened.

Cole might be an idiot, but he was an observant idiot. "You and Marit, huh?"

"Yeah." Lars propped himself up on an elbow. "How did things go with Isabelle?"

"Isabelle has made it very clear that I had one chance and I blew it."

"I don't know about that. I saw a few sparks flying between you two."

"Don't mistake gunfire for fireworks," Cole said, even though he couldn't deny the sizzle he still experienced every time Isabelle was near.

"Want to talk about it?"

Cole had to remind himself that his social life wasn't classified. "You know how I've been traveling a lot the past few months?"

"Yeah."

"I wasn't the greatest about keeping in touch with Isabelle while I was gone."

"When you say you weren't the greatest, are you talking about not answering a few texts and calls or did you give her the silent treatment?"

"I didn't think of it that way, but Isabelle seems to think I was ghosting her."

"No wonder you were getting the cold shoulder."

"Yeah." Cole ran a hand through his hair. "I just spent a fortune on roses, but I'm not sure that's going to be enough."

"Maybe Marit will have some ideas. She knows what women like."

The goofy grin was back.

"You really like this girl."

"Can you blame me?" Lars's whole expression brightened. "You know how people say beauty comes from within? Marit is even more gorgeous on the inside than on the outside."

"You're really hooked."

Lars laced his fingers behind his head, laid back, and let out a contented sigh. "Yeah, and I'm pretty happy about it."

A little envious of his cousin's good fortune, he asked, "Do you really think Marit will know how I can set things right with Isabelle?"

"Only one way to find out."

"Then call your girlfriend and see if she's on board," Cole said.

"It's after midnight. I don't think waking her up is a good idea."

"If she's anything like you, she's lying in bed, staring up at the ceiling with an identical grin on her face."

"I told her I'd call her in the morning." Lars rolled over on his side and propped himself up on his elbow again. "Oh, also, I knew you were anxious about getting the information on that diamond, so I emailed the serial number to my contact in case he was working late."

"Any luck?"

"Not yet. I got an automatic reply that he was out of the office through tomorrow. I should hear back from him by the next day at the latest."

"Thanks for trying."

"We'll get the information. It just might take a day or two," Lars said. "In the meantime, when did you want to try to see Isabelle?"

"I asked her to lunch tomorrow, but she turned me down."

"Maybe we can get her to change her mind."

"How?"

"I have no idea."

The lift came to a stop, and the doors opened. Marit stepped out into the hotel lobby, her eyes immediately drawn to the grand piano in the corner. A smile teased her lips. After Lars had left the night before, she'd virtually floated up to her suite on the fourth floor. One kiss. One incredible, earth-shattering kiss and everything had changed.

Sleep had been practically impossible. And when the digital clock on the bedside table had announced the arrival of 1:00 a.m., she'd resorted to counting sheep. Sometime after two hundred sixty-seven, she'd finally succumbed to exhaustion, and she'd awoken almost seven hours later to a room full of daylight and the ringing of her phone.

Hearing Lars's voice had been a welcome way to start the day, but his call had been both brief and cryptic. Cole needed her assistance, and if she was up for it, he and Lars would meet her in the hotel lobby within the hour. Marit's curiosity had been piqued, and she'd readily agreed. Fifty rushed minutes later, she was showered, dressed, and ready to discover what she could do for Cole.

She scanned the vast lobby. The three hotel employees working the front desk were busy with customer checkouts. A line of overflowing luggage carts waited nearby, and the gaffer from Marit's recent photo shoot was talking to a bellboy. Yvette LeBlanc, the head stylist, waved at her from across the room before turning her attention to Marco, who was standing at her side. The day before yesterday, Yvette had offered Marit tickets to a high-brow event this weekend. Even though Marit would probably still be in Vienna, it was unlikely that Lars would want to go to anything like that. Besides, asking the stylist about the tickets now was definitely not worth initiating another encounter with Marco.

Marit turned away. Experience told her that the organized chaos would continue in the lobby until the crew headed to the airport.

Two men entered through the revolving door, and Marit's heart lifted. Lars and Cole. Lars saw her immediately, a smile lighting his face as he crossed the distance between them in long strides.

"Good morning," he said, pulling her into his arms.

She smiled. "Good morning to you too."

He brushed her lips with a soft kiss, leaving them tingling. "You look amazing."

Behind him, Cole cleared his throat. Lars rolled his eyes, and Marit chuckled softly.

"Hi, Cole," she said. Lars stepped aside so she could see Cole more clearly. He didn't look nearly as happy as his cousin. "What's going on?"

"He has girl trouble." Lars answered for him.

Cole gave him an irritated look. "Lars thought you might have some ideas for how I can fix things with Isabelle. She's pretty upset with me right now."

"What did you do?"

"I think it's more a case of what I didn't do."

Marit raised her eyebrows. "Okay. What didn't you do?"

"Call. Text." He shrugged. "Keep in touch while I was gone."

She looked at Lars. "Is this a family thing?"

"Maybe." Lars had the grace to look uncomfortable. "It kind of looks that way, doesn't it?"

She pointed to a small grouping of armchairs near the window. "Let's go over there, and you can fill me in."

Cole's details were sparse. But it didn't take long for Marit to pick up on the depth of his desire to make things right with Isabelle.

"Well," she said when he finished telling her about the two dozen roses he'd had delivered to Isabelle's office that morning, "I have good news and bad news for you."

A line creased Cole's forehead. "Go ahead."

"The good news is I'm pretty sure Isabelle's attitude toward you right now comes from her having been badly hurt."

"That's good news?" He shot an uneasy glance at Lars, who returned it with a sympathetic look.

"Definitely." Were all men this dense or only these two? "Isabelle wouldn't be so upset if she didn't care about you."

Cole looked thoughtful. "What's the bad news?"

"It's going to take considerably more than roses to win her back."

"Like what?"

"Like a grand romantic gesture followed by consistent follow-up."

"I was under the distinct impression that two dozen red roses *was* a grand romantic gesture," he said.

"It was a good start."

"A good start!" He ran his fingers through his hair. "Is there a price limit to these grand romantic gestures?"

Marit grinned. "Nope."

He turned to Lars. "How come you didn't have to do one of these?"

"I'm starting small and working my way up."

"Small, like gingerbread?" Cole asked.

Lars raised his hands, his lips twitching as he fought back a smile. "Hey, I may be an idiot, but I didn't mess up as badly as you."

Cole looked unconvinced and turned his attention back to Marit. "I don't know what you see in this guy."

Marit laughed. "If I'm lucky, he'll pick up a few pointers after watching you win back Isabelle."

"I'm listening." Lars reached for her hand, his touch causing havoc with her heart rate. "What did you have in mind?"

She was silent for a moment, mentally reviewing the tourist information she'd read before arriving. "It would be a lot easier to come up with suggestions if I was more familiar with Vienna, but—" She broke off to look through the window. A taxi had pulled up outside the hotel, and a couple waiting by the front doors stepped forward to claim it. "How cold is it out there?"

"Warmer than yesterday," Lars said. "And the sky's clear."

"What about a ride in one of those white, horse-drawn carriages I've seen driving around the city?"

"The fiakers?" Cole asked. "They're just tourist traps."

"They're romantic," Marit corrected.

"People who live in Vienna don't go anywhere near them."

"Exactly." She gave him a knowing look. "What's your bet Isabelle has never taken a carriage ride around this beautiful city?"

"She's right, Cole," Lars said. "And if you hit a bakery or a deli first, you could make up a lunch and take it with you."

Cole folded his arms. "It won't work."

"Why?"

"I already asked her to have lunch with me, and she turned me down."

"Then I'll ask her," Marit said.

"It won't matter who asks her," Cole said. "She doesn't want anything to do with me."

"How about if we go together?" Lars asked. "Marit could ask Isabelle to lunch without mentioning that either of us would be there."

"Yes," she said. "You two could wait outside with the carriage while I go into the bank to get her."

"And then what?" Cole asked. "Isabelle arrives outside, sees me, and does a U-turn back into the bank?"

Marit smiled. "I don't think so. Don't forget the white carriage and picnic basket will be there too."

"The grand romantic gesture," Cole muttered.

"That's right." Marit gave him an encouraging smile. "I really think it will help."

He sighed. "All right. At this point, I don't have anything to lose except more money."

"Great," Lars said, coming to his feet. "There are some brochures in a stand by the door. I'll see if they have any on the carriage rides. Marit, why don't you give Isabelle a call, and once you've persuaded her to join you for lunch, we'll come up with ideas for the picnic."

Isabelle breathed in the scent of roses and fought against her embarrassment and irritation. The simple glass vase filled with two dozen red blooms had arrived only minutes after she had walked into the bank. All the tellers had gushed over the flowers, and Isabelle had been inundated by questions about who they were from.

"An old friend" had been her simplified answer, even though she wasn't sure Cole even qualified to be a "friend" at the moment.

His weak apology last night had done little to chase away the hurt that had deepened with each passing day over the past few months. Now he was sending her flowers, thinking it would make it all better? And at work, no less. The man really was clueless. Embarrassing her in front of her colleagues wasn't helping his case.

At least she would be able to escape the office when she left for her midday meal. When Marit called to invite her to lunch, Isabelle had accepted without hesitation. She truly enjoyed spending time with Marit, and she rarely had the opportunity to develop friendships that didn't have anything to do with work. Besides, after receiving the roses this morning, Isabelle wouldn't put it past Cole to show up and ask her out again.

She released a frustrated sigh. Even though her mind tried to downplay the effect of his presence, a little seed of regret planted deep inside her at the idea that she might miss him. Isabelle shook that thought away. Cole wasn't ever going to make her a priority, and she needed to learn to let go of the ridiculous idea that they could build a future together.

Focusing on work once more, she did a quick search of an account that had higher-than-normal activity. After verifying that the transactions were valid and justified, she moved to the next line item that fell into the suspicious category.

A knock sounded on her open door. Gerhart stepped inside, an iPad in his hand. "Did you see the activity level report? The Klaussen account had over four times the volume this quarter than usual."

"I just finished looking at that." Isabelle picked up her notepad. "The family is remodeling their home in Salzburg. The extra activity is primarily payments to contractors and for the purchase of supplies."

Isabelle didn't mention that she'd gone the extra mile and verified that the payments were going to valid contractors and that the rates were within the normal range for the specified work. Part of her job with the CIA was to ferret out transactions disguised as something other than what they really were. Construction projects were among the more common tricks used by smugglers, money launderers, and terrorists.

"Don't forget to write up your notes and put them in the file in case the auditors ask about it," Gerhart said.

Did he really think she would ever forget to do her job? Isabelle didn't dignify the comment with a response.

"I'll be at the Landstrabe branch all afternoon," Gerhart continued. "Call me if anything comes up that needs my immediate attention. Otherwise, I'll see you tomorrow."

"Okay." Isabelle waited for his footsteps to fade down the hall before she turned back to her work. Her gaze lingered on the roses, and her traitorous heart lifted for a moment before she reminded herself that she was still mad at Cole. She couldn't afford to open her heart to him again, could she?

Footsteps approached again, but this time when they stopped, Marit appeared in her doorway.

"Marit. Come in."

"I hope you don't mind me coming up to your office." Marit stepped inside. "The woman at the reception desk said it would be okay."

"You have perfect timing." Isabelle waved at the chair across from her. "Have a seat. I just need to shut everything down, and then we can go."

Marit sat in one of the two padded chairs upholstered in a deep forest green. "I'm so glad you are able to get away for a little while today."

"Me too. I eat lunch at my desk far too often." Isabelle logged out of her computer. "How did things go with Lars after I left last night?"

Color rushed into Marit's cheeks, and her lips twitched. "Good."

"You're blushing. What happened?"

Marit rubbed her lips together as though debating what to say. "It's not polite to kiss and tell . . ."

"If there was a kiss, you have to tell."

Marit laughed. "Let's just say I wasn't the only one thinking, 'It's just that.'"

"I'm happy for you." And she was. Isabelle couldn't resist asking, "So how was the kiss?"

Marit's smile won out. "Incredible."

CHAPTER 8

"If you don't stop pacing, the driver's going to think you're afraid of getting into a slow-moving carriage," Lars said.

"He wouldn't be far off." Cole glared at him. "This was a stupid idea."

The two men were standing in front of the bank where Isabelle worked. Behind them, the carriage Cole had hired stood ready for its passengers. The two horses at the front waited patiently, occasionally flicking a tail or twitching an ear. The driver was equally relaxed, sitting on his perch in the traditional long coat and top hat of the fiaker drivers.

Lars placed his hand on his cousin's tense arm. "Relax," he said. "It's going to be okay. Marit will bring Isabelle out, and Isabelle won't be able to resist the opportunity to tour the city in a horse-drawn carriage."

"If she turns it down, I might send her the bill."

Lars raised an eyebrow. "That comment is barely worth a response, but you might want to seriously rethink which ideas you think are stupid."

Cole grunted. Given the man's current mood, Lars guessed it was the closest he would come to offering an apology. He felt bad for Cole. Isabelle wasn't making this easy on him. But, like Marit, Lars was optimistic that this gesture would make a difference.

"Here they come," Lars warned.

The two women stepped out of the bank, wearing warm coats, but whereas Marit was dressed casually in form-fitting jeans and low-heeled boots, Isabelle had on black trousers and high heels. Marit laughed at something Isabelle said, and Lars's heart warmed to see the joy on her beautiful face. How had he ever gotten so lucky?

"Any minute now." Cole's voice was low, but it was as though Isabelle heard the cue. She looked up, spotted the men standing beside the carriage, and stopped.

Marit didn't miss a beat. Slipping her arm through Isabelle's, she said something and tugged her forward. Reluctantly, Isabelle complied.

"Hi, Isabelle." Lars greeted her with a welcoming smile. "Glad you could join us."

"Thanks. This isn't exactly what I had in mind when Marit called, but it's good to see you again, Lars." She eyed the carriage curiously. "You've actually reserved this fiaker for lunch?"

"Not me. Cole."

Surprise lit her eyes, and she turned to Cole. "This doesn't seem like something you'd sign up for."

"Have you done it before?" he asked.

"No. Have you?"

"Nope." He raised one eyebrow as though offering her a dare. "It might be fun. And going with a couple of Dutch tourists gives us an airtight excuse for doing something so un-Viennese."

A small smile tugged at her lips. "Is acting like a sightseer such a terrible thing? We are Americans, after all."

At that moment, a herd of tourists crossed the plaza in a cloud of excited chatter. They each wore matching orange sweatshirts and were following a man carrying a raised umbrella.

Cole watched them go, his expression unreadable. "For the record," he said, eyeing Lars sternly, "if you and Marit had been wearing the same color shirt, this excursion would have been off."

Lars spotted mirth shining in Isabelle's eyes. If she could find humor in Cole's grumpiness, they had even greater reason to hope.

"Well, since my coat is blue and Marit's is gray, the carriage ride is still on," Lars said. And before Isabelle could back out, he added, "Let's go. I'm hungry."

"Climb in, Isabelle," Marit said. "I'll follow you."

Marit gave Lars a knowing look, and he stifled a grin. Having Isabelle go first was a masterstroke. Not only was she trapped in the vehicle, but those coming in after her could choose their seats. Neither he nor Marit would take the one next to her. And that left Cole.

Isabelle hesitated. "I have to be back at the bank in an hour."

"The tour lasts forty minutes," Cole said. "And we'll eat as we go."

She peered into the carriage. A bag lay in the center of the floor. "What's for lunch?" she asked.

"Doner kebabs from the stand across from the Rathaus," Cole said. "Your pocket bread is filled with rice, lamb, red cabbage, tomatoes, yogurt sauce, and no onion."

Isabelle's eyes widened. "You remembered."

"Yeah, I remembered." He smiled. It was the first genuine smile Lars had seen on Cole in over an hour. "It's your favorite."

Isabelle nodded, and without another word, she climbed into the waiting vehicle. Marit took the seat opposite her. Lars sat beside Marit, and Cole entered last, taking the seat beside Isabelle.

"We're ready, Paul," Cole called to the waiting driver.

"Very good, sir."

With a snap of the reins, the fiaker started forward. Lars slid his camera strap off his shoulder and set the instrument down before reaching for the red-and-black plaid blanket beneath the seat. He unfolded it and offered one end to Marit. Out of the corner of his eye, he saw Cole doing the same thing. Isabelle had yet to relax in her seat, but she accepted the blanket and laid it across her knees.

Lars put his arm around Marit and drew her close. This ride might be intended for Cole and Isabelle's benefit, but he was more than happy to take full advantage of it.

They rode out of Stephansplatz, leaving the Gothic architecture of the magnificent cathedral behind and entering streets lined with tall baroque-style buildings. The white and cream stone walls contrasted with colorful doors and an occasional green copper roof.

"Tell us what we're seeing," Lars said.

"Old Town, Vienna," Cole replied. "Packed with history and hidden gems."

"Hidden gems?" Marit said. "What do you mean?"

Cole shrugged. "Sometimes people walk past these buildings never knowing what's inside."

"Give us examples," Lars said. Isabelle had yet to join the conversation, but the stiffness in her posture had eased. She was watching Cole, listening to what he was telling them.

"The Spanish Riding School." Cole pointed to the imposing building fronted by columns and statues on their left. "People drive by here all the time without realizing that it houses a stable for the famous Lipizzaner stallions."

"My little sister was horse-crazy," Marit said. "She had a poster of the Lipizzaner stallions on the wall in her bedroom. I didn't realize they were trained in Vienna."

Lars studied the building as they passed. Cole was right. He never would have guessed what lay behind the grand facade.

They turned a corner onto another street, and Cole reached for the bag. "We should eat." He removed the individually wrapped doner kebabs and handed them out. "I had the guy put an initial on each one, so make sure you get the one you ordered." He glanced at Isabelle. "Or would have ordered."

"Thanks," she said, taking the one he offered her.

He nodded and gave her a bottle of water too.

"These are great," Lars said. He hadn't been convinced that Cole was making the best choice when he'd insisted on buying lunch from the doner stand.

"Another Viennese triumph over McDonalds?" Isabelle asked.

He caught her teasing tone and played along. "Well, I'm not sure about rice over fries, but . . ." He took another bite. "It's close."

Isabelle laughed. Cole shot him a surprised look but it was Marit who spoke first.

"Your turn, Isabelle. Which of these buildings we're passing is your favorite?"

"There are so many." She gazed out at the park they were passing. The trees were bare, but vast lawns and evergreen shrubs brought color to the wintery scene. "This is MuseumsQuartier. There are several art galleries and museums within this huge block." She thought about the question a little longer. "But I think if I had to choose my favorite hidden gem in Vienna, it would be the State Hall in the Austrian National Library."

"Will we see that building?" Marit asked.

"I think so." Isabelle leaned a little closer to Cole to see past the driver's perch. "If we turn right at this next corner, we'll pass it."

"Why do you like it best?" Cole asked.

Isabelle met his eyes and immediately scooted back a few inches. "Have you been inside?"

"No."

"It's one of the most beautiful libraries in the world."

Cole frowned. "Why haven't I heard about it?"

"It wouldn't be a hidden gem if everyone knew about it." Isabelle took another bite of her doner, but she couldn't quite hide her smile. "Besides, when was the last time you went out of your way to visit a library?"

"What makes it special?" Marit asked, cutting off any riposte Cole might make.

"When you walk in, you feel like someone has taken the library in Disney's movie *Beauty and the Beast* and dropped it into a cathedral."

"It sounds amazing. I'll have to visit it before I leave." Marit watched the building go by. "I'm coming to understand why you both love Vienna so much."

She leaned her head against Lars's shoulder, and he tightened his hold around her.

Isabelle nodded. "Even if you're a transplant, it's easy to feel that you belong here."

They rode past beautifully tended parks and ancient churches. The opera house, Rathaus, Karlsplatz, and The Hofburg all came and went. Lars itched to open his camera and take photos of the iconic structures, but that would mean moving his arms and relinquishing Marit. It wasn't worth it.

After her one slip, Isabelle kept her distance from Cole for the rest of the ride. But by the time the carriage rolled back into Stephansplatz, her icy tone when speaking to him had melted into cool wariness.

"Thank you," she said as the driver brought the vehicle to a stop outside the bank. "I had a good time."

"I'm really glad you came," Marit said.

Isabelle smiled. "Me too. But I have a big report to file before three o'clock, so I'd better get going."

Cole stepped out of the carriage and offered her his hand. She ignored it, choosing to step down on her own instead. Lars and Marit joined them.

"All set?" the driver called down to them.

"Yep. Thanks, Paul," Cole said.

"My pleasure." The driver raised his hand, and with another flick of the reins, the carriage moved away.

"I was hoping to pick up the diamonds while I was here," Cole said. "Do you have time to get me into the vault?"

Isabelle glanced at her watch. "If we're fast."

"Great." Cole turned to Lars. "I'll be right back."

"Maybe I'll take advantage of this wait time to use the toilet," Marit said. "Are you going to stay here?"

"Yeah," Lars said. He lifted his camera off his shoulder again. "I'll take some photos while you're away."

She smiled. "In other words, you won't even know I'm gone."

He leaned in and pressed a brief kiss to her lips. "I'll know," he said. "Hurry back."

Isabelle led the way into the bank and pointed Marit in the direction of the restroom. She still couldn't believe Cole had gone to so much trouble for a lunch date she hadn't even agreed to. For all he knew, she could have turned around and gone back into the bank when she'd learned he was coming with her and Marit.

She'd thought about it, but she'd always wanted to ride in one of the horse-drawn carriages. The chance to see Vienna that way had been too tempting to turn down.

How had Cole known? Maybe he hadn't. The thoughtful gesture seemed more in line with something another woman would suggest.

She glanced over as Marit crossed the lobby and headed for the ladies' room. Isabelle would have to interrogate her new friend later.

Isabelle slowed and took the time to scan the lobby. A man waiting outside the manager's office, his back to her. Another man at the new accounts desk, his eyes searching the room as well.

Cole stepped beside Isabelle and put his hand gently on her back. A sense of connection seeped through her. What was wrong with her? She'd decided against dating Cole. She was supposed to be getting over him, not letting him sneak in under her defenses.

A teller finished helping one of the patrons at the counter and spotted her. Before motioning the person next in line forward, the teller nudged the woman at the next station. A whispered comment, a gesture in Isabelle's direction. No doubt they had connected the dots that Cole was the sender of her roses.

Embarrassed, Isabelle averted her eyes and moved toward the elevator. Still curious about who was behind today's outing, she opted to take the direct approach and question Cole. Not that she expected a fellow CIA operative to cave to her interrogation tactics, but she was up for a challenge.

They reached the elevator, and she pressed the Up button.

"Who's idea was it to hire the fiaker?" she asked.

"That was Marit."

So much for a challenge.

Cole must have sensed her surprise because he said, "You didn't really think I would lie, did you?"

Isabelle stepped inside the empty lift and waited until they were enclosed inside before speaking. "You do lie for a living." She pressed the button for the second floor.

"I don't lie to you."

"So you say."

Cole took her by the arm and stepped in front of her so his back was to the lift doors. Sincerity and an intensity she rarely saw in him filled his expression. "I haven't lied to you."

"Would I know if you had?"

"Probably not," Cole admitted.

An honest answer. He had her there.

Before the conversation could continue, the lift dinged and the doors opened.

As though a curtain had been closed, all evidence of Cole's emotions disappeared.

He stepped to her side once more and motioned for her to exit the lift first.

She glanced back at him, both impressed and irritated that he could transform himself so quickly. Would she ever know the real Cole Bridger? Did she want to? And was she willing to let her guard down long enough to give him the chance to know the real her?

CHAPTER 9

COLE FOLLOWED ISABELLE DOWN THE hall toward the vault. His hand still tingled from when he'd taken her arm. How could the woman have such an effect on him when he barely knew her? But he did know her, at least enough to understand the strain of living a double life, of always censoring your words and carefully avoiding close relationships that could jeopardize your cover.

He doubted Marit or Lars had noticed the brief flash of vulnerability on Isabelle's face when she'd come out of the bank earlier or the almost imperceptible hesitation as she'd debated her next move. But he'd noticed. He'd been trained to notice. What he hadn't been trained to do was open himself up to the risk and pain a relationship could cause.

Isabelle cast a questioning glance in his direction, as though she sensed his inner turmoil. A man in his forties approached and passed by them with a nod in greeting to Isabelle.

Adopting a professional tone, Isabelle asked, "Are you sure you want to transport the diamonds yourself? I can arrange for an armed vehicle."

"I don't think my employers will appreciate the attention that would come with having an armored car pull up in front of the embassy."

"Good point." Isabelle paused at the entrance to the safe-deposit boxes and greeted the guard stationed there. "Hi, Leon."

"*Fräulein* Roberts."

Isabelle stepped aside so Cole could sign the log to access his box. As soon as he completed his task, they entered the long, narrow room together. Safe-deposit boxes lined three walls, the overhead light reflecting a golden glow from the metal compartments. A single bar-height counter occupied the center of the room.

Isabelle stepped toward the box Cole had rented yesterday. "Do you have your key?"

"Yeah." Rather than retrieve it from his pocket, he fumbled for words. "I really am sorry I didn't call or text while I was gone."

Isabelle turned to face him. The vulnerability he had glimpsed in her expression earlier returned. "Why didn't you?"

"I don't know. I thought about it." Cole could make excuses about how busy he had been or how he'd been undercover and couldn't risk making a call. His eyes met hers, and he opted for the truth. "Since I joined the agency and until I met you, I hadn't even considered being in a serious relationship. I'm not sure I even know how one works."

"We were hardly in a serious relationship." Isabelle said the words, but Cole didn't miss the way her face shuttered, a sure sign she had chosen to hide her inner feelings. He'd practiced that skill often enough in his own life.

"Seems to me we were heading toward serious before I went out on assignment." Cole took a step forward. "I messed up. I thought about you while I was gone, but when I saw you again—" He broke off, searching for words. After a moment, the truth tumbled free. "Now I can't stop thinking about you."

"Cole, relationships are built on trust, and you broke mine."

"What will it take to convince you that this time will be different?"

"You're assuming I'll give you a second chance."

"I'm hoping you will." Cole took another step. "Forgive me? Please?"

The shield fell away, the depth of the pain he'd caused reflected in her eyes. "You hurt me. That's not something that's easy to forget."

"I know, but if you'll let me, I'll make it up to you." Cole lifted his hand helplessly. "And I'm not talking about sending you roses."

"They were beautiful." She paused briefly before adding, "But for future reference, my favorite are yellow roses."

Encouraged, Cole took her hand. "Then I'll send you yellow roses next time."

Both elegant eyebrows lifted. "Next time you mess up?"

"No. The next time I want you to think of me."

Surprise flashed in her eyes, and he sensed her wavering. His gaze locked with hers, and he leaned closer.

His lips were only an inch from hers when the familiar electrical zapping sound of a Taser echoed from the hall. A heavy thud followed.

Cole instinctively stepped between Isabelle and the door and reached for his gun. It wasn't until he discovered it missing that he remembered he'd left his weapon secured at his apartment.

Two men rushed into the vault, both wearing ski masks and gloves. One carried a Taser in one hand and the safe-deposit box log in the other. The other man lifted his gun and aimed, but this weapon wasn't a Taser.

"Hands up," the man said in German.

Cole could disarm the man if he came a step closer, but he couldn't guarantee the man's partner wouldn't disable him or Isabelle with the Taser or, worse, draw the pistol in the front of his waistband. Unwilling to risk Isabelle's safety, Cole slowly complied.

"You." The shorter of the two men waved his Taser at Isabelle. "Over here."

Isabelle moved slowly. She cast a glance at Cole, a glint of determination visible on her face. She was ready to act. They just needed to wait for the right opening. Then these two would learn they were messing with the wrong people.

Marit turned off the tap in the small sink and pushed the button on the hand drier. The loud whirring filled the small room. She shook her hands beneath the blower. They were dry enough. She wanted to get back to Lars. A small smile played across her lips at the thought of spending the rest of the day with him. When he'd put his arm around her and pulled her close in the carriage, she'd not wanted the ride to ever end. It was going to be hard to top this morning's activity.

She hoped the outing had been good for Isabelle and Cole too. Isabelle had not been happy about Cole's inclusion in their lunch plans, but perhaps now that they'd spent a pleasant hour together, she'd be willing to consider giving him another chance. If Cole were smart, he'd make the most of the one-on-one time afforded him by going to the vault to plead his case.

A muffled thud reached her through the closed door. Puzzled, Marit pulled it open and stepped into the small alcove that separated the bank's toilets from the front lobby. A couple of meters in front of her, the security guard who'd greeted her with a polite nod only minutes before lay prostrate on the floor. Beside him stood a masked man.

Marit froze. Behind her, the toilet door clicked shut. The sound echoed through the unnaturally quiet alcove.

"Hands up!"

The masked man stepped in front of her, his gun raised. He was tall, dressed in jeans and a navy sweater, and through the slits in the gray fabric, his dark eyes were trained on her. Marit reached behind her for the doorknob.

"Up!" he yelled.

With her heart hammering in her chest, she slowly raised her hands.

"Now, move!" The man jerked his head toward the lobby. "In there."

Marit walked into the lobby. The four bank tellers and three customers who'd been in the bank when she'd entered were now sitting on the floor, their backs to the counter. Their expressions ranged from fear to anger to incredulity. One woman was quietly sobbing. A second gunman stood over them, wearing a blue ski mask.

The guard had not moved. Was he dead?

"Your phone and watch go over there," her captor barked.

Marit looked to her left. A small pile of phones and digital watches sat heaped on the end of the counter.

"I'm not wearing a watch," she said.

With her arms raised, it was easy to see that her wrists were free of anything.

"Phone," he said. "And don't even try to tell me you haven't got one of those."

Knowing she'd be searched if she denied it, Marit lowered one arm to reach into her coat pocket and withdrew her phone. She held it out.

He ignored her outstretched hand. "I told you to put it on the counter."

Beneath his irritation, Marit caught something else. There was an inflection in the way he pronounced his words that tagged him as a foreigner. He may be speaking German, but she was willing to bet it wasn't his first language.

She moved to the counter and set her phone down. She worked with people from all over Europe. If she could hear him speak a little more, she might be able to narrow down where he was from.

"Hurry it up!" the other gunman yelled. "Get her on the floor with the others."

That one was a German speaker. But not Austrian. His accent came from farther north. Somewhere closer to her home in the southern region of the Netherlands.

Marit had worked hard to minimize her Dutch accent when she spoke English and German. She knew firsthand how difficult it was. For many, it wasn't worth the effort. If these two didn't care enough to hide their backgrounds, she was going to take advantage of it.

Her horror at what was happening around her gave way to determination. Taking her place on the floor a meter from the young teller whose face was almost as white as his shirt, she studied the gunmen. Eyeing them the way the stylists on set analyzed the models, she gauged their height and weight, neck size, and waist before studying their feet. She may not be able to stop these thugs herself, but she could give the authorities the best description of masked men they'd ever received. All she had to do was stay alive long enough to share it.

CHAPTER 10

A BANK ROBBERY? SERIOUSLY? IRRITATION rather than fear flowed through Isabelle. She and Cole could disarm these two men, but they needed a distraction to make sure no one got shot.

She and Cole had been relegated to the far side of the safe-deposit vault, the counter situated between them and their captors. The taller of the two men, his brown eyes visible beneath his green ski mask, stood a few meters away, reciting box numbers as his black-masked partner broke open the corresponding safe-deposit boxes.

Four boxes already littered the floor, personal documents, deeds, and passports spilling out of them.

Other than pocketing cash and jewels, the robbers hadn't bothered with any of the other contents. They were clearly looking for something specific, but what?

Isabelle's stomach clenched when the numbers were read for the Falcon Point jewels.

"No." The muttered whisper escaped Cole, barely audible.

Isabelle quickly checked their captors to make sure they hadn't noticed his reaction. How had he even known which boxes belonged to his family? Her eyes landed on the log currently in Green Mask's hand. Cole must have read the box numbers when he'd signed it yesterday.

She put a hand on his elbow, the movement gaining unwanted attention. The pistol raised a fraction of an inch higher. "Don't move."

Isabelle's hand dropped back to her side.

One by one, the Falcon Point boxes were broken free of their individual metal compartments and laid out on the counter.

"These have secondary locks on them," Black Mask said.

"Break them open," Green Mask demanded with a wave of his gun.

Black Mask inserted lock picks into the side-by-side locks. A little jiggling was all it took before the locks snapped open. He pulled the lid up, opened a velvet box, and let out a low whistle. "We hit the jackpot."

"Is that them?"

"No, but if the rest of the stuff in these boxes is like this, we have a small fortune here."

Green Mask leaned forward to examine the pink diamond necklace.

Isabelle bent her knee so her foot lifted directly behind her. Moving slowly, she reached her hand back and removed her heel. She nudged Cole and handed him the shoe.

Confusion lit his features, but he accepted the offering.

Black Mask removed his lock picks and reached for the next box.

Green Mask stopped him. "We don't have time for that. We only have one more box to check. Get it first." He recited the number. This time, it was Cole's safe-deposit box.

Isabelle shifted her weight onto her stockinged foot. As soon as Green Mask's attention strayed to his partner's efforts to break open the last box, she quickly removed her other shoe and gripped it in her hand like a weapon.

Black Mask pulled Cole's box free and opened it. He retrieved the black velvet bag and looked inside. "Found them."

"Give them here." His partner dropped the log on the counter and stretched out his hand. As soon as Black Mask passed him the diamonds, satisfaction gleamed in his eyes. He slid the stones, still encased in the bag, into his pocket. "Grab those two boxes. I'll take this one."

Anticipation hummed through Isabelle. The moment the men picked up the safe-deposit boxes, she lifted her arm and sent her shoe flying.

Although there was no obvious sign of blood, the guard on the floor had yet to move. Marit had no way of knowing if the gunman had killed him. She only knew that he was not in any position to help them.

She glanced at the wall to her right. The light above the lift door indicated that it was stationed on the second floor. That had been Cole and Isabelle's destination. And as soon as they'd accessed the diamonds in the vault, her friends would ride it back down to the lobby. She took an unsteady breath. There was nothing she could do to warn them or to prevent them from stepping out as soon as the doors opened.

And then there was Lars. Would he notice how long she'd been gone? Would he assume she'd joined Cole and Isabelle, or would he come looking for her?

Behind her, the gunman with the gray mask was emptying the cashiers' drawers. Based on the steady thuds, he was rapidly working his way along the row of desks. At this rate, he'd be finished in no time. Then what? It was hard to believe that he and his sidekick would just walk out of the bank with a bag full of stolen euros and leave half a dozen witnesses behind.

The sounds of the gunman's progress stopped abruptly. He slammed something hard. "This last one's still locked."

The blue-masked gunman who'd been standing guard over them swore and stepped closer to his hostages. "You were told to unlock your drawers," he said, aiming his gun at the tellers one at a time. "Which of you didn't follow orders?"

The young man sitting near Marit swallowed loudly. His pale face now held a tinge of gray. She glanced at him anxiously, but the gunman's attention was on the older woman sitting in the center of the group.

He pointed his weapon at her chest. "You, Fräulein?"

She did not deny it.

"Did you really think you could get away with it?" he jeered.

Her shoulders tensed, and she closed her eyes.

The young man beside Marit flinched. "Leave Liselotte alone!" he yelled. "It was me. I left my drawer locked."

Instantly, the gunman swirled to face him, his gun raised.

Marit saw the gleam of satisfaction in his dark eyes and reacted before she had time to think through the ramifications. "No!" she screamed and threw herself at the young man, knocking him sideways as the gunshot sounded.

Cole's muscles tensed. Isabelle's aim was off. The shoe she hurled at the weapon-wielding robber clipped his wrist, but his pistol remained firmly gripped in his hand.

The green-masked robber dropped the safe-deposit boxes he held. Jewelry cases spilled out onto the floor.

Cole's heart seized when the man swung his pistol toward Isabelle. Too far away to grab the weapon, Cole threw Isabelle's other shoe. It caught Green Mask in the chest, and he aimed his gun toward Cole instead.

Two more safe-deposit boxes crashed to the floor when the gunman's partner freed his hands and reached for his weapon. As though by unspoken agreement, Isabelle struck the black-masked thief at the same time Cole kicked the gun from Green Mask's hand. The pistol skidded across the floor toward the vault entrance. Green Mask scrambled after it as Isabelle threw a wicked left jab at the other robber.

Cole grabbed Green Mask from behind before he could reach the fallen gun. The man thrust his elbow into Cole's ribs.

In a move aimed at self-preservation, Cole ignored the throbbing in his side and yanked Green Mask's arm. He succeeded in putting more distance between his opponent and the gun, but they had barely squared off before Green Mask's fist flew toward Cole's jaw.

Cole blocked the punch with one hand and delivered a punch of his own to the man's midsection.

Green Mask crashed against the table in the center of the room, and Cole checked on Isabelle just as her hand jutted out, palm first, and connected with the other man's nose. Satisfied that she could handle herself, Cole turned his back to Green Mask in the same moment another punch swung toward his face.

Cole ducked, the man's gloved knuckles grazing his jaw. Pain pulsed through Cole just as he lifted his own fist and plowed it into the other man's face. Cole swept his leg out to knock him off his feet, but Green Mask jumped up and avoided the contact. An instant later, Green Mask's leg extended, and he kicked Cole in the chest.

His balance compromised, Cole fell against the wall of safe-deposit boxes. The metal hinges gouged into his back, and he darted to the side to avoid the punch that followed.

Green Mask's fist whizzed past him and impacted the metal wall instead. He cried out, and Cole threw an elbow at his head.

Behind him, Isabelle's opponent grunted. An instant later, a gunshot fired. Cole turned, relieved that Isabelle was still vertical. Unfortunately, so was the man she was grappling with, and the man now had his gun in his hand. Isabelle threw another punch and sent Black Mask stumbling back a step.

Black Mask thrust his leg out, and his foot connected with Isabelle's stomach. The force of the kick sent her back several feet and knocked her to the ground.

With Green Mask still reeling, Cole rushed forward as Black Mask lifted his weapon and aimed. Cole knocked his hand sideways as another shot exploded through the air.

Cole grabbed the man's wrist and ripped the pistol out of his hand. Cole took a step back and aimed at his new opponent.

"Watch out!" Isabelle cried out.

Cole ducked. A bullet whizzed past. He returned fire, but Green Mask was already ducking out of the vault, his gun in one hand and a safe-deposit box in the other.

Black Mask started to follow, but Cole fired a warning shot, and he reconsidered.

"Hands where I can see them," Cole said in German.

Isabelle scrambled back to her feet and rushed after Green Mask.

"Isabelle! Wait!" Cole took a step toward the door, angling his body to make sure his weapon stayed trained on the remaining robber.

Before Cole reached the vault entrance, Isabelle reappeared. "I hit the silent alarm. The police should be here any minute, but this guy's partner got away."

Cole looked pointedly at their prisoner. "Maybe our friend here can tell us where we can find him."

Isabelle's eyebrows lifted, and she spoke in English. "I wouldn't count on it."

CHAPTER 11

LARS TOOK ONE MORE PHOTOGRAPH of St. Stephen's spire against the backdrop of the clear blue sky before turning his attention to the little girl chasing pigeons in front of the cathedral's steps. The child's cheeks were pink, her eyes sparkling with delight as the birds fluttered around her. He crouched to get a better angle, smiling at the little girl's giggles.

In the distance, a siren wailed, and the pigeons took flight. He snapped picture after picture, rising to his feet as the flock swooped around the plaza and took off over the cathedral.

When the last bird disappeared, Lars lowered his camera, his focus returning to the sirens. They were significantly louder now. The little girl who'd been chasing the birds covered her ears. Three men with their hands full ran across the plaza and disappeared into the entrance of the U-bahn station. At the nearby market, shoppers stopped what they were doing to watch four police cars with flashing lights peel around the corner and come to a screeching halt outside the bank.

Officers piled out of the cars, pedestrians scattered, and Lars's stomach clenched. Some of the policemen dropped into defensive positions behind their vehicles, weapons trained on the bank's doors. Two others started across the plaza, clearing the open area of people as they moved. With a few urgent shouts and a baby's cry, a cloud of fear and danger descended.

More distant sirens filled the air, but Lars didn't wait for their arrival. He took off running. Directly toward the bank.

"Stop right there!" One of the police officers stepped into his path.

Somewhere deep in his subconscious, Lars knew that forcing his way across the police blockade would not help Marit. Or Cole. Or Isabelle. But that did nothing to lessen his frustration. He slowed his steps, his chest tightening as the echo of Marit's parting laughter filled his mind.

Two ambulances pulled into the plaza, their sirens obliterating all other sound.

"What's going on in there?" Lars yelled.

The officer ignored him. His attention was on the garbled message coming through the walkie-talkie attached to his shoulder. The sirens turned off. The door to one of the ambulances popped open. Someone shouted an order, and half a dozen policemen wearing bulletproof vests and helmets started toward the bank doors.

"Tell me," Lars demanded.

The police officer's gaze was on his fellow officers' furtive progress up the stairs. "Someone triggered the bank's silent alarm. That's all I know."

Lars tried to move forward, but the policeman grabbed his arm.

"My girlfriend's in the bank." He spoke in German. "So's my cousin."

"And our job is to get them out safely," the officer said. "You can't—"

The walkie-talkie crackled to life again. The officer turned his head to listen. Lars could only hear his heart pounding. If anything happened to Marit now . . . He couldn't finish the thought. Instead, he focused on Cole. He'd witnessed his cousin disarm a hired gun at the hospital in Amsterdam. If Cole was with Isabelle and Marit, there was a good chance they'd make it out unscathed. *If.* With clenched fists, he watched the officers approach the bank's doors. He'd never pinned more hope on that unreliable word.

An unnatural hush fell over the plaza. Vaguely aware that a crowd had gathered at the edge of the market, Lars stayed crouched behind the police car. Watching. Waiting.

The bank doors opened. Two armed officers went in. Seconds later, four more followed. Silence. Lars forced himself to breathe. A voice came over the walkie-talkie, the words fast and urgent. Four paramedics took off, medical bags in hand. They raced up the steps and disappeared into the bank. Lars had waited long enough. If unarmed paramedics could go in, so could he. He started around the vehicle.

"Hey!" The police officer followed, but before he reached Lars, the bank doors opened again. A woman exited. She hurried down the steps, scanning the area as though looking for someone. Lars's mouth went dry. It was Isabelle. But where was Marit?

"Isabelle!" he called.

She spotted him and veered in his direction. The policeman stepped between them. Undeterred, Isabelle acknowledged the man's presence with a professional nod. "He's with me," she said, flashing her ID at the officer. "And he's needed in the bank."

The policeman's eyes narrowed. "Just because you work at the bank doesn't mean you can invite a civilian into a crime scene, Ms. Roberts."

She glanced at the name badge on his uniform. "Understood, Sergeant Schneider. But your supervisor, Detective Meyer, has requested his help to identify items stolen from the bank vault."

Lars stared at her. The bank vault. Did she mean Cole's bag of diamonds, or was she referring to the Falcon Point jewelry?

Sergeant Schneider's expression remained skeptical, but he pushed the button on his walkie-talkie and spoke into it. The response was instant. Squaring his shoulders, he stepped aside. "You're free to go," he said curtly.

Lars didn't need a second invitation. He took Isabelle's arm and propelled her toward the bank. "What happened? Is Marit okay?"

"An armed robbery. And, yes, Marit is fine."

Relief made his limbs weak. "What about Cole?"

"He's talking to the detective inside."

They'd reached the bank doors. Lars reached for the handle. He needed to see Marit—to hold Marit—for himself.

"Lars." Isabelle's voice was strained.

He paused, turning to face her.

"Before you go in," she said. "You need to know. Three of the four perpetrators got away. And they took some of your family's jewelry with them."

Cole escaped the bank the moment he finished giving his statement to the police. No matter what the police thought, the men behind the robbery weren't typical bank robbers. They were connected to Rogers's kidnapping. What Cole didn't know was how.

Maybe with his access to CIA resources, he could identify who was behind the recent criminal activity and recover the stolen Falcon Point jewels.

His gut twisted at the memory. He had watched it happen. If he hadn't stayed with Isabelle, he might have caught the other thief. Then again, he could have gotten shot for his efforts. Either way, he'd made his choice. Isabelle's safety had taken priority over recovering his family's treasures.

Even though he hated to leave Lars and Marit behind, he couldn't delay in reporting the incident to his superiors. He made it as far as the U-bahn station before an unsettling question broke through his thoughts: How had the men in the vault known the jewels were there? Cole hadn't put that detail into his official report. The only person he had shared it with was Jasmine.

The idea that Jasmine could have compromised the information surfaced only to be discarded. No way he believed for a minute that she had leaked intelligence, and the possibility of her working with the people who had kidnapped Rogers was downright ludicrous. The woman's loyalty to the United States ran as deep as anyone's he'd ever known, including his own family.

Cole replayed his last conversation with her. She knew where the diamonds were stored as well as when he planned to transport them. When he'd spoken to her on the phone, she hadn't repeated anything he'd said, and Cole's office in Vienna had been empty at the time of their conversation. She must have put the details in a report. The question was, Who had seen it? If it had stayed in-house at the CIA's Budapest station, the number of suspects would be minimal. If not, the possibilities would increase dramatically. Regardless, the CIA had a mole somewhere within her midst.

Determined to assess the possibilities, Cole made his way to the Vienna field office. He had barely walked in when his boss approached with Zoe, their finance officer, right behind her.

"Where have you been?" Gwendolyn asked. "We need to coordinate the transport of the diamonds you confiscated and get them to the embassy."

"How did you know about the diamonds?" Cole asked.

"It was in the incident report from the hostage rescue," Gwendolyn said. "The Budapest chief of station called me this morning to find out if we had inventoried the diamonds yet."

Technically, Lars had a detailed inventory of the gems as well as the serial number on the one diamond, but Cole wasn't about to share that information. Not until he knew who was leaking intel.

"I'm afraid we won't be able to do a detailed inventory," Cole said. "The bank was robbed today. The diamonds were among the items stolen from the safe-deposit boxes."

"What?" Gwendolyn's tone sharpened with accusation.

Zoe's eyes widened. "You secured a million euros' worth of diamonds, and now they're gone?"

"Yeah." Cole's jaw clenched, and a new wave of frustration snaked through him. "They're gone."

"How am I supposed to report this?" Zoe looked from Cole to Gwendolyn, clearly distressed.

"Pull the police report and add it to my statement of fact," Cole said. "This isn't the first time evidence has disappeared."

"But I've never had to report it before," Zoe said. "And for this much money, you can be sure there will be an audit."

"Sorry, Zoe." Cole headed for his desk.

Gwendolyn followed. "Are you sure the diamonds were stolen?"

"I was in the safe-deposit vault to retrieve them when the robbery went down." He pulled out his desk chair. "And yes, I have a witness."

"I want the full police report on my desk by close of business today."

"The police are still questioning witnesses, but I'll put in the request," Cole said.

"Make sure you cc me on all correspondence."

"Yes, ma'am." Cole offered a mock salute.

Irritation flared on Gwendolyn's face, but Cole ignored it. The woman was a micromanager to a fault. She couldn't help it, but he didn't have to like it.

He booted up his computer and put in the request for the police report. After he completed that task, he retrieved the after-action report Jasmine had filed last night. Sure enough, she had included a detailed description of the diamonds. She also noted where Cole had secured them and when he planned to deposit them in the embassy vault.

Cole grabbed the secure phone on his desk and dialed Jasmine's number. As far as he could tell, her report had been sent only to the Budapest and Vienna offices, but he needed to know if she had shared the contents with anyone else.

Jasmine's phone rang once and went straight to voice mail. Cole's eyes narrowed. She hadn't mentioned traveling today, and that was the only reason her phone should be off this time of day.

He searched his CIA directory and dialed again, this time calling the chief of station in Budapest.

"This is Don."

"I'm sorry to bother you," Cole began before introducing himself. "This is Cole from the Vienna station. I'm trying to get in touch with Jasmine Reynolds. She was working out of your office yesterday."

"Yes. She filed her report last night, but I haven't seen her since this morning."

"When we were on our stakeout, she said she wasn't heading back to Germany until tomorrow. Any idea where she might be?"

"None. Her travel order is out of the Frankfurt station, so I'm not sure what her plans were."

"How's Rogers doing?"

"The hospital kept him overnight, but he should get released today."

"Good to hear."

"Since I have you on the phone, can you tell me how I ended up with a bunch of operatives in my backyard without my people knowing about it?"

He could, but he wasn't going to. Cas's involvement had dictated the need to use only operatives who were aware of the guardian program. Apparently Don and his people didn't fit that requirement.

"We were just following a lead," Cole said. "When we found out Rogers was inside, we didn't have time to call for backup."

"Do me a favor and let me know next time you're in my city. I don't like being in the dark and getting my intel from reading reports about what happens in my area."

"Understood," Cole said. "If you do see Jasmine, could you please have her call me?"

"I'll pass the message on to my secretary."

"I appreciate it." Cole hung up. He put in a leave request to take the rest of the day off, logged off his computer, and headed for the exit. He wasn't about to wait for Gwendolyn to tell him he had to stay at work. He needed intel, and he needed to work with people he could trust.

CHAPTER 12

COLE ENTERED HIS APARTMENT. EMPTY. He had expected Lars to be back by now. Guilt tugged at him. Maybe he should have waited at the bank until they could all leave together. He grabbed his phone, but instead of dialing, he continued into his bedroom and unlocked the safe tucked away in the bottom of his closet. He pulled out his second cell phone, the one he carried with him only when on assignment so he could contact Cas if he got into trouble.

He dialed her number.

"This is Ghost."

"Cas, it's Cole."

"You'd better be alone if you're using my real name."

"I'm alone," Cole confirmed before muttering, "but not by choice."

He'd come so close to bridging the gap between himself and Isabelle today. He would have succeeded had it not been for the ill-timed robbery. Then again, when was it a convenient time to get robbed?

"What's going on?" Cas asked, pulling him out of his thoughts.

"The diamonds we recovered in Budapest were stolen today."

"What happened?"

"I had my cousin check them out last night at the bank where he was inventorying some other jewelry," Cole said. "Since it was getting late, I locked the diamonds in a safe-deposit box. When I went back to get them, a couple thugs showed up."

"Were they looking for the diamonds specifically?"

"Oh yeah." Cole described how they had used the sign-in log to narrow their search to the boxes accessed yesterday. "Unfortunately, they also got away with a large box filled with jewelry from my family's estate."

"Sorry, Cole. Any idea how these guys knew to look for the diamonds at the bank?"

Cole loved how Cas could get right to the heart of the problem. "That's what I need your help with. Jasmine put the details in a report last night, but she's the only person who knew about the diamonds."

"What about the bank staff? Could someone have leaked it?"

"Highly unlikely. The bank employee who rented me the safe-deposit box is NOC," Cole said, using the shorthand term for a CIA operative under a nonofficial cover. "She was with me when the burglary happened, and there's no way she was involved. Beyond her, only my cousin and his girlfriend have seen the diamonds, but I never told them where they came from."

"You think the leak came from inside the CIA?"

"Yes. Not only that—Jasmine's phone is off. I hoped you could run a search to see if she's on a flight back to Frankfurt."

"That's easy enough. Hold on." The clicking of computer keys carried over the line. "No. She isn't on any flights, at least not under her name or her CIA alias."

Cole fought back his rising concern. "I have no idea where she is or why she isn't answering."

"You don't think she's the leak, do you?"

"Not a chance." Focusing on the other possibilities, he said, "I know my boss accessed Jasmine's report. Any chance you can see who else did? If it's only been seen in the Budapest and Vienna offices, the list of suspects is limited."

"I'll see what I can find and call you back."

"Thanks." As an afterthought, Cole said, "One more thing."

"What's that?"

"I want you to clear my cousin and his girlfriend so they can help me in my search."

"You want me to what?" Disbelief punctuated Cas's words. "I can't just clear civilians to access classified material."

"I can keep their access to classified material to a minimum, but Lars has connections to the jewelry industry that may help us find answers we can't get on our own."

"What kind of name is Lars?"

"Dutch. He's from the Netherlands. His full name is Lars Hendriks."

"Your cousin isn't even American?"

"Nope. His girlfriend is Dutch too. Marit Jansen."

Cas sighed. "You really are a challenge."

"Yeah, but you love me anyway."

"You keep telling yourself that." She blew out a frustrated breath. "I'll get back to you."

"As soon as possible," Cole said.

"In my job, that's always the case."

Lars tightened his grip on Marit's hand. She hadn't let go since they'd walked out of the bank together. Not that he was complaining; he wouldn't want it any other way. But she'd hardly said a word on the U-bahn train, and now that they were within half a block of Cole's flat, Lars was starting to wonder if it would have been better to meet Cole at Marit's hotel. At least there she had a comfortable bed and room service.

If it weren't so important that he speak with Cole right away about the loss of the Falcon Point jewelry, he wouldn't have brought Marit to his cousin's flat at all. But by the time Lars had finished giving the detective a full list of all the items missing from the vault, Cole had left and he wasn't answering his phone. Lars guessed he was reporting the diamonds' theft to the powers that be at the embassy. He didn't envy him that job. Then again, Cole may make Lars inform the rest of the family of the significant loss to the family's estate, and he suspected that telling their cousin, Anna, might be worse than confessing to an outside authority.

His mounting concern over Marit's well-being wasn't helping the sick feeling associated with the loss of such irreplaceable items either. He glanced at her. The light in her eyes had yet to return.

"You okay?" he asked. It was a stupid question. Of course she wasn't. But his brain was devoid of a post-hostage-situation conversation starter.

She managed a weak smile and nodded.

Lars mentally relegated "You okay?" to *non*conversation-starter status and tried again. "Would it help to talk about it?"

"I don't know."

"You could try, and if it's too hard, you can stop."

Marit caught her bottom lip between her teeth, and Lars had a sinking suspicion she might be fighting tears.

"The same scenes from inside the bank keep playing over and over in my head. And even though you're with me and we're nowhere near Stephansplatz anymore, they won't go away."

Lars had noticed the splintered wood on the front of the counter as soon as he'd walked into the bank's lobby. It didn't take a forensic expert to know a bullet had caused it. And given the paramedics' feverish activity around the guard lying on the floor, it was obvious that his condition was serious.

"Marit, what you went through today . . ." He stopped walking and turned to face her. "You wouldn't be human if it didn't affect you. You don't have to try to push the experience aside or block it out like nothing happened. It did happen. And it's okay to give yourself time to get over it and to admit that you were scared. I was scared too."

Her lower lip was definitely quivering now, and tears had filled her eyes. Without a word, he released her hand and wrapped his arms around her, pulling her close. Clutching his jacket, she laid her cheek against his chest.

"The gunman was going to shoot one of the tellers because he left his cash drawer locked," she said. "I . . . I was sitting next to him. I pushed the teller over, and the bullet hit the counter behind us." She shuddered. "It was so loud. So close. The gunman probably would have tried again, but another one burst out of the stairwell and yelled at the two in the lobby to get out of there. When they opened the doors, I heard the sirens."

"And that's when Cole and Isabelle showed up."

Isabelle had told Lars that they'd reached the lobby soon after the gunmen had fled.

"Yes." Marit raised her head. She was crying. "And then the police and the paramedics. And you."

Lars released a tense breath. He'd crossed the foyer at a run to reach her, gratitude that she appeared uninjured threatening to overwhelm him.

"Thank goodness Isabelle got me in." He pressed a kiss to Marit's forehead before gently wiping the tears off her cheeks with his thumbs. "Not sure the officer could have kept me behind police lines much longer."

She smiled. It was small, but it was an improvement over her last attempt.

"Come on," he said, taking her hand again. "I think I remember seeing Belgian hot chocolate packets in one of Cole's kitchen cupboards. According to my sister, that makes everything better."

CHAPTER 13

MARIT FOLLOWED LARS UP THE stairs to Cole's flat and waited while he unlocked the door. She wasn't sure what she would have done without his steadying presence the last hour or so. She'd held it together at the bank—during the robbery and the police questioning afterward. It had only been when she'd removed herself from the situation and had taken the time to reflect on how close she'd come to not making it out alive that any emotions had set in.

"It looks like Cole's beaten us here," Lars said, pushing open the door and gesturing her inside ahead of him.

Marit entered a small living room divided from an even smaller kitchen by a short counter. Two sofas took up most of the space in the living room. They looked to be relatively new, but one was a bit more faded than the other and was almost completely hidden beneath an untidy heap of bedding.

The overhead light was on, and as Lars followed her inside, Cole appeared in the doorway that she assumed led to a bedroom.

"Hi," he said. "I'm glad you're here. Sorry I had to leave the bank so fast."

"No problem." Lars was hurriedly relocating the bedding onto one corner of the sofa. "It took me a while to go through the Falcon Point inventory. I figured you needed to be somewhere else."

"Yeah." Cole rubbed the back of his neck, his stress obvious. "After what happened at the bank today, we've got some pretty big issues to deal with."

"Like how long we wait to tell your grandfather, Tess, and Anna about the robbery," Lars said.

Cole grimaced. "Among other things."

"How bad is the loss of the diamonds, Cole?" Marit asked.

"Pretty bad," he said. "My boss isn't happy, obviously. The stones were worth a lot. But the bigger concern is, How did those men know they were in the vault?"

Lars walked into the kitchen and started rummaging through the cupboards. "What makes you think they did?"

"Because Isabelle and I were there when they arrived. They had an agenda."

Lars set two mugs on the counter. "What d'you mean?"

"They were after the safe-deposit boxes that had been accessed in the last twenty-four hours."

"Couldn't that mean they were looking for the Falcon Point jewelry rather than the diamonds?" Marit asked.

"Not likely. Based on their reactions when they opened the boxes, I'd say the jewelry was a bonus. They were searching for the bag I brought in."

"Well, the bonus is worth a lot more than your diamonds," Lars muttered. He emptied a hot chocolate packet into each cup.

Cole raised an eyebrow. "Help yourself," he said dryly.

"Marit needs one."

Cole's look of exasperation melted into one of contrition. "Sorry, Marit. I should've asked. How are you doing?"

Shaky. Empty. Afraid of being alone. She wasn't ready to admit those things in front of Cole even if Lars already suspected them. "I guess I'm still trying to wrap my mind around what happened," she said.

"I think we all are."

"Lars said hot chocolate would help."

Cole turned back to Lars. "You'd better make that three cups."

Lars grabbed another mug and filled the kettle with water. "It seems to me that you're messing with the wrong people if they're willing to stage an armed bank robbery to get the diamonds back."

"That's a given," Cole said grimly. "Where did the gems come from, and where are they going? That's what's more to the point."

"I don't know if it's helpful or not, but the two gunmen in the bank lobby weren't locals," Marit said.

She had Cole's full attention immediately.

"How do you know?" he asked.

"Their accents. They both spoke fluent German, but one of them spoke like a Berliner. And I think the other was from Slovakia."

"Slovakia? Are you sure?" For some reason, this seemed really important to Cole.

Marit allowed her thoughts to dwell on the man who'd pointed a gun at the teller. She attempted to block out the vision of his cruel sneer and focused on his voice. "Yes," she said. "It was the way he pronounced his vowels. He sounded like one of the makeup artists who sometimes works with me. She's from Bratislava."

Cole paced across the small room, his expression thoughtful. Lars pulled his phone out of his pocket and scrolled through a few pages before stopping to read something. "My contact at Coster Diamonds wrote back," he said.

Cole stopped pacing to listen.

"The certification associated with the serial number on the diamond in your bag was verified at the Munich Jewelry Show last month."

"Did he give you a name?" he asked.

"Hans Koch is the seller, but no buyer's name is listed." Lars frowned. "If it wasn't registered under a new name, there's no way of knowing who left with it."

Isabelle downloaded the security tape for the bank for the past twenty-four hours and pulled the memory stick out of her computer. After she slipped it into her purse, she logged out and made her way to the parking garage. At least she had driven to work today instead of taking the U-bahn, though her plan to stop by the market on her way home no longer held any appeal. After going through her statement with the police, filling out a report for her superiors, and sending a more detailed report to the CIA, she was mentally and emotionally exhausted.

She should go home, yet when she pulled out of the parking garage, she turned toward Cole's apartment rather than her own. She was perfectly capable of reviewing the security feed herself, but she suspected Cole had a good idea of who the bank robbers were and why they had been after the diamonds in his safe-deposit box.

She pulled up to a stop light, and her cell phone rang. She pressed the button on her steering wheel to answer it. "Hello?"

"Isabelle, it's Gerhart. I just heard what happened. Are you all right?"

"I'm fine, but both of our guards were injured."

"Yes, I heard. They are both at the hospital, but it appears they will recover."

Isabelle had already received that information before she'd left, but she said, "That's good to hear."

"Yes, it is." He paused. "There is another matter I'm reluctant to bring up." Another pause. "Because you were present in the safe-deposit vault at the time of the robbery, you will need to be placed on administrative leave until after the police investigation concludes."

Isabelle absorbed the implication and the sting that came with it. It was standard policy, she reminded herself. "I understand. Do you have any idea how long the police investigation will take?"

"At least a week. If you have anything you need from your office, let me know, and I can arrange for one of the guards to escort you up there."

Cut off from her resources. Great. "Thank you, I will."

She maintained her professional tone while she said her goodbyes, but she couldn't fight the unsettled feeling that churned in her stomach.

Her fingers tightened on the steering wheel. This afternoon had started with so much promise, and now the day was ending with her being sidelined for one job and ineffective for the other. She could hardly help the CIA monitor suspicious money transfers if she couldn't access her bank's financial systems.

She forced her thoughts away from her phone conversation with Gerhart and tried to focus on her unexpected outing with Cole. The roses had been out of character for him but not completely surprising after their talk last night. She had been determined to ignore his attempts to break through the wall she had built around her heart, but the grand gesture of a picnic lunch in a carriage ride had chipped away a few pieces.

Maybe more than a few pieces.

She couldn't believe she'd nearly kissed him in the vault. What had she been thinking? One pleasant outing and she was ready to let him scale her defenses? Had he really missed her while he'd been gone, or was she simply a challenge he wanted to overcome to prove he could win? She wasn't sure, nor did she know him well enough to gauge his sincerity. The man was as good at hiding his inner thoughts and feelings as she was.

Needing a distraction, she flipped on the radio. The local news station cut from a commercial to the next segment. Not surprisingly, the bank robbery was the lead story.

After listing the basic facts, the newscaster segued into the next story. "New reports have surfaced about the bombing in Frankfurt. Authorities suspect a band of refugees from Syria are behind the attack. A second bombing occurred two hours ago in Berlin. The police have taken more than two dozen Syrian refugees into custody for questioning."

A bank robbery *and* two bombings. Isabelle let out a sigh. What would be next?

CHAPTER 14

COLE SIPPED THE LAST OF his hot chocolate. Lars was right. Hot chocolate did make things better. Since drinking hers, Marit's color had improved significantly, and the stark terror Cole had seen in Lars's eyes when he'd first entered the bank had faded.

Cole had already sent a secure text to Cas with the update of Marit's description of the bank robbers who had been in the lobby. Rogers had been kidnapped from Bratislava. If Marit was right, one of the men at the bank today was from there. Cole couldn't ignore the common theme running between the two events.

His secure cell phone buzzed in his pocket. He stood and pulled it free. "Excuse me for a minute." He headed into his bedroom and closed the door. Certain Cas was the caller, he answered and asked, "Anything new?"

"I'm afraid so," Cas said. "Eight people accessed the after-action report from Budapest before the robbery. I emailed you their names."

Eight. Not a huge number but still larger than he'd hoped. "I guess it could be worse."

"I'm afraid it is. Jasmine has gone dark."

"Excuse me?"

"You heard me. She's disappeared, and it's clear she doesn't want to be found," Cas said, obviously frustrated. "She didn't claim her cell phone when she left the Budapest station this morning. She isn't using public transportation. She's vanished."

"You don't think she's involved with the diamond theft." Cole shook his head even though Cas couldn't see him through the phone. "There's no way."

"I'm not sure if the diamonds are connected to her disappearance, but you have to admit the timing is suspicious."

"Very suspicious, but how do we know Jazz wasn't taken hostage by whoever grabbed Rogers?"

"It's possible, but why wouldn't she have taken her cell phone with her when she passed through security?"

"Can you get the video feed from when she left?" Cole asked. "Maybe someone from inside the station is responsible for her disappearance."

"I already looked. When she walked out, she was alone. She waved at the guard and acted like everything was fine."

"If Jazz went dark, she has to have a good reason."

"I agree," Cas said. "The only two reasons I can think of are she is either involved in the diamond robbery—"

"Not a chance."

"Or she's hiding from whoever leaked the location of the diamonds to the guys who hit the bank."

"But how did she know?" Cole asked. He lowered his voice and added, "The station chief said he hadn't seen her since this morning, but the robbery didn't happen until this afternoon."

"That's a good question," Cas said. "For now, we need to do some searching without the CIA being involved."

"Easy for you to say. You're set up to access information at home. I'm not."

"You're about to be," Cas said.

"I'm not following."

"Walk out of your apartment. I left a package for you."

Cole left his bedroom and passed Marit and Lars on the couch.

"Everything okay?" Lars asked.

"I'm about to find out." With the phone still pressed to his ear, Cole opened the door. A shipping box lay outside his apartment, his name printed on a shipping label. He picked it up. "This is from you?"

"Yes," Cas said. "You have three secure laptops, and they're marked for who can use which one. I already loaded this morning's surveillance feed from the Budapest station on yours."

Cole closed the door and carried the package back into his room. As soon as he closed himself inside, he said, "You know I have two civilians with me right now."

"I cleared your civilians like you asked. You have three laptops because you need help beyond what I'm going to be able to provide."

"They can help me?" Cole asked. He hadn't expected Cas to grant his request.

"Yes, but you need to avoid giving them access to information about agency personnel," Cas said. "See if they can help you trace the diamonds. I also already loaded the surveillance feed from the Munich Jewelry Show last month. Maybe your cousin and his friend can figure out who bought the diamond Lars was tracing."

"How did you know about that? Lars just got the email a few minutes ago."

"He read it a few minutes ago. It was sent two hours ago."

"You're reading my cousin's email?"

"You did ask me to clear him," Cas reminded him.

"Okay, good point." Cole blew out a breath. "Where do I need to focus my attention?"

"We need to find out what those diamonds are funding and what's going on in Bratislava that we don't know about."

"What about you?" Cole asked. "Are you joining in the search?"

"I have to deal with these latest bombings first. Something isn't quite right about them."

"There's never anything right about a bombing."

"I know, but the news keeps hitting sooner than it should."

Concern rose inside him as memories of an old case surfaced. "You don't think Steven Powell is behind this?"

"I have to consider the possibility," she said.

Cole thought through the impact of Cas's words. It had been only a few months ago that they had put a stop to Powell's recent reign of terror. As far as they could tell, the reason for that string of bombings had been two-fold: to eliminate an old professional rival and to build his news empire. Deep down, Cole suspected the man was just as interested in playing with world events for his own amusement as he was for anything else.

"The man is a narcissist," Cole said, "but I thought we had cut off his finances."

"So did I," Cas said, her voice grim. "I'll call you when I know more. In the meantime, answer your door."

"Why? Not another package."

"No, but your girlfriend is there."

"Isabelle?" Cole asked, but the line went dead.

A knock sounded, and a moment later, Isabelle's voice joined Lars's. Cole picked up the box and carried it back into the living room. He set it on the counter and studied the woman who had only hours earlier helped him fight off two armed men. Their eyes met, but her expression didn't reveal her emotions about what had almost happened in the vault or the conflict that had followed their almost kiss.

As much to satisfy himself as to comfort her, he crossed to her and drew her into his arms. "I'm glad you're here."

Her arms came up to rest on his back. "Me too."

Cole held her for a moment, and when he pulled back, he caught a glimpse of frustration in her eyes. "Are you doing okay?" he asked.

"Yeah, except I just found out that I'm being placed on administrative leave until after the police investigation."

"Why?" Marit asked.

"Standard procedure," Isabelle said. "I accessed the safe-deposit vault right before the robbery took place, so that means I need to be cleared of any wrong-doing before I can go back to work."

"That's so unfair."

"I agree, but there's nothing I can do about it." Her gaze landed on the box, and her eyebrows lifted.

Though Isabelle didn't voice a question, he could hear it as if she had spoken. Her curiosity of whether he was expecting a package and what it contained was written all over her face. He ripped off the brown packaging tape and opened the flaps. Then he pulled out a box with a picture of a laptop on it. Cole's name was written on the outside. He set it aside and pulled out the other two, one with Lars's name and the other with Isabelle's.

Cole glanced at Isabelle. "Looks like someone knew you were coming."

Lars crossed to the counter, a confused expression on his face. "New computers? I don't understand."

"These are secure laptops so we can research the diamonds and where they came from," Cole said. "The laptop with your name on it has the surveillance feed from the jewelry show in Munich."

"How did you get that?" Lars asked.

Cole shrugged. "I guess I have friends in the right places."

CHAPTER 15

LARS LEANED BACK AND ROLLED his shoulders. He and Marit had been hunched over the laptop Cole had given him for hours. At this point, he wasn't sure what ached more, his back or his eyes.

"Need a break?" Marit asked.

"Yeah."

She pressed a key to pause the grainy video. The progress bar showed up at the bottom of the screen. It was discouragingly short.

"At this rate, we'll be here for weeks," she said. She'd obviously noticed it too.

"If we're still doing this weeks from now, you'll have to check me into a padded cell," Lars said.

She laughed softly. "I'll join you."

He looked over at Cole and Isabelle. They were sitting on the opposite sofa, each fully engrossed in whatever was on their respective computer screens. Lars had no idea what they were working on. Based on the fact that they had yet to raise their heads, it had to be more captivating than the video feed of people wandering around a jewelry show.

"Can we switch movies?" he said. "Yours must be better than ours."

"Hmm?" Cole's distracted grunt was only marginally better than Isabelle's continued silence.

"They're definitely watching something more exciting than us," Lars said. "I've never known Cole to forget about dinner."

Marit glanced at her phone, her eyes widening when she saw the time. "We've been at this for hours."

"Tell me about it. My stomach's going to start eating my liver pretty soon."

"What was that?" Cole said. "Are you guys hungry?"

Lars rolled his eyes. "It's been about five hours since our hot chocolate break."

Cole shut his computer with a snap. Startled, Isabelle looked up from her screen.

"Time to eat," he announced. "What sounds good? Chinese, pizza, or Indian?"

"Whatever's fastest," Lars said.

"Chinese." Cole picked up his phone and opened an app. "The restaurant is three doors down the street. What does everyone want?"

Isabelle didn't know how Cole had gained access to secure laptops, and she didn't dare ask the question in front of Lars and Marit. Regardless, for the past several hours she had scoured through surveillance video tapes from the bank and tried matching the identities of the burglars to known associates of the men who had been involved in the recent kidnapping of a CIA agent from Bratislava. Marit's descriptions from the bank had helped her narrow her suspect list, and she hoped by compiling a lineup of photos that Marit would be able to help shorten it further.

Beside her, Cole stood. "Our food should be ready in a few minutes. I'll be back."

Isabelle debated whether she should offer to pick it up so she could stretch her legs. Lars must have had the same idea. He stretched his hands above his head. "I could use some fresh air. Want me to pick it up?"

"That would be great, if you don't mind," Cole said.

"Want to come with me, Marit?"

She hesitated briefly before nodding. "I think a walk would do me good."

"Where is the Chinese food place again?" Lars asked.

Cole gave him the directions to the restaurant where Cole had taken Isabelle the first night they'd met. Maybe it was just as well that she wasn't picking up their food. She wasn't sure she wanted to relive good memories when so many bad ones had followed.

Cole handed Lars some euros, and a minute later, Isabelle and Cole were left alone. Then again, maybe she should have offered to pick up the food.

Cole settled back beside her, and his arm brushed against hers. Her heartbeat quickened, but she forced her breathing to remain steady.

"Any luck with IDing our guys from today?" Cole asked.

"Nothing definitive." She rolled her shoulders to combat the tightness that had settled there. "How did you get these computers? Did Gwendolyn approve you working from home?"

"No. I'll have to either take leave or see if I can fake a travel order so I can stay out of the office for the next few days."

Isabelle turned to face him. "Why would you do that?"

"We have a leak in the agency. No one besides the two of us, Lars, and Marit knew where those diamonds were being stored except the people who read the after-action report from when we went in after Rogers."

"Is that what you've been working on? Trying to find the leak?"

"Yeah. Unfortunately, we've only managed to narrow it down to someone in either the Budapest or the Vienna field offices. I'm down to seven people who saw the report who could have been involved."

"That's not a lot of people."

"No, but it's a long way from eliminating everyone but one."

"True." Isabelle set her laptop aside and stood. "Is it okay if I get some water?"

"It is, but I'll get it for you." Cole rose and crossed to the kitchen.

"How much do Lars and Marit know about what you do for a living?" Isabelle followed him, stopping at the counter that separated the living room from the kitchen.

"They both think I'm an embassy worker," Cole said.

"You never answered my question. Where did the laptops come from? They have the same encryption as what the agency uses."

Cole poured both of them a glass of water. He handed one to Isabelle and leaned against the counter behind him with his own. "Have you ever heard of the guardians?"

"Guardians? No."

"They're a group of undercover operatives. They help out agents who get into trouble, particularly in sensitive situations."

"I heard someone talk about a ghost one time when I was at headquarters, but it sounded like some kind of myth to me."

"Ghost is the name they go by, but they aren't a myth," Cole said. "One of them is working with me. She's the one who delivered the laptops and fed us the intel we're going through."

"She?" Unwanted jealousy flared.

Cole set down his water and skirted around the edge of the counter so there were no longer any barriers between them. "I'm not interested in her or any other woman except you." He reached for her hand, and Isabelle's heart hammered in her chest.

"Cole, I can't go through another six months of you toying with my emotions."

"I have no intention of messing this up." He edged closer and leaned in. "I missed you."

"I missed you too." The truth escaped her. "I was mad at you for making me miss you."

"Give me a second chance?" Cole asked. "Please?"

Isabelle hesitated. She wanted Cole in her life but not if another heartbreak was going to follow. Before she could formulate a decision, Cole's lips brushed against hers.

Her heart bounced into her throat, and her stomach flip-flopped.

Cole's free hand slid around her waist to draw her closer. A shiver rippled through her, and for a moment, the months apart faded from her mind. Unable to resist, she let herself fall into the kiss, the sensation even sweeter than she remembered.

The door opened, and Isabelle pulled away.

Cole groaned. "We really have to work on our timing."

Her heart still hammering in her chest, she fought back a smile. If Cole was this annoyed at being interrupted, maybe he did care. A ray of hope sparked inside her. Maybe this time would be different.

Cole checked the time on his laptop and set the device aside. "I think we should call it a night. I can't see straight anymore."

"Good idea," Lars agreed.

Isabelle yawned. "Is it really midnight?"

"It is," Cole said. "We could all use some sleep."

Marit glanced from Lars to Cole and back to Lars again. "I hate to ask, but would one of you mind escorting me back to my hotel? After what happened today, I'm a little nervous about going on the U-bahn alone."

"Maybe you should stay here tonight," Lars suggested. "We can kick Cole out of his room and let you sleep in there."

Cole started to protest but thought better of it. If it were Isabelle in the same situation, he wouldn't want her sleeping on a lumpy couch. Plus, women tended to appreciate privacy, especially in such cramped quarters.

"I have my car with me," Isabelle said. "I had to park a couple blocks away, but if you don't mind a little bit of a walk, I'll take you to your hotel." She yawned again.

Cole put his hand on her knee as an unexpected wave of concern surfaced. "You shouldn't be driving. You can barely keep your eyes open."

"I'll be okay." She blinked several times as though trying to remind herself that she was still awake.

"Stay here tonight," Cole said. "I have a futon mattress in my closet. You and Marit can have my room. Lars and I can sleep out here."

"My apartment is only twenty minutes away."

"Even if it were five minutes, you're exhausted," Cole said. "We all had a long day. Besides, if you both stay here, we can start on the surveillance video again first thing in the morning."

Isabelle exchanged a glance with Marit. "Just like a man to think we'll want to stay in the same clothes for two days in a row."

"Fine. You can go home and change in the morning," Cole said. "After you get some sleep."

"Cole is right," Lars added. "Besides, I'm sure between me and Cole, we have something the two of you can use for pajamas."

"I even have extra toothbrushes." Cole squeezed her knee. "I bought a four pack last time I was at the store."

Marit looked at Isabelle. "What do you think? Are you up for a slumber party?"

"I have to admit I am pretty wiped out," Isabelle said.

"What can you offer us for pajamas?" Marit asked.

"I'll go check." Cole stood and started toward his bedroom. As an afterthought, he turned back. "Lars, I get the couch by the window."

"But that's the one I was going to sleep on. The other one's lumpy."

Cole grinned. "I know."

CHAPTER 16

MARIT WOKE TO THE SOUND of rustling sheets. She opened her eyes. There was just enough light in the room to make out a figure straightening the bedding on Cole's bed.

"Isabelle," she whispered.

The figure turned. "Marit. I'm sorry. Did I wake you?"

"It's okay." Marit raised herself into a sitting position on the futon mattress. "What are you doing?"

"I'm going to run home and change," she said. "I figured if I went early enough, I could bring breakfast back with me." She paused. "Do you want me to drop you off at your hotel on my way?"

Taking a shower and putting on clean clothes did sound appealing, but Marit knew a detour like that would slow Isabelle down considerably.

"You go ahead," she said. "I'll head over there later this morning."

"If you're sure." Isabelle picked up her purse from beside the bed. "I'm going to try to slip out without waking the guys. Let them know I'll be back soon."

"I will."

Marit watched her open the door and close it quietly behind her. She waited a couple of minutes. No sound came from the adjoining room. It appeared that the men slept more soundly than she did. She picked up her phone. Six twenty-two. After going to bed so late last night, it was unlikely that the men would be up anytime soon. She should probably try to get more sleep too. But the terrifying images of the bank robbery that had kept her awake until the early hours of the morning lingered.

She'd been grateful for Lars's invitation to stay here. Having Isabelle in the same room and knowing that he and Cole were next door had helped immeasurably when darkness had left her alone with her thoughts. She shook her head. Closing her eyes again was not worth the very real risk of a nightmare.

Tossing the blanket aside, she climbed off the futon and tugged Cole's sweatpants up. They were warm and comfortable but about ten sizes too big. Lars's T-shirt dwarfed her too. She lifted a handful of the blue fabric to her nose and breathed in the faint scent of his detergent mingled with aftershave. The smell had kept him close and had helped her make it through the night.

Crossing the bedroom on silent feet, she opened the door and peered into the living room. The faint gray light of early morning was peeking through the blinds. A mound of blankets lay on each sofa. From one, she heard faint snores. From the other, a tuft of disheveled blond hair was barely visible against the armrest. Marit smiled. The hair could belong to either cousin, but based on the fact that it was the lumpy sofa, she guessed it was Lars.

She tiptoed to the counter and unplugged the computer she and Lars had been using the night before. They still had hours of jewelry show video footage to review. There was no point putting off starting the tedious job if she was going to be up anyway.

Returning to her makeshift bed, she slipped her feet back under the covers, set her pillow behind her back, and opened the laptop.

"All right, Mr. Koch," she muttered as she pushed Play. "Let's see who you spoke to in the afternoon."

Thankfully, the German jeweler was fairly easy to spot in the grainy video. His bald head reflected the large conference center's ceiling lights, and his plaid button-down shirt stood out among the more conservative clothing of the other vendors.

Marit watched as he spoke to the man at the table next to his, as he ate bratwurst and onions from a paper plate, and as he showed three women and one man an assortment of jewelry. Two of the women left with a ring box inside one of Mr. Koch's distinctive silver drawstring bags.

She glanced at the progress bar at the bottom of her screen. Five more minutes and she'd switch to the video feed from one of the other cameras.

A tall man in a gray suit approached Koch's table. The two men spoke, and then Koch reached for a metal box beneath his chair. Marit moved the computer a little closer. This was something new. She watched as Koch opened the box. Using a pair of jewelers' pliers, he withdrew three gems from the box and set them on a black cloth in front of the man.

The newcomer held each stone to the light before setting them back on the cloth. A conversation ensued. Then Koch placed all three stones in a tiny plastic bag before putting the plastic bag into one of his silver drawstring bags. The man handed him something—a credit card, perhaps—and Koch made a phone call. He didn't stay on the phone long, and whatever he heard must have been satisfactory, because he gave the tall man back his card, along with the silver bag containing the gemstones. The man put his hand in his jacket pocket and pulled out a slightly larger black drawstring bag.

Marit did a double take, her heart rate kicking up a notch. The black jewelry bag looked just like the one Cole had brought to the bank. She paused the video, studying the bag in the still picture. It was the right size and had no obvious markings. She took a deep breath and started the video again.

The tall man opened the black bag and dropped the silver one inside. He returned it to his pocket, shook Koch's hand, and walked away.

Marit paused the video again. Yesterday, she hadn't really known what she and Lars were looking for when Cole asked them to review this tape. Instinct told her this was it.

Kicking off the bed covers, she scrambled to her feet. With the computer in her hands, she hurried into the living room.

"Lars." She knelt in front of the lumpy sofa and reached out her hand to gently shake his shoulder. "Lars."

His head moved, and his startling blue eyes appeared above the blanket. He blinked as he registered her appearance beside him, and then his eyes crinkled. Without seeing his mouth, she knew he was smiling.

"My T-shirt's never looked so good," he said.

Warmth flooded Marit's cheeks. She'd completely forgotten how she was dressed. Thankfully, she had a perfect distraction. She lifted the computer so he could see it. "I've been watching the video feed. I think I've found something."

Lars's expression changed. He swung his legs off the sofa and sat up. "Show me," he said, patting the spot next to him.

She sat down beside him and set the computer on her knee, angling the screen so he could see it.

"I'll rewind it a few minutes. Watch what happens when the tall man with the white hair approaches Koch's table."

"Hang on." Cole untangled himself from the blankets on the other sofa. "I want to see this too."

Marit waited until Cole was standing where he could see the screen, then she pushed Play. She sat silently, watching the encounter again. When the tall man walked out of the screen, she pressed Pause, and Lars released a low whistle.

"It was the same bag," he said.

"Sure looks that way," Cole said. "Nice work, Marit." He moved to the counter to grab his computer. "Use your photographic magic to get the best possible angles on the guy, Lars. Then send me screenshots."

"It's a security feed," Lars said. "We'll be lucky to see his face at all."

Cole dropped back onto the sofa and opened his laptop. "I'll take whatever you can give me."

"Looks like we've found our suspect," Cole said. "Peter Brinkerhoff. Age fifty-eight. Owner of three jewelry shops: two in Vienna and one in Salzburg. Specializes in diamonds."

Lars stared at him. It had been less than ten minutes since he'd sent the final image of the man from the security feed to Cole's computer. "Want to tell me how you did that so fast?"

"The embassy has a pretty extensive data bank."

Lars was quite sure the embassy had a list of known terrorists and felons they consulted for visa applications, but to identify an Austrian businessman from an indistinct photo so quickly seemed beyond the scope of American diplomatic personnel. "Not buying it. Try again."

Cole looked up from his computer. Lars caught something in his eyes, but whatever it was disappeared before Lars could identify it.

"Okay," Cole said. "His name is Hubert Pinkerton, and he's a butcher from Portugal."

At Lars's side, Marit giggled. She'd been snuggled up against him while he and Cole had been on their computers. Having her there had completely made up for having to sleep on the lumpy sofa. He tightened his arm around her and rolled his eyes. Cole had made a smooth recovery, but Lars was pretty sure he was hiding something.

For now, he'd play along. "Not all my family members are this obnoxious," he said.

"I know," Marit said. He could hear the laughter in her voice. "Your sister is lovely."

"Hey!" Cole said, but his defense was interrupted by a knock on the door.

"That must be Isabelle," Marit said.

"Isabelle?" Cole glanced from the bedroom door to the door cam picture on his watch. "I thought she was still asleep."

Marit slipped out of Lars's embrace and started toward the door. "She went home to change before you guys woke up."

Cole ran his fingers through his hair in a vain attempt to tame it.

Lars chuckled. "You may as well give up. It's a lost cause."

Cole scowled at him, and Lars laughed harder. He knew his hair looked just as bad, but Marit didn't seem to mind.

"Good morning." Isabelle walked in, bringing the smell of warm bread with her. "I brought kolaches and juice for breakfast."

"You must have read my mind," Lars said.

"Either that or I went with whatever was fastest," she teased.

Cole crossed the room to meet her. He put one arm around her and brushed her cheek with a soft kiss. "Thank you," he said.

She blushed and held out the bag. "Where do you want them?"

He took the bag and set it on the counter before opening a cupboard to pull out some cups.

Lars glanced at Marit. She was standing near the door, a small smile on her face. She caught his look, and he winked. Her smile widened. Despite all the awful things that had happened at the bank afterward, maybe yesterday's carriage ride had done some good after all.

CHAPTER 17

ISABELLE SAT BESIDE COLE ON the couch while she ate her breakfast. He'd finally added a second chair to his kitchen table, a luxury he hadn't indulged in until shortly after they'd started dating months ago, but with four of them eating together, it made more sense to use the coffee table for their morning meal.

Lars relayed the discovery Marit had made this morning, pride filling his voice as he described her success.

When Cole announced the identity of the jeweler who had purchased the stone in question, Isabelle set her breakfast aside. "Peter Brinkerhoff?"

"How do you know him?" Cole asked.

Not *if* she knew him but *how*. It was amazing how observant Cole could be in some situations and so clueless in others. Then again, he had been sweet to insist she stay at his apartment last night. Maybe he was improving.

"I've never met him, but Brinkerhoff is a client at my bank."

"If you recognize his name, he must be a big-dollar client," Marit said.

"Yes. He's part of the seven-figure club." Isabelle turned her attention to Cole. "And he keeps several safe-deposit boxes at my branch of the bank."

"Which means he knows the layout," Cole said.

Isabelle nodded. "The more I think about the robbery, the more convinced I am that these guys had a detailed layout of the bank. Brinkerhoff would know enough to give them that information."

"I was leaning toward there being an inside man, but this would make sense." Cole retrieved his laptop.

"What are you doing?" Marit asked.

"Pulling the GPS on Brinkerhoff's cell phone."

Marit's eyebrows lifted. "You can do that?"

"I have a friend at the embassy who owes me a favor," Cole said without missing a beat.

Nice recovery. Cole was getting a little too comfortable around these civilians. If he wasn't careful, they were going to discover he was far more than a simple embassy employee. That wouldn't bode well for either of them maintaining their cover stories, especially if this new relationship between them continued. The seed of hope inside her sprouted. Could she and Cole make it work this time around?

Lars's voice broke into her thoughts. "I hope your friend is already at the office." He checked the time on his cell phone. "It's only eight."

"We'll find out soon enough," Cole said.

"Why do you want to tap into Mr. Brinkerhoff's GPS?" Marit asked.

"If we can figure out which of his stores he's working at today, one of us can make an appointment to go see him." Cole tapped a few keys on his keyboard. "We need to figure out where that diamond went after he bought it. I also want to see if a friend of mine can enhance the video feed."

"The same one who provided the laptops?" Isabelle asked. Surely he didn't plan to involve the CIA until they had identified the source of the intel leak.

"Yeah. If she can't do it, I'm sure someone in her department can," Cole said.

Yesterday, Isabelle had full access to both her banks' databases and CIA resources. Now she was relying on people who were the inspiration behind the vague ghost story she'd heard only in passing years ago. She was ready to get back on solid footing, where she knew the players and who she could trust.

She slid closer to Cole so she could see his screen just as he finished typing in his request to Ghost. Then he opened the video feed segment Marit had viewed earlier.

"This is all we've found for the visual of Brinkerhoff so far," Cole said. "Do you recognize him?"

"The quality of the image is pretty bad, but that looks like him." Isabelle straightened when a card of some sort passed from Brinkerhoff to Koch. "What was that?"

"The credit card?" Cole asked.

"That's not a credit card." Isabelle motioned to the screen. "Back it up."

Cole did as she asked.

"Can we see too?" Marit stood and moved beside her.

Cole set his laptop on the coffee table, and everyone crowded around so they could see the screen. He pressed Play.

"Look." Isabelle pointed when Brinkerhoff passed the card to Koch. "He didn't swipe the card through any kind of credit card reader."

"You're right," Cole said. "He made a phone call instead."

"Looks to me like it was a prearranged transaction," Isabelle said.

"Assuming that jewelry bag Brinkerhoff was carrying really is the one the diamonds were in, Brinkerhoff may be into more than selling jewelry."

"You think he's involved in some sort of smuggling?" Lars asked.

"I don't know if it's smuggling or acting as the middle man for payments between buyer and seller, but either way, I want to have a chat with him," Cole said. "Koch too."

"You don't even know where Hans Koch lives," Lars said. "Jewelers come from all over the region for these jewelry shows."

"I'll ask one of my coworkers to check him out. I'm sure someone can figure out where he's from." Cole typed in yet another request on his laptop. "For all we know, the buyer and seller could both be involved with whatever's going on."

"Buyer and seller," Marit repeated. "What are they buying and selling?"

"That is the fundamental question I need to answer," Cole said.

Isabelle cocked an eyebrow. "It's the fundamental question *we* need to answer."

Cole emerged from the bathroom, his hair no longer an unruly mess after a restless night. After Lars had showered and changed, he had left to escort Marit back to her hotel room so she could freshen up and get some clean clothes. Whether Cole would be giving up his bed for another night remained to be seen, but he suspected Marit would bring an overnight bag with her when they returned. He needed a bigger apartment.

Isabelle glanced up from her laptop, a flicker of uncertainty flashing on her face.

A tug of guilt surfaced. He'd gone to bed last night thinking everything was good between them, but if her expression was any indication, he still had a long way to go to repair the damage he had done to their relationship.

Suspecting his words wouldn't do much at this point, he simply asked, "Anything new?"

"No movement on Brinkerhoff's phone. I did find some information on Koch though."

"What do you have?"

"He's from Munich, and he's been working these jewelry shows for years," Isabelle said. "His financials don't show any unusual activity, nor do his communications."

"Thorough," Cole said, impressed. "What about Brinkerhoff?"

"He opened his first jewelry store over twenty years ago, but over the past five years, he's expanded to three. Over the same time period, his revenue has increased tenfold."

"That's quite a jump."

"I agree. It's hard to say if his improved finances are a result of a booming business or if he has an outside money stream coming in."

"You've been busy. Did you get the chance to look at the CIA employees who accessed Jasmine's report?"

"A bit." She tilted her head and gentled her voice. "I know you have a long friendship with Jasmine, but are you sure she isn't the one behind the leak?"

"Not a chance." Cole shook his head. "She was the senior agent when we found the diamonds. If she wanted them, she could have insisted on securing them herself."

"But if she wanted to avoid suspicion, it makes more sense that she would let someone else have them first so she could shift the blame."

Cole couldn't disagree with her there. "But why go to that effort only to go dark? She knows she's the prime suspect right now. She wouldn't have put herself in that situation unless it was absolutely necessary."

"Any luck on tracing her?" Isabelle asked.

"No. I assume you haven't either." He sat beside her.

"Not a trace. It's like she was never in Budapest."

"Like riding a bike," Cole muttered.

"What?"

"Nothing." He leaned back on the couch and stretched his arm across the back of it as he slid closer to Isabelle. Even though the scent of her shampoo tickled his senses, he focused on her laptop screen, which was split between the GPS locator for Brinkerhoff's phone and the man's website for his jewelry stores.

"Maybe we should try calling one of the stores and setting up an appointment," Cole suggested.

"What do we say is the purpose of needing to meet with him?" Isabelle asked.

"Your bank did just have a robbery yesterday, and he does have safe-deposit boxes there."

"True." She checked the time. "And the stores are open."

She picked up her phone off the coffee table, searched her contacts, and dialed. Cole could barely make out the ringing followed by a woman's voice on the other end.

"Yes, I need to make an appointment to see Peter Brinkerhoff as soon as possible."

The indistinct mumble buzzed in Cole's ear as he strained to make out the woman's words.

"It's quite urgent." A pause. "I see." Another pause. "I did also want to come in and look at some loose diamonds. Is there someone else who can help me with that?" Isabelle tapped a finger on the couch impatiently. "No, thank you. I'll try him at home."

Isabelle hung up.

"What?" Cole asked.

"Apparently Mr. Brinkerhoff won't be back in the store until next week," Isabelle said. "He's also the only person who sells loose stones. His employees are not authorized to access that section of their vault."

"Interesting." Cole contemplated their options. "Could he be working at one of the other stores?"

"No. He's entertaining some out-of-town guests. Apparently, they are all attending Vienna's annual benefit ball for the performing arts on Friday."

"Maybe we should go too," Cole suggested. "It would be one way to talk to him."

"That's a great idea," Isabelle said. "But it isn't going to be as easy as you think."

CHAPTER 18

Marit watched Lars unlock the door to Cole's flat, marveling at how quickly this small space had come to feel like home and the people within like family. It hadn't taken much for Lars to persuade her to pack an overnight bag when she'd gone back to the hotel to shower and change. Regardless of the hotel's opulence and amenities, she'd much rather be on a futon mattress at Cole's place than by herself in her spacious, lonely hotel room.

He opened the door and ushered her inside.

Isabelle looked up as they entered. "Hi," she said. "Welcome back."

"Yeah." Cole's focus remained on his computer screen, but when a fresh page loaded, he leaned back against the sofa with a disgruntled grunt. "Someone explain to me why an invitation to an exorbitantly expensive ball would be the most sought-after ticket in Vienna."

"It's where the elite go to see and be seen," Isabelle said.

"Someone should clue them in," Lars said, dropping onto the opposite sofa. "You can see and be seen by thousands more people if you go to a football match. And—huge bonus—you don't have to go dressed like a penguin."

"See," Cole said. "Lars gets it."

Isabelle rolled her eyes, and Marit bit her lip to prevent a laugh from escaping.

"What's the event?" she asked.

"It's Vienna's annual benefit ball for the performing arts," Isabelle said. "While you were gone, we found out that Peter Brinkerhoff won't be available all week, but he is planning to attend the ball on Friday. Cole was hoping we could crash the party so he could talk to him about the diamonds." She shrugged. "Finding tickets is proving difficult."

Marit took a seat next to Lars on the sofa. Was this the ball her stylist, Yvette LeBlanc, had been telling her about on their last day on location? "Are they holding it at Schönbrunn Palace?"

"Yes. They have it there every year. I think that's one reason why it draws such a crowd." Isabelle paused and gave her a curious look. "How did you know that?"

"That's where I was working earlier this week. Preparations for the ball were well underway when we finished our photo shoot." Marit's mind raced, and she reached for her phone. Was it possible that Yvette still had her tickets? It was a long shot, but it was worth pursuing, especially if Cole's search had come up short. "Give me a second. I need to make a call."

Ignoring Isabelle's questioning look, Marit dialed Yvette's number. She had no idea where the stylist would be now. Not Vienna, certainly.

"Hello."

"Hi, Yvette. It's Marit."

"Well, this is a nice surprise. Where are you calling me from?"

"I'm still in Vienna," Marit said. "Where are you now?"

"Back in Paris, *ma petite*. Where I belong." Her throaty laugh was distinctive. "You know how it is. I can't be gone from this city too long."

Truth be told, Marit didn't know. She'd been to Paris on numerous occasions and felt no great yen to return. But this wasn't the time to tell Yvette that.

"I'm sorry you weren't able to stay in Vienna long enough to attend the ball," she said. "Did you end up giving your tickets to someone else?"

Cole shifted to the edge of his seat, and Marit knew she had his attention.

"They're not the sort of tickets you can offer to anybody," Yvette said. "You were the only one I knew who was staying on until the weekend, but you told me you didn't want to go alone."

"So you still have them?" Marit held her breath.

"Are you asking, or is Marco? Has he finally persuaded you to go out with him?"

"I'm asking. This has nothing to do with Marco. I don't even know where he is."

"Good. Stay away from that preening magpie, *ma petite*. He just likes to collect pretty things to make his own nest look better."

Yvette spent a great deal of time with her models. Marit should have known the savvy Frenchwoman would have taken Marco's measure.

"You have no need to worry on that score." Marit glanced at Lars. He smiled at her—a slow, sweet smile that set a hundred butterflies free in her stomach. "There's someone else in my life. And I think you'll approve."

"Well now, that is news. Is he ballworthy? He has to look good in a tux, you know. If you use my tickets, my reputation is on the line."

Marit would have laughed, except she knew that Yvette was completely in earnest. "I've never seen him in a tux, but I think he'll clean up well."

Cole snorted, and Marit didn't dare look at Lars. She should have been smart enough to place this phone call in the bedroom. Alone.

"Then the tickets are yours," Yvette said. "It's ridiculous to have four tickets go to waste. Two is far more acceptable."

Four. Yvette had four tickets. Marit clenched the phone more tightly. "How would you feel about me using all four?" Before Yvette had a chance to respond, she continued. "Two good friends. Completely ballworthy."

"And your dresses? Where are they from?"

Marit's heart sank. She should have known one of Paris's foremost stylists would ask that question. There was nothing remotely gown-like in her suitcase. "Well—"

"You will go to Monique Martin," Yvette said, not waiting to hear more.

Marit had modeled Monique Martin's designs before. Her gowns were stunning—as were her price tags. "Yvette, as beautiful as they are, I cannot afford a Monique Martin original."

The Frenchwoman clicked her tongue. "Nonsense. If you use my tickets, you will wear Monique's gowns. I will call her. She can loan you two gowns for the night. A free modeling session for her, and my reputation remains intact." She paused. "But I will want pictures. Lots of pictures."

Marit could hardly believe it. "I'll text them to you before the evening is over," she promised. "Thank you so much, Yvette."

"I am glad you called." Her voice softened. "Enjoy your magical evening at Schönbrunn, *ma petite*. I will have the tickets overnighted to your hotel. And I shall call Monique's salon this morning so they will be ready when you and your friend arrive. *Au revoir*."

There was a click, and she was gone. Marit lowered her phone from her ear and turned to face the others.

"Did you just do what I think you just did?" Isabelle asked.

Marit grinned. "Four tickets to the ball and two gowns on loan from Monique Martin."

Isabelle gasped. "Monique Martin? Seriously?"

"Who's Monique Martin?" Cole asked.

"Wait. Does this mean I have to wear a tux?" Lars said.

Marit and Isabelle took one look at Lars's horrified expression and burst into peals of laughter.

"Sorry to break it to you, cuz," Cole said. "But I think you should take that as a yes."

Cole used a trip to the market as an excuse to leave his apartment so he could have some privacy to check in with Cas. Rather than go downstairs to the lobby, he climbed the three flights to the roof.

He stepped toward the outdoor tables that created a picnic area during the summer months but were rarely used this time of year.

The wind whipped through his coat, and he shivered. Tucking his scarf more firmly around his neck, he checked the roof and ensured he was alone. Then he quickly pulled off his glove and dialed Cas's number.

"Anything new?" Cas asked.

"I was about to ask you that." Cole used his shoulder to hold his phone to his ear so he could put his glove back on.

"Still no sign of Jasmine," she said, giving him the detail he most wanted. "What about you? Have you had any luck with your research?"

"I haven't had time to look into activity in Bratislava, but we tracked down the diamond with the serial number." A gust of wind whipped over him, and his breath caught. He paced the length of the roof to keep his blood moving. "The diamond was sold to a local jeweler. Peter Brinkerhoff."

"Have you questioned him?"

"Not yet. His staff said he's not going to be at work for the next week . . ."

"We can't wait that long," Cas insisted.

"You know something."

"There was a bombing in the train terminal in Amsterdam this morning. The news broke on social media within minutes of the attack."

"That's what happened with the recent bombing in Frankfurt," Cole said, again thinking of the Steven Powell case from a few months ago. Hoping to boost his news empire to the top, Powell had orchestrated several terrorist attacks as a way to create a public dependence on the news he reported. "What's the latest on Steven Powell? Any updates?"

"He was last traced to Italy, but that was months ago," Cas said. "He doesn't have access to the funds we froze in the US, but it's possible he had a stash somewhere in Europe that we didn't manage to identify."

"Like a stash of diamonds."

"It is one of the best currencies for criminal activities. Hard to trace, easy to transport."

"And no money trail," Cole added.

"Exactly."

"The question is, What would be his motivation this time?" Cole rubbed his gloved hands together in a futile attempt to warm them. "His news networks have all been taken over by other companies."

"I have no idea. Logically, he would only spend whatever money—or diamonds—he has in order to make more," Cas said.

"Maybe there was a news station somewhere that he owned and we missed."

"It's possible," Cas said. "On a different subject, I questioned Rogers this morning. According to him, when his kidnappers interrogated him, they asked who sent him and what he was doing there."

"What else?"

"Nothing. They didn't ask about money or weapons. They didn't ask about intel or the US government."

"You don't think they knew who he was." Cole walked across the roof again, dead leaves crunching beneath his boots. "It's possible they took him because they thought he saw something that would compromise them."

"Or compromise whatever they're planning," Cas said.

"Rogers is lucky they didn't kill him on the spot."

"I had a similar thought. He said he couldn't really hear what they were saying, which makes me think they were afraid he would be able to identify them."

"Or they thought he was sent by someone they're dealing with. I can't think of another reason to keep him alive unless they thought he had information they needed or was worth something to one of their associates," Cole concluded. "Where is Rogers now?"

"On a flight to Paris. I want him to work with the FBI sketch artist there to see if we can identify the men who left before we got there."

"Why the FBI?"

"I don't want our mole to get wind that we're onto them. In the daily report, Rogers's transfer will be called medical leave and will show him going back to the States."

"How do we get the intel from the Bureau?"

"The guardians can access the information once it's in the FBI's system. I'll forward it to you as soon as I get it," Cas said. "In the meantime, Rogers will work with our FBI agent in Paris to help us track Steven Powell's movements."

"Good. It will be nice to have the extra help. If Powell is involved, who knows what he's really up to." Cole paced back toward the door. "Any chance you also have access to the IDs on the kidnappers we neutralized or the bank robber we captured yesterday?"

"The kidnappers were guns for hire, all Ukrainian," Cas said. "So far, no leads stemming from them, but we're searching financials."

"If they were getting paid in diamonds, you won't find anything." Cole sighed. "What about the robber?"

"He was from Salzburg. He's been linked with a crew that has worked all over Switzerland, Germany, Austria, and France."

"These guys were clearly pros. Want to send me the IDs of the other suspects?"

"We can let Interpol handle that."

"Send me the information anyway. I don't want to take any chances that these guys might want to eliminate witnesses." Even though Isabelle's image was the one that popped into his head, he said, "Especially when I have civilians helping me."

"Now that you've tracked the diamonds, you don't need them to be involved anymore."

"Actually, they're still helping me with that."

"How?"

"Remember how I said Brinkerhoff is out of the office for the next week?"

"Yes."

"Turns out he's going to some fancy ball tomorrow with some out-of-town guests. Marit was able to get tickets for all of us."

"If you're planning to question Brinkerhoff, they shouldn't be there. If he's involved, there's no way to know how he might react if he's cornered or if his guests cause problems."

"I had the same concern, but if I'm going to find a way to get Brinkerhoff alone, I may need their help. They speak his language. I don't know jewelry. They do."

"It's risky, especially if they don't know what they're getting into."

"I know, but we're going to be in a public place with a lot of people," Cole said. "I'll make sure Marit and Lars are enjoying the ball while Isabelle and I question Brinkerhoff. After all, how dangerous can dancing be?"

CHAPTER 19

LARS ENTERED THE FINAL PHOTOGRAPH into his inventory of items stolen from the Falcon Point jewelry collection. His great-grandmother's wedding ring. Frustration mingled with regret. After all he and his cousins had gone through to uncover their family legacy, to lose those treasures now was a bitter pill to swallow.

The sound of a key entering the door distracted him from his work.

He looked up as Cole walked in. "How was the market? Did you find what you needed?" Lars asked, noting Cole's empty hands.

"No. Apparently, I'm not the only one who likes Muller's whole wheat bread. They were sold out. I'll have to try going earlier tomorrow."

Lars hadn't thought Cole was that picky about food. It seemed to him that if his cousin's favorite loaf was gone, he would have settled for a different one. "Must be amazing bread."

"It is." Cole stepped up behind him and studied his computer screen. "What are you working on?"

"Cataloging the list of items stolen from the Falcon Point collection," Lars said.

Cole scanned the photos, his expression grim. "The emerald earrings and the tiara."

"Among many other things, yeah." Lars released a tense breath. "When are we going to tell the others?"

"Let's give the authorities a couple of days to see what they can find," Cole said. "I don't especially want Anna pounding on my door, demanding answers we can't give her. I'm hoping that if Brinkerhoff can give us a lead on the diamonds, it will also help us locate the jewelry."

Brinkerhoff. Lars's heart sank. "Are we really going to have to go out and rent tuxes for that event?"

"You will, not me," Cole said. "I already have a tux."

Lars stared at him incredulously. "You own a tux? Are you secretly an American version of James Bond or something?"

Cole moved into the kitchen, took a glass out of the cupboard, and opened the fridge. "Embassy dress code," he said. "We host more than our fair share of these black-tie events."

"Great. Next, you're going to tell me that you know how to waltz."

Cole set his glass of milk down and grinned at him. "You don't?"

"Of course I don't. How many twenty-something men out there actually know how to waltz?"

Cole chuckled. "More than you think."

Like a rapidly rising tide, panic surged within Lars. Was he going to be the only man at the ball who didn't know how to dance? He couldn't do that to Marit. She deserved better. "Show me," he said, coming to his feet. "Right now. Before Marit and Isabelle get back from dress shopping."

"If you think I'm going to dance with you, you have another thing coming."

"You don't have to dance with me. Just show me the steps."

"Not happening."

"Cole." Lars ran his fingers through his hair. "Marit got you the tickets you wanted. The least you can do is help her partner not look like a complete klutz on the dance floor."

Cole eyed him warily. "If I show you, you have to be the girl."

"How am I supposed to learn the guy's part if I'm the girl?"

"I thought you were smart."

"Obviously not smart enough. If I were, I'd have taken clandestine dance lessons like every other guy must have done."

Cole rolled his eyes. "Fine," he grumbled. "I'll be the girl. But if one word of this reaches anyone else—especially Isabelle—you'll be off the lumpy sofa and sleeping on the landing outside."

"Deal," Lars said.

Isabelle couldn't believe she was not only going to Vienna's annual benefit ball for the performing arts but would also be wearing an original Monique Martin gown. She pulled out of her parking space outside the designer's studio and headed into the flow of traffic. At least since she had driven to Cole's this morning, she and Marit wouldn't have to carry their gowns on the train.

"Cole's eyes are going to pop out of his head when he sees you in that dress," Marit said from the passenger seat.

"I don't know about that. You, however, are going to be a showstopper when we walk into Schönbrunn Palace tomorrow night."

"If using our looks to distract Peter Brinkerhoff is what Cole needs us to do, I'm happy to oblige." Marit shifted in her seat, and the humor in her voice faded. "Can I ask you something?"

"Sure." Isabelle answered automatically, even though she mentally prepared to evade Marit's question. Such was the life of a CIA agent. Too bad. She suspected Marit and she could become close friends if she didn't have to hide her true identity.

"Who does Cole really work for?" Marit asked.

"He works at the US embassy," Isabelle said. "Why?"

"I don't know. It just seems odd that he's doing all of this research at home when I have to imagine the embassy has better resources and they would have a vested interest in recovering the diamonds."

Isabelle debated briefly how much to say. If Cole's guardian friend had really done a background check on Marit and Lars, she was relatively certain there wasn't anything nefarious in their backgrounds. Regardless, that didn't qualify them to enter their circle of need-to-know.

"Cole hasn't said much," Isabelle began, "but he's concerned that the robbers were specifically interested in his diamonds."

"How is that even possible? He only brought them to your bank the night before. It didn't even look like he'd planned to leave them there." The words were barely out of Marit's mouth before she came to her own conclusion. "He thinks someone at the embassy is involved."

"He needs to rule out that possibility."

"I can't imagine what that would be like, suspecting people you work with of doing something illegal."

"I'm sure it isn't easy." Isabelle glanced in her rearview mirror and memorized the make and models of the various cars behind her. Out of habit, she turned three streets too soon to make sure she wasn't being followed.

A silver Audi and a black Volkswagen also turned.

"How are things going with you and Cole?" Marit asked. "Have you had a chance to talk?"

"A little bit." Isabelle switched lanes and took the next right. The Volkswagen continued past her. The Audi slowed, and a delivery truck merged between her and the silver sedan.

"He seems to really be trying," Marit said.

"Yeah, but Cole is the type who likes a challenge. It's hard to know if he's trying because he can't stand losing or if he's really interested."

"I don't know him as well as you do, but he looks pretty interested to me."

Isabelle made another turn to put herself back on course with her intended destination. The truck behind her rumbled past. A moment later, a glimpse of silver appeared in her rearview. Was that the same car she had noticed earlier?

It pulled behind a blue hatchback before Isabelle could confirm the sedan was an Audi. Not willing to take any chances, she made a left at the next light.

"Where are you going?" Marit asked. "Isn't Cole's apartment the other way?"

"Yes, but there's a road closure I want to avoid." Isabelle switched lanes, hoping to get a better look at the silver sedan. "I got stuck there when I drove back from my apartment this morning."

"Isabelle?" Concern filled Marit's voice. "What aren't you telling me?"

A silver Audi. Isabelle took the next turn.

Marit swiveled in her seat to look behind them before training her gaze on Isabelle again. "What's going on?"

As much as she hated to worry Marit, Isabelle opted for the truth. "I think that silver Audi is following us."

"Are you sure?"

"We're about to find out." Isabelle spotted an open parking space on her right. She slowed and flipped on her blinker to signal her intentions and took her time parallel parking her car.

"What are you doing?" Marit asked.

"If that guy is really following us, he'll park too or circle around the block until he finds a spot."

"What if he's one of the men from the bank yesterday?"

Then those men had an insider working with them. Isabelle didn't verbalize her thoughts, instead adopting a soothing tone. "Don't worry. We aren't getting out of the car. As soon as we know what he's doing, we'll get out of here."

"How would someone even know to look for us?"

"Good question." It was. How could she have been located? She had disabled the GPS on her car right after she bought it, and she had a scrambler on her cell phone to prevent people from being able to monitor her movements. "Stay here." She put the car in park and climbed out.

"But . . ." Marit started to protest, but Isabelle closed the driver's side door as though preparing to go into one of the nearby apartment buildings.

The Audi slowed and pulled to the side of the road a few cars in front of her. Her stomach clenched. If she were alone, she would disappear into the crowd, but Marit wasn't the type to go unnoticed. Isabelle would have to evade, but first, she needed to find out how this guy knew how to find her.

While the driver parked, Isabelle ducked and ran her hand under the wheel well. Nothing. Still suspicious that someone had placed a tracker on her car, she repeated the process with the rear wheel.

After a quick check to make sure the person following her wasn't approaching, she circled behind the car to check the passenger side. Her fingers brushed against a button-sized object. She peeked at it and identified the tracker as one commonly used by both criminals and law enforcement.

She pulled it free and walked to the car behind her. She dropped her glove, and when she leaned down to pick it up, she pressed the tracker to the underside of the other car.

A man emerged on the sidewalk twenty meters in front of her. She took a moment to assess him. The collar of his overcoat was flipped up, and his scarf covered half his face. His attire was similar to the few other pedestrians on the street, but the way his gaze swept over the sidewalk, pausing when it reached her, gave the man away. He wasn't here for a stroll, and Isabelle would bet he didn't live here.

Moving at a deliberate pace, she started forward. When she reached the front of her car, she jumped into the driver's seat.

The man started running toward them.

Isabelle cranked the wheel and pressed on the gas. Her car whipped within a fraction of an inch of the BMW in front of her as she pulled onto the road.

Marit gasped. She jerked around to look behind them. "He's running back to his car."

"Tell me if he follows."

"He's following." Marit kept her gaze behind them. "What are you going to do?"

"We're going to lose him." Isabelle took the first turn.

"He's gaining on us." Trepidation hummed through Marit's words.

Isabelle checked her mirrors. Irritation bubbled inside her. Marit had gone through enough yesterday. So had she. The last thing they needed was a high-speed chase through the middle of Vienna.

A right turn, followed by a left, then another right. The Audi matched her every move.

"He's not giving up," Marit said. "Maybe we should drive to the police station. I heard that's what you're supposed to do if someone is following you."

The wisdom was sound, but the kind of people who were likely to follow Isabelle weren't the sort who would worry about the police or witnesses.

She increased her speed and headed toward the Christmas market. Maybe the crowds there would give her the obstacle she needed to separate herself from the man behind her.

When a group of tourists crossed the street and impeded her progress, she gritted her teeth. This wasn't what she had in mind.

Marit pressed her hand against the dashboard. "We're trapped."

"Not exactly. Hold on." With half a block still between her and the pedestrians, Isabelle slammed on the brakes and turned the wheel. Her body leaned into the turn as the car spun around until it was facing the opposite direction. Isabelle gunned the engine, and her car shot forward.

They passed the Audi, the man's face now visible.

"I've seen that man before," Marit said.

"Where?" Isabelle asked. "Where have you seen him?"

"At the bank." Marit turned her head back toward Isabelle. "He was the detective who questioned me."

"He's a cop?" Isabelle asked.

"I'm afraid so."

CHAPTER 20

"You were pursued around Vienna by a police officer?" Lars did nothing to hide his incredulity. "Why?"

"I have no idea." Isabelle sat on the sofa next to Cole. "They have my phone number. Calling would have saved them a lot of trouble."

"And us a lot of stress," Marit added. She was still trying to process how an afternoon of trying on designer gowns had morphed into a frightening car chase. "He obviously didn't know that Isabelle can handle a car like a grand prix driver."

Cole exchanged a look with Isabelle. "Commuting on the Washington Beltway will do that to you."

"I'm glad it turned out okay," Lars said. "And it looks like you found dresses."

"We did." Marit smiled at the memory of her time in the designer's showroom with Isabelle. It had been so much fun to share that experience with someone who'd never been pampered by a stylist before. "But we're not telling you anything more. You'll have to wait until tomorrow to see them."

Lars eyed the two oversized garment bags lying across the other end of the sofa. "I don't suppose you picked up a tux for me while you were out, did you?"

"Oh, no," Marit laughed. "You're not getting out of it that easily."

Lars sighed. "Okay, Cole. Give me the name and address of your tux guy."

"Cole has a tux guy?" Marit asked.

"Apparently."

"For the record," Cole said dryly, "I also have a dry cleaning guy, a building custodian, and a mailman." He pulled out his phone and sent Lars a link. "The shop's only a few blocks away."

"Great," Marit said. "We can walk there."

Lars's head shot up from studying the street map on his phone. "Are you volunteering to come with me?"

"Yes." She paused, suddenly uncertain. "If you'd like me to."

"Are you kidding?" He got to his feet and reached for her hand. "You've just thrown a drowning man a life preserver."

She smiled, threading her fingers between his and loving the instant connection that hummed between them. "It won't be that bad."

"Not anymore," he said, his gentle kiss on her cheek making her skin tingle. "Let me grab my jacket and we can go."

Two minutes later, he was ready. Marit slipped on her gloves.

"Good luck," Isabelle called as Lars opened the front door.

"Thanks," Lars replied. "We'll see you soon."

They walked down the stairs, and when they reached the pavement, he took Marit's hand again.

"Which way?" she asked.

"Left two blocks and then a right."

The wind had picked up since she and Isabelle had returned. Leaves swirled in the gutter. A woman walked by with a poodle on a leash, and the smell of Chinese food wafted down the street from a nearby restaurant. Marit's thoughts turned to the impromptu dinner they'd shared at Cole's flat the night before—a dinner that had come after hours of working on computers that had mysteriously appeared on Cole's doorstep.

"Lars," she said. "What exactly is Cole's job at the embassy?"

"I don't think he's ever told me. I know he travels quite a bit. And evidently, he sometimes has to go to events in a tux." He glanced at her. "Why do you ask?"

Marit couldn't really put her finger on it. "I don't know. It's just a feeling I have." She'd hoped that talking to Isabelle would settle her unease, but having their conversation interrupted by a high-speed chase hadn't helped at all. "Maybe he's higher up in the ranks there than he lets on."

"He might be. We could ask him."

They turned the corner, and Marit spotted the small menswear shop across the road. She pointed to the window where a mannequin wearing a gray suit stood beside a table covered in ties. "There it is."

Lars nodded and led her to the pedestrian crossing. They stopped, waiting for the light to change, and he gave her an apologetic look. "You know I have no idea what to ask for in there, right?"

She smiled and squeezed his hand. "Don't worry, I've got this."

The moment Lars and Marit left, Cole had pulled up his suspect list again. Now able to speak freely, he and Isabelle had split up the names, each of them taking half of the CIA employees who could have possibly leaked information about the location of the diamonds.

"You can cross Alex Schumacher off the list," Isabelle said. "He didn't access the report until nine yesterday morning, and then he immediately went into a meeting with the Budapest station chief. I don't show any outgoing calls from the Budapest station between eight fifty-four and nine eighteen."

"Looks like that clears Gregor too. He opened the report at eight fifty-seven, and he was in the same meeting."

"That's two more down."

A secure message popped up on Cole's screen. "My guardian friend just sent me new intel."

"What is it?"

"A suspect list from the bank robbery." Cole skimmed the list and the bios. "Based off the height and weight of the suspects and with the detail Marit provided on their accents, Ghost is pretty confident these are our guys." Cole turned his laptop toward her. "All three of these are known associates of the man we captured in the vault."

"One from Berlin, one from Bratislava. Marit is good."

"Yeah." Cole motioned to the fourth man in the crew. "This looks like the guy who was in the vault with us."

Isabelle leaned closer, and her arm brushed his. "I think so too."

Cole resisted reaching out and pulling her close. Barely.

Work first. "Look at the last known addresses on these guys. Not one of them lives less than an hour from here."

"Then we can also eliminate these two from our list." Isabelle straightened and focused on her screen again. "Litton and Brenchley didn't access the report until after ten. Even if they made a call right away, I don't think there's any way the bank robbers could have mobilized quickly enough to prep and hit the bank in less than three hours."

"I agree. Plus, neither of them left before lunch, so they wouldn't have had access to their personal cell phones," Cole added. "Both of their desks are in the open area in our offices. They wouldn't have been able to make a call without being overheard, and I didn't see anything in their email correspondence that looked suspicious."

"That leaves us with four. Two analysts out of the Budapest office, the finance officer in Vienna, and the station chief in Vienna."

Cole studied the remaining names. "I have a hard time believing Zoe or Gwendolyn is involved."

"Assuming you're right, that Jasmine isn't the leak, I have to think it's one of these two. Adams and Font both accessed the report the night before, and they both work in Budapest. One of them must have done or said something that spooked Jasmine."

"I agree, but I don't see anything that points to either one." Cole hit Reply on the message from Cas. "Maybe the guardians will have better luck with figuring out which one it is."

"Now what?" Isabelle asked. "Has Ghost already notified the police of the identities of the bank robbers?"

"Yeah. She passed that along." The mention of the police brought a grin to his face. "You really evaded a cop this morning?"

"Don't laugh. I had no idea who the guy was."

"I figured as much. He must have been tailing you to see if you were involved."

"Maybe we should be tailing him to make sure he's not involved," Isabelle said. "He could have been following me because he wants me out of the picture."

"Then he's messing with the wrong woman." Despite Cole's confidence in Isabelle's abilities, an uncomfortable protectiveness swept through him. "Ghost might have a way to check him out. If we get lucky, she might even be able to plant the seed that you're innocent."

"I doubt anything she does can help. The way I lost him today didn't do much for proving my innocence."

Cole chuckled. "Poor Marit. She has no idea what she's gotten herself into."

"Neither does Lars, although I think they're starting to suspect what you really do for a living."

"What do you mean?"

"Marit was asking about you." Isabelle lifted her laptop. "Having these miraculously show up with video feed already loaded didn't exactly help your cover story."

"Yeah, I know," Cole admitted. "I have to keep reminding myself that Lars isn't in our circle of need-to-know for anything beyond the jewelry."

"Maybe it's time you put in the request to at least let him know who you really work for."

"He's a foreign national. The agency will never approve that."

"It's worth asking. After all, he's already cleared to work with us on tracing the diamonds."

"Yeah, but that was through the guardians. Until we know who the mole at the CIA really is, I'm not giving them any reason to pay attention to Lars."

Isabelle put her hand on his knee. "I don't blame you."

A ripple of attraction jolted through him. He put his hand on hers, and her eyes darted up to meet his. Unable to resist, Cole leaned forward. Her breath shuddered out, mixing with his. Anticipation fluttered in his stomach.

His lips were an inch from hers when the doorknob rattled. Isabelle pulled back, and Cole groaned in frustration when the door opened a second later.

Marit walked in, followed by Lars.

Lars held out his garment bag. "Okay, I'm all set for tomorrow. Is it okay if I hang this up in your closet?"

Cole motioned to the coat closet by the front door. "There's probably more room in there."

Lars opened the coat closet door and hooked the hanger on the rod. "Marit, do you want to hang your dress up in here too?"

"Are you sure you don't mind my staying here again tonight?" Marit asked. "I feel silly asking, especially since I have an empty hotel suite."

Lars glanced at Cole expectantly.

"It's fine," Cole said.

"Marit, why don't you stay at my place?" Isabelle suggested. "I have a spare bedroom, and it will be a lot easier to get ready for the ball tomorrow if we don't have to share a bathroom with these two."

"That's true," Marit said, clearly considering.

Cole felt the unexpected disappointment at the idea of Isabelle not sleeping in the next room. "Isabelle, you can stay tonight too."

"Thanks, but I'd prefer to sleep in my own bed. Besides, I kind of want to see if the cops are staking out my place."

"You want them to follow you?" Marit asked.

"Not particularly, but if they're still trying to find me, we know they aren't any closer to finding the real suspects."

"I guess that's true," Marit said.

Uneasiness settled over Cole. "I'm not crazy about you staying at your place if the cops are watching you."

"I'll be fine. I have a traditional deadbolt and electronic locks," Isabelle said. "No one is getting in my apartment without me knowing about it."

"Most people would take comfort in knowing there was a policeman parked right outside," Lars said.

"I'm not most people," Cole said.

"Yeah. I'm starting to realize that."

CHAPTER 21

Lars watched the streets of Vienna pass by through the car window as Isabelle drove to her flat. Historic buildings housing modern shop fronts, horse-drawn carriages competing with cars and buses. Somehow, despite the encroachment of modernization, the unique character and charm of this old city remained intact.

Up ahead, a large green area lined with trees came into view. Isabelle slowed the car, driving alongside the park until she spotted a tiny gap between a white delivery van and a red Fiat. With the competence borne of experience, she slid her car in between them and parked alongside the curb, with inches to spare on each end of her vehicle.

Lars whistled through his teeth. "Marit wasn't kidding about your driving skills, Isabelle. That parking job was pretty impressive."

She laughed. "In this city, if there's a parking spot—no matter how small—you claim it."

"Is your flat nearby?" Marit asked.

"Right across the street."

They all climbed out of the car. Lars noticed Cole eyeing the other vehicles parked along the side of the road. They were obviously of a similar mindset. Isabelle's flat might be more comfortable for the two women, but if there was any sign of a silver Audi, he was pretty sure they'd all be sleeping at Cole's place again.

With a computer under one arm and Marit's cumbersome garment bag balanced over the other, Lars followed the others across the street to a tall white-stone building similar in architecture to the one Cole lived in.

"These old buildings are all so beautiful," Marit said.

"Unless you're hoping for an elevator." Cole's face was barely visible over the top of Isabelle's voluminous garment bag.

"When I've spent a day sitting behind a desk in the bank, I like the exercise," Isabelle said, starting up the narrow stairs. "But bringing in groceries can be a workout."

Cole gave a resigned sigh, and four flights of stairs later, Lars was in complete agreement with him. Lifts and escalators had never sounded so good.

"Tell me it's easier to go down," he said.

Cole chuckled. "The view's worth it. That's what Isabelle tells me anyway."

Isabelle opened the door and led them inside. "Take a look."

They entered a pleasant living room furnished with a couple of sofas, a coffee table and a crowded bookshelf. A large painting of Vienna at night hung on one wall. On the other side of the room, a wide window displayed a magnificent view of the park and Vienna's skyline beyond.

Marit moved to stand by the window. "Wow. It's amazing, Isabelle."

"I'm glad you like it." She smiled. "Come with me. I'll show you where the guest room is."

The two women disappeared, and Lars laid Marit's dress across the back of one of the sofas.

"I think you may need to up your game," he told Cole, pointing to a couple of plants thriving in pots on the windowsill. "Compared to this, your flat is seriously lacking in the decor department."

Cole shook his head. "I'm not even going to try to compete. Besides, I'm not home enough to keep a plant alive."

"Yeah, about that . . ." Lars took a seat. "What exactly do you do when you're traveling?"

Cole set Isabelle's garment bag beside Marit's. "It varies," he said.

Lars's phone rang. He pulled it out of his pocket and glanced at the screen. "Hold that thought," he said. "I want to hear the details, but this is Tess."

An expression that looked suspiciously like relief crossed Cole's face. "Tell your sister hello for me," he said.

Lars nodded and accepted the call. "Hey, Tess."

"Lars," she said. "I'm glad I caught you. I just wanted you to know that I'm okay."

"That's great." Lars glanced at the clock. Tess should still be at work in the Van Gogh Museum in Amsterdam. Why was she calling to tell him that now?

There was a pause. "You haven't heard, have you?"

"Heard what?" His stomach tightened as the first inklings that something was very wrong settled over him.

"There was a bombing at Centraal Station."

Centraal Station was the main train station in Amsterdam. Thousands of people came and went through it every day.

"When?"

"Eight thirty this morning."

Lars dropped onto the nearest sofa as shock shot through him. "Eight thirty. That's when your train from Haarlem arrives."

"I know." Tess's voice cracked. "I took the early one today. I needed to be at the museum for a meeting at eight."

"Tess." Lars released a ragged breath as the magnitude of what could have happened hit him. "I'm so glad you're all right. Were there many injured?"

"Three deaths so far," she said. "And over twenty injured. Bram's been involved since it happened. He . . . he said it was really bad."

Tess's boyfriend, Bram, was a paramedic in the city. He saw more than his fair share of accidents. If he said it was bad, it undoubtedly was.

"Have they closed the station?"

"Yes. They're hoping to reopen some of it later tonight, but I don't know yet if they'll have the Haarlem line running. Bram has offered to drive me home, but I may just stay in the city. He'll be exhausted by then."

"Use my flat," Lars said. "You know where the spare key is."

"Thanks." Her voice warmed. "I was hoping you'd offer."

"Of course. And, Tess, keep me updated. You were right. I need to know that you're okay."

"I will. Take care yourself."

Tess ended the call, and Lars slowly lowered his phone. "There's been a bombing at the main train station in Amsterdam," he said.

Cole frowned. "I heard something about that earlier today."

"Why didn't you say something?" Emotion filled Lars's voice. "It happened at the time that Tess usually arrives in the city by train."

Cole's face paled. "Usually? Does that mean she wasn't there today?"

"She took an earlier train this morning." Was it wrong to feel such relief when others had not been so fortunate?

Isabelle and Marit appeared in the doorway.

"What's going on?" Isabelle asked.

"There was a bombing at the main railway station in Amsterdam this morning," Cole said.

"Another bombing?" Isabelle reached for the computer she'd set on the coffee table. "Something weird is going on."

Marit took one look at Lars's face and joined him on the sofa. "Is Tess okay?"

"Yes. She just called." He pulled Marit into his arms, grateful when she held him tight. They both had many friends and colleagues in Amsterdam.

"Let's see what we can find out about it," she said softly. "Maybe they will have released the names of the casualties by now."

He pressed a kiss to her forehead and released her. She opened the laptop he'd set on the sofa and started opening Dutch news sites.

"It doesn't look like they have a lot of details yet," she said, sharing the screen with him. "And the only photos taken inside the station are coming from social media sites."

"Which ones?" Isabelle asked. Cole had moved to sit beside her and was watching as she clicked away on her computer.

"RTL 4 is crediting Pulse with the photos and the quotes from eye-witnesses," Lars said.

"Have you ever heard of that social media site?" Cole asked. "Is it a popular one in the Netherlands?"

"I'm not familiar with it," Marit said, looking puzzled. "And in my profession, we need to be aware of the big ones."

Cole appeared thoughtful, but before Lars could ask him what he was thinking, his phone rang again. He stiffened. Was it someone else from Amsterdam? He looked at the caller ID. "I don't recognize the number," he said. "But I'd better take it."

The others sat quietly, watching as he answered the call.

"Hello."

"Is this Mr. Hendriks?" It was a man's voice, and he was speaking German not Dutch.

"It is."

"This is Detective Meyer. We spoke at Bankhaus Steiner at the time of the recent bank robbery."

"Yes," Lars said. "I remember." Was this the same policeman who'd been tailing Isabelle? Had Lars made the suspect list now?

"I'm calling to give you an update on the theft of your family's jewelry."

Lars felt the muscles in his jaw relax. He pushed the button for speakerphone so the others could hear. "What have you learned?" he asked.

"Not much, I'm afraid. We've identified two of the gunmen, thanks to Miss Jansen's excellent descriptions and the bank's security feed, but they're still at large. We have men checking pawn shops around the city in case any of the items show up at one of them."

"Detective Meyer." Lars worked to keep his voice even. He could have done without this after Tess's news. "As I told you at the bank, the jewelry in that safe-deposit box is worth millions of euros. If the thieves are willing to risk selling one-of-a-kind items of that value, they're going to do it on the black market, not at a local pawn shop."

"I agree, but we also have to operate on the premise that the perpetrators don't realize the value of the pieces they stole. In which case, we must not rule out the possibility of a pawn shop sale," the detective said. "It would be helpful if you would send me photographs of the missing pieces."

Lars could not argue the point. "I can do that," he said.

"I appreciate it." The policeman rattled off his email address, and Marit typed it into the computer. "I'll be in touch as soon as I have an update for you."

"Thanks."

The connection ended, and Lars set down his phone with a sigh. "Well, you heard him. No progress on the jewelry yet—which I assume means no progress on finding your diamonds either, Cole."

"Except for Peter Brinkerhoff," Marit said.

"Yes." Cole was looking thoughtful again. "We need to figure out how to corner the jeweler at the ball so I can ask him some pointed questions in private."

Lars pulled up the first photos he'd taken of the Falcon Point jewelry. This batch was still in the bank. He'd have to scroll further to get to the ones the detective needed. He looked at the picture of the stunning pink diamond necklace on his screen, and an idea began to form.

"Isabelle," he said. "Would the bank allow me access to the two safe-deposit boxes still at the bank?"

"I would think so," she said. "Enough time has passed since the robbery. They should be functioning normally by now."

Cole eyed him curiously. "What are you thinking?"

"We need something that will attract Brinkerhoff's attention at the ball," he said. "I know what it's like to walk into a room full of strangers with Marit. She's beautiful enough that even if she were dressed in a potato sack, she'd garner attention."

Marit shifted uncomfortably beside him. Lars took her hand. He knew she did her best to ignore the extra attention, but this time, it might work to their advantage.

"Brinkerhoff will notice her," Lars continued. "And if Marit is wearing the Falcon Point pink diamond necklace, he'll notice that too. No jeweler of his caliber would miss it. Marit and I can approach him to talk diamonds, and then I can suggest that he take a look at some other diamonds from the same collection and introduce him to you and Isabelle, who'd be wearing the pear-cut diamond earrings."

Cole nodded, a spark of interest in his eyes. "I think you might be onto something. What do you think, Marit? Are you willing to act as bait?"

"If it helps you get back your great-grandmother's wedding ring, I'll do it."

Lars squeezed her hand, touched by her answer. The gold ring was likely the item of least monetary value in the collection, but Marit had made a connection to his great-grandmother through it.

Cole turned to Isabelle and raised an eyebrow. "How would you feel about wearing invaluable diamonds tomorrow night?"

"That's quite an offer," she said. There was a hint of teasing in her voice. "Does this mean you trust me more than the Vienna police do?"

"Absolutely."

CHAPTER 22

Isabelle sat on one of the stools beside her kitchen counter, a wide assortment of cosmetics covering the previously clear surface. When she had offered to let Marit move in with her for the remainder of her stay in Vienna, she hadn't anticipated that Marit would bring with her an arsenal of beauty products. Didn't models have makeup artists and stylists for this? At least the tickets to the ball had already arrived when they'd stopped by the hotel.

"I really don't think all of this is necessary," Isabelle said. She had offered the same opinion when Marit had insisted on twisting her hair into a complicated up-do. Isabelle had to admit she loved the results, but she doubted she could replicate the look if her life depended on it.

"Look up." Marit picked up an eyeliner pencil and uncapped it to reveal the pointy tip.

Isabelle resisted the urge to defend herself, instead forcing herself to remain still. She wasn't opposed to wearing makeup. She put on a light dusting every day before work, but spending the better part of an hour painting her face seemed like overkill. At least Marit had let Isabelle stay in her jeans and blouse to do it.

Marit traded the eyeliner for mascara. After she applied it to Isabelle's eyelashes, she stepped back and gave a satisfied nod. "Okay. You're all set."

Isabelle stood and crossed to a large rectangular mirror hanging on her wall. "Wow. I didn't know I could look like this."

"I just enhanced your eyes a bit and gave your lips some color."

"I think you did a bit more than that. Doing makeup is your superpower."

"It's not the same as racing around city streets so well that even the police can't catch you, but I do all right."

"You do better than all right." Isabelle blinked, making sure the movement reflected in the mirror. Yep. The woman staring back really was her.

"Come on." Marit tapped Isabelle's shoulder. "Let's get dressed. The guys should be here in a half hour."

Marit collected her makeup and carried it into the guest bedroom.

Isabelle retreated to her room and changed into the borrowed dress.

Navy-blue silk overlaid with lace fell to her ankles, a slit up one side stopping just past her knee. Isabelle wasn't about to wear something that would restrict her ability to walk . . . or run. She eyed the impractical bone-colored heels. Her feet would be killing her by the end of the night, but the reputation of Marit's friend would remain intact.

Isabelle collected the cream wool coat that also sported a Monique Martin label. She held it up in front of her, approving of the classic lines and the way the color enhanced her complexion. Owning such an item would be in character for someone of her position at the bank, and as impractical as the price tag might be, Isabelle suspected she would end up purchasing the coat rather than returning it.

She stepped out of her bedroom at the same time Marit emerged from the guest room.

"Wow." Even though Isabelle had already seen Marit in the cream-colored draped gown, with her hair twisted up into a stylish chignon bun and her features accented even more than usual, she was truly stunning. "You are going to be the center of attention tonight."

"That's what I'm good at."

Isabelle caught the hint of regret in her voice. "That may be, but Lars sees you as far more than a pretty face."

Marit's expression softened, and a smile played on her lips. "He does, doesn't he."

Isabelle nodded. "The man is head over heels for you."

"Do you really think—"

A knock sounded at the door.

Isabelle crossed the room. After looking through the peephole, she pulled the door open. Cole and Lars stood in the hall, looking like they could have been on the red carpet of a Hollywood event.

Cole took in her appearance, and his jaw dropped.

An unexpected satisfaction crept through her. She smiled and forced herself to look at both men instead of staring at Cole. "You both look very dapper tonight." She stepped back. "Come on in."

Cole's eyes locked on hers. Lars nudged him through the door, but Cole's gaze didn't falter.

Isabelle's cheeks heated.

Marit stepped forward, an absolute vision with her sleek gown and gorgeous features.

Now Lars's jaw dropped. "Wow. You look incredible."

"Thank you." Marit reached out her hand and placed it in Lars's.

"Cole and I are going to be the envy of every man at the ball tonight."

"As long as we get noticed by Brinkerhoff, we'll be happy," Marit said.

"If he doesn't notice you, he's blind," Lars said. "Right, Cole?"

Cole didn't respond.

"Cole?" Lars waved his hand in front of his cousin's face.

Finally, Cole snapped out of the trance he was in, and he looked at Lars. Lars grinned. "I think this is the first time I've seen you speechless."

Cole motioned to Isabelle and Marit. "With the way they look tonight, I'm surprised you can form a coherent sentence."

"I'm used to this." Lars motioned to Marit. "She looks like this all the time."

Now Marit's cheeks heated. "Are you ready to go?"

"Almost." Lars reached into his pocket and drew out a black velvet jewelry case. He set it on the counter and opened the lid. Inside, the pink diamond sparkled beneath the overhead light.

"It really is beautiful," Marit said.

"So are you." Lars lifted the necklace from the case. "May I?"

Marit nodded. She turned around so Lars could slip the necklace into place. After he fastened the clasp, she put her hand up to the jewel now hanging from her neck. "What do you think? Will Brinkerhoff notice it?"

"I don't know how he could miss it."

Cole pulled a smaller jewelry case from his pocket and held it out to Isabelle. "I believe these are for you."

"It's a good thing Marit was here to help me put my hair up." Isabelle retrieved one earring and slid it into place. After she put the other one on, she lowered her hand.

"You're stunning." Cole leaned forward and brushed his lips across her cheek. "Truly stunning."

Another blush rose to her cheeks. Was this the same man who had forgotten she existed during the months he was away? The connection between them sparked, and Isabelle managed a smile. "Thank you."

Lars offered his arm to Marit. "Shall we?"

Marit nodded.

Cole helped Isabelle with her coat and settled his hand at her waist. "Let's get this party started."

When Cole drove Isabelle's car into the vast courtyard of Schönbrunn Palace, Marit could only stare. She'd worked here during daylight hours, when the sandy-colored stone walls and hundreds of windows had reflected the sun and cast a warm glow over the open square. It had looked magnificent then. Now, silhouetted against the dark sky by myriad glowing lights, it looked magical.

"I'm beginning to understand why people wanted to come so badly," Lars said. "This place is amazing."

"I love visiting in the summer, just to walk through the grounds," Isabelle said. "There's even a zoo."

They joined the slow line of cars crawling around one of the large circular fountains and inched toward the grand staircase that marked the entrance to the palace. Valets darted back and forth, taking car keys from elegantly dressed guests and driving cars to a parking area on the other side of the courtyard before running back to claim the next vehicle.

The system appeared as seamless as it was efficient, and it wasn't long before Cole pulled up in front of the palace. Leaving the car running, he nodded to the nearest valet and went around to join Isabelle. Lars appeared at Marit's door to help her out.

"I feel like Cinderella arriving at the palace ball in my borrowed gown," Marit whispered.

He smiled at her. "Do me a favor. Don't go looking for Prince Charming or losing your shoes. Neither of those possibilities bode well for me."

"Why would I need to find Prince Charming? I'm arriving with him." Marit tucked her arm through his, the warmth of his smile wreaking havoc on her attempted calm. "And do you really care that much about my shoes?"

"Only when it comes to protecting your feet from a partner who's had one dance lesson with a pretty useless teacher." They started after Cole and Isabelle, who were crossing the short distance to the stairs. "I feel like I should apologize ahead of time."

"No apology necessary," she said. "There's no one else I'd rather dance with." She caught the uncertainty in his eyes and stopped walking. "I mean it, Lars."

His eyes searched hers. "You really do, don't you?"

"Yes."

He reached out to touch her face, and a wisp of white floated down between them, landing on the sleeve of his black jacket. Another one followed. Marit looked up. The dark sky was filled with spiraling snowflakes.

"Snow," she said, unable to contain her wonder at the sight. "Look at how beautiful it is."

"It is beautiful." Lars smiled at her delight. "Unfortunately, it's also wet." He brushed the rapidly accumulating flakes off his jacket and grabbed her hand. "Come on, Cinderella. It won't do to have you soggy for your grand entrance."

Cole and Isabelle were waiting for them at the main doors.

"Everything okay?" Cole asked.

"Yep," Lars replied. "Just admiring the snow."

Cole accepted Lars's response without comment. He held the tickets in his hand. "Once we're in the ballroom, everyone keep an eye out for Brinkerhoff."

They crossed the entrance hall together. Footsteps, voices, and laughter echoed off the marble-tiled floor and vaulted ceiling. Enormous paintings in gilded frames hung on the walls, and lights flickered from chandeliers. Cole offered their tickets to a man at the door to the ballroom. The man eyed the numbers on the corner of each ticket and glanced at a list of names on a clipboard in his hand.

"We're Yvette LeBlanc's guests," Marit said, stepping up. "She sends her regrets that she could not be here tonight."

The man took one look at Marit and straightened his shoulders. "Yes, of course. Welcome to Schönbrunn Palace's Great Gallery." He inclined his head and moved aside to allow them to walk into the room beyond.

The ballroom was breathtaking. An intricately pieced wood parquet floor ran the length of the long room. Cream-colored walls were decorated with gold molding. Light shone from the many wall sconces, reflecting off the crystal and gold of the elaborate fixtures and spotlighting the room's focal point—the magnificent oval murals on the ceiling.

In the far corner, a string ensemble was playing a Strauss waltz. Several couples—the men wearing tuxes and the women in elegant gowns—danced in the center of the room. Other guests milled around the edge of the dance floor. Some were seated at the beautifully appointed tables positioned along the walls, while others were standing, talking in small clusters. A few people were already partaking of the drinks and appetizers waiters were carrying around on circular gold trays.

"In case you were wondering," Lars muttered, "we're not in Cole's flat anymore."

Cole gave him a withering look, and Marit stifled a giggle. She understood Cole's stress. She felt it too. But she was grateful for Lars's ability to lighten the mood.

"I think I see him," Isabelle said. "On the right, near the far wall. He's sitting at a table with half a dozen other people, talking to a woman wearing a red gown. There are a couple of men standing between him and us."

Cole took a few steps to the left to look that way without being too obvious. "I see him," he said. "And it looks like his male guests have some muscle."

"You think they're bodyguards?" Lars asked.

"They have the right vibe," Cole said. "But looking intimidating is no match for looking stunning." He turned back to face Marit. "Are you ready?"

Her stomach was a tangled knot. Did that count for anything? Lars placed his hand on her back. It was a simple touch, nothing more than a reminder of his presence, but it gave her the courage she needed. "Yes."

The music filling the ballroom came to an end, and couples cleared the floor.

"That's our cue," Cole said. "Lars, when the next dance begins, lead Marit across the floor toward Brinkerhoff. Try to position yourself so that you're near him when the music stops. Isabelle and I will stick close."

Marit felt Lars's arm tense, but he nodded and said, "We've got this." He took her hand to guide her into the center of the room. She felt the stares as they left the safety of the wall, but she kept her focus on Lars. He winked at her, and she smiled. He was right. They had this.

CHAPTER 23

COLE LED ISABELLE TO A spot on the dance floor where they could see Brinkerhoff without being in his direct line of sight. Typically, he would have opted to watch from a dark corner where he wouldn't be noticed, but with Isabelle on his arm, there was no chance of that. Between her and Marit, he doubted there was a single man in the room who hadn't looked their way. Not that he could blame them. His pulse still hadn't steadied even though nearly an hour had passed since Isabelle had first opened her door.

She stepped into his arms as a new song began, and for a brief moment, they were the only two people in the room. Her gorgeous green eyes met his, and whatever reservations Isabelle had harbored about him seemed to melt away. He drew her close and had to remind himself of the reason he was here.

Isabelle's fingers brushed against the skin above his collar, and another jolt rocketed through him.

He looked down, but she was discreetly scanning the room. She leaned closer and whispered, "You aren't supposed to be looking at me."

"It's hard not to."

A faint blush tinted her skin. "I told Marit that her skills as a makeup artist are her superpower."

"I can agree with that," Cole said. A little flash of disappointment surfaced on her face. He leaned closer and added, "But I doubt I'd be able to keep my eyes off you even if Marit hadn't done your makeup."

The blush deepened. "We aren't here for you to stare at me."

"I guess you're right," Cole conceded. "But it's a nice side benefit."

Isabelle looked over his shoulder. "Do you recognize anyone with him?"

Him. Brinkerhoff. Right. The reason they were here.

Cole twirled her around until he had a better view. Four men and two women sitting together at a round table set for eight. The other two seats were unoccupied, but if the half-filled glasses of wine at each place setting were any indication, the other couple was currently on the dance floor.

"I don't think I've ever seen any of them before," Cole said, his voice low. "What about you?"

"No, but it's hard to see the two with their backs to us."

"We'll try for a better angle." Cole guided Isabelle closer, moving toward the edge of the dance floor.

A short distance away, Marit and Lars danced near Brinkerhoff's table.

Cole swallowed, his neck straining against his bow tie as he fought back the memory of teaching Lars to dance. At least his cousin was a fast learner. Looking at him now, no one would ever suspect this was Lars's first time waltzing with a woman.

The song ended, and several couples exited the dance floor. Out of the corner of his eye, Cole glimpsed a man who looked vaguely familiar. Before he could get a good look at him, however, a man in his late fifties stepped into his line of sight.

"Isabelle?" His eyes wide, the newcomer stepped closer. "My goodness. I hardly recognized you."

"Gerhart." Isabelle nodded politely. "I wasn't aware you would be here tonight."

"I come every year." He motioned to the woman beside him. "My wife has been on the planning committee for years. I don't think you've met. Lina, this is Isabelle Roberts. She works with me at the bank."

"Oh, yes. I believe Gerhart has mentioned you. You are much younger than I expected."

Isabelle ignored the comment and offered her hand. "It's nice to meet you, Frau Wimmer."

"And who is this?" Lina motioned to Cole.

"Cole Bridger." Cole shook each of their hands in turn. "It's good to meet you."

"Gerhart is one of the senior vice presidents at Bankhaus Steiner," Isabelle said.

"And what do you do for a living, Mr. Bridger?" Gerhart asked.

Another song started, and Isabelle put her hand on Cole's arm. "I love this song." She turned to the Wimmers. "Will you excuse us?"

"By all means." Gerhart stepped back.

Isabelle stepped into Cole's arms and leaned in close. "Should I be suspicious that he's here tonight?"

"I don't know," Cole said. "Should you?"

"Maybe." Isabelle's gaze lifted to meet his. "The day of the robbery, Gerhart wasn't at the bank."

Cole's eyes narrowed. "Where was he?"

"He said he had a meeting at another branch."

"Does he have meetings like that often?"

Isabelle shook her head. "No. He doesn't."

Lars had stopped counting steps less than half a minute into the dance. How could he possibly be expected to do something so mundane when he held Marit in his arms? It wasn't happening.

Avoiding the couples closest to them, he trusted in the music's tempo to dictate their movement and pulled her closer. She looked up. Her warm brown eyes met his, and his breath caught. She was so incredibly beautiful—inside and out.

"How did I ever get so lucky?" he whispered, reverting to Dutch to verbalize the feelings of his heart.

Her smile was slow and sweet. "I was just thinking the same thing."

Her fingers brushed his neck, the brief touch on his skin upending his footwork.

"Sorry," he murmured.

"No apologies, remember? You're doing wonderfully."

He found his place again and guided her around another couple. He twirled her forward. She laughed softly as her gown flowed around their ankles in a cloud of silk. Guests glanced her way. She ignored them.

They danced until the music came to a close. Reluctantly, Lars released her from his arms. Light from the nearest wall sconce caught the pink diamond at her neck, painting her cream-colored gown with miniature rainbows—an ethereal reminder of why they were there.

He took a moment to situate himself. They'd ended the dance within a few meters of Brinkerhoff's table. If they walked off the dance floor at just the right angle, the jeweler could not help but see them.

"Looks like it's showtime," he said softly.

She nodded, slipping her hand into his. Raising her chin, she set her sights on their target and turned on a well-practiced smile. Lars matched it with a smile of his own, and they walked off the dance floor toward Brinkerhoff.

Making sure that Marit and the diamond necklace remained clearly visible from where the jeweler sat, Lars approached the table. The prickling sensation that they were being watched followed them, but he kept his eyes averted until they were within a meter of Brinkerhoff's chair. At that point, Lars looked over at him and caught the jeweler's gaze glide from Marit's face to the necklace.

Brinkerhoff pushed back his chair and rose to his feet. "Pardon me for being so forward," he said, "but I couldn't help but notice your necklace. Am I right in thinking it's a pink diamond?"

"Yes." Marit touched the diamond at her neck and offered the man a stunning smile.

To Brinkerhoff's credit, he maintained his wits well enough to continue speaking. "Remarkable. I'm not sure that I've ever seen such a large cushion-cut pink diamond before."

"I believe it's close to three carats," Lars said, entering the conversation for the first time.

Brinkerhoff turned his attention from the necklace to Lars. "If you've not had it officially appraised, I would be happy to offer you my services." He extended his hand. "Peter Brinkerhoff. I own a couple of jewelry shops here in Vienna."

"Nice to meet you," Lars said, shaking his hand. "Lars Hendriks, and this is my girlfriend, Marit Jansen."

Brinkerhoff shook Marit's hand. "Stunning."

Not sure whether the jeweler was referring to the necklace or to Marit, Lars placed a protective hand on her back. "My cousin is with us this evening," he said. "His friend is wearing a pair of pear-cut diamond earrings from the same collection. If you are a man who appreciates exquisite jewelry, you must see them."

"Are they also pink diamonds?"

Lars could almost hear the man calculating the earrings' worth. "No, but as far as I can tell, they're virtually flawless. And at least two carats apiece." Brinkerhoff hesitated, and Lars turned to flattery. "I'd be grateful to have a man of your expertise take a look at them. And perhaps we could arrange a time to have you appraise a few other pieces from the collection in the next week or so."

Brinkerhoff considered his suggestion a moment. "I believe that can be arranged."

"Excellent," Lars said. "Let me introduce you to my cousin."

Cole had to give it to Lars. Not only had the man avoided stepping on Marit's toes while they were on the dance floor, but now, talking to Brinkerhoff, he also didn't appear the least bit nervous. Maybe talking jewels relaxed him. Weird.

Cole tugged at the edge of his jacket to make sure his waistband holster wasn't visible beneath the clean lines of his tuxedo. Coming to a ball armed wasn't his first choice, but with two civilians putting themselves in front of a potential criminal, he hadn't been willing to risk their safety.

Lars and Marit approached with Brinkerhoff, the older man already eyeing Isabelle. Cole's protective instinct flared only to relax a second later. As stunning as Isabelle looked tonight, Brinkerhoff's gaze had zeroed in on her earrings.

"Lars, you didn't exaggerate. These are stunning. I haven't seen a setting like that outside of pictures."

"Cole, Isabelle, this is Peter Brinkerhoff of Brinkerhoff Jewelers," Lars said.

"Good to meet you." Isabelle extended her hand.

Cole offered a brief nod and handshake.

"Peter is interested in seeing Isabelle's earrings," Lars continued.

"Yes. I've always had a fondness for diamonds," Peter said.

"Perhaps you'd like to go out there where the light is better." Cole waved at the doorway behind him.

"That's not necessary." Brinkerhoff glanced at Cole briefly before turning his attention back to the pear-cut diamonds dangling from Isabelle's ears. "The way the stones catch the light in here is perfect."

So much for easy.

The orchestra began a new song.

Cole took a half step back.

"These are part of a family collection," Isabelle said. Following Cole's lead, she edged closer to the door. "We don't know much about how old they are though."

Brinkerhoff moved forward for a closer inspection. "My guess is late eighteen hundreds."

"Perhaps we should step into the hall," Isabelle suggested. "The music is rather loud."

"I'm afraid I can't tell you much beyond the time period without my loupe," Brinkerhoff said. "If you'd like to come by my store, I'd be happy to give you an appraisal."

"I may do that." Isabelle put her hand on Brinkerhoff's shoulder, angling her body so she was between Cole and the other guests. "But I'd rather talk about it now."

"I'm afraid I need to get back to my wife." Brinkerhoff turned to Lars and Marit. "Lars, it was nice talking to you."

"Mr. Brinkerhoff, I have another matter I would very much like to discuss," Cole said, taking his best manners out for a spin. "Could you please spare a few moments that we might speak privately?"

"I'm sorry. Not tonight." He started to take a step back.

Resigned that he couldn't take the easy route, Cole drew his weapon and pointed it discretely at Brinkerhoff.

"I think we should have a talk first," Cole said in a low voice. "I'm sure your wife won't mind."

Marit's gaze dropped to the gun, and her face paled. Lars's jaw tensed, but his expression was more of a here-we-go-again look rather than surprise.

Isabelle held her position, but she spoke calmly to Lars and Marit. "Maybe you two should go back and enjoy the ball. I'll stay with Cole."

Lars nodded. "Come on, Marit. Let's see if we can make it through another waltz without me stepping on your toes."

Marit recovered from the unlikely scenario of seeing a weapon drawn in a palace ballroom. "I'd like that."

"We'll see you both later," Cole said. He reached out his free hand and placed it on the jeweler's shoulder as though they were friends about to share an intimate conversation. In fact, they were going to share an intimate conversation. It just wasn't one that his current companion was likely to enjoy.

CHAPTER 24

"WHAT IS THE MEANING OF this?" Brinkerhoff asked with indignation rather than fear. "Who are you, and what do you want from me?"

Cole escorted him toward the small gallery, away from the single security guard down the hall. "We just want to talk."

"About what? I don't keep money on me, if that's what you're looking for."

"We aren't planning to rob you," Isabelle said quietly. "Like my friend said, we just want to talk."

She waited for Cole to escort Brinkerhoff through the gallery's open doorway. As soon as they were inside, Isabelle closed the door behind her.

"You don't need to point a gun at me if you want to have a conversation," he said.

"I told you in the ballroom that we had something important to discuss," Isabelle said calmly. "You weren't interested."

Fury flashed in the other man's eyes. His lack of concern sent alarm bells ringing in Cole's head.

Cole took a step back so he wasn't in arm's reach of Brinkerhoff. "You were at the Munich Jewelry Show last month."

"So? Nearly every jeweler in the region was there."

"You purchased some diamonds from Hans Koch," Cole continued. "One of those stones was recovered from a crime scene a few days ago."

"What does that have to do with me?"

"We need to know who you sold it to."

Brinkerhoff looked pointedly at Cole's pistol. "Did it ever occur to you to visit me at my store? That's where I keep my records."

"It did," Cole said.

"You have been unavailable," Isabelle said, her tone much more polite than Cole's. "This is a rather time-sensitive matter."

"Time sensitive enough to pull a gun on me."

"Yes." Cole's eyes met Brinkerhoff's, and the other man flinched.

"My records are at my store. There's nothing I can tell you tonight," Brinker-hoff insisted.

"Do you ever buy and sell uncertified diamonds?" Cole asked.

Brinkerhoff's eyes darted to the side. "Absolutely not."

Cole's suspicions heightened. "Do you sell loose stones?"

"It's not common, but it does happen."

"Great. Then you should remember selling this particular stone. It would have been sold within the past three weeks."

"I don't remember selling any loose diamonds this month. Perhaps one of my associates sold it," Brinkerhoff said. "I would have to check my records."

"Interesting." Isabelle exchanged a look with Cole before focusing on the jeweler once more. "When I spoke with your store manager, she said no one was authorized to sell loose stones but you."

Brinkerhoff clenched his jaw. The likelihood of this man being involved in illegal activity increased a thousand percent.

"Who are you working with?" Cole asked. "And what are the diamonds paying for?"

Brinkerhoff simply stared.

Cole sighed. This might take longer than he'd thought.

Cole has a gun. Cole has a gun. The words repeated through Marit's head in time to the waltz. Isabelle hadn't even flinched when he'd drawn it. Lars had looked unsurprised. What on earth was going on?

Misreading Lars's lead, she stepped to the right and collided with his chest. He gripped her more tightly, waiting until she was steady before continuing with the dance.

"You okay?" he asked.

"Yes. No." Marit met his eyes. "Cole has a gun."

Lars grimaced. "Yeah, I noticed that."

"And you're not shocked?"

"I've seen him with a gun before."

Memory came flooding back. Lars had told her of his first meeting with Cole at the hospital in Amsterdam. It was an introduction that had ended in a chaotic shoot-out.

"Lars, he's in Schönbrunn Palace." Panic welled within her. She'd told Yvette that her friends were ballworthy, not brawlworthy. "He can't use a gun in here."

"I'm sure he's aware of that. He's not going to shoot an unarmed man, and it's extremely unlikely that Brinkerhoff is armed—especially since he has those bodyguards watching out for him."

Marit turned to look at the table where Brinkerhoff and his guests had been sitting. Her heart stuttered. "They're gone. Those men aren't at the table anymore."

Lars tensed. "Are you sure?"

"Yes."

"Keep looking," he said, spinning her in a slow circle. "See if you can spot them somewhere else in the room."

Marit scanned the crowd as she turned.

"The door," she said. "They're heading through the door Cole, Isabelle, and Brinkerhoff just left through."

Lars gave up all pretense of dancing. Taking her by the hand, he plowed through the swaying couples and headed directly for the exit.

"Where are we going?"

"We need to warn Cole. If those thugs find him, things are likely to get ugly."

Marit's heart pounded. This couldn't be happening again. "What are you going to do?"

"I don't know yet," he said. He glanced at her. "I'm open to suggestions."

Up ahead, the two men disappeared through the door. Lars lengthened his stride, reaching it seconds later and pushing it open. At the far end of the hall, a palace security guard stood monitoring the comings and goings at the great gallery's main entrance. The two bodyguards glanced that way before turning toward the door directly across from them that led into the small gallery. That had to be where Cole and Isabelle had taken Brinkerhoff. And if they were that close, she and Lars had no time to lose.

"Excuse me," Marit called. She let go of Lars's hand and hurried to catch up with the men. "I wonder if you two gentlemen could help us."

The men stopped. The shorter of the two ran his gaze over her from head to toe. She suppressed a shudder, grateful when Lars stepped up beside her.

"What is it?" the man asked.

The man wouldn't win any points for polite conversation, but Marit was more interested in stalling for time. If Cole and Isabelle were half as smart as she thought they were, they'd have picked up on how many men were about to enter the small gallery.

"We're looking for the toilet. Is there one on this floor, or do we need to go downstairs?"

"I have no idea, lady," Shorty said. "Why don't you ask the guy who works here?" He pointed down the hall toward the distant security guard.

"Sorry," Marit said. "We didn't recognize you from behind. I don't think we were introduced when we met Mr. Brinkerhoff."

"No. We weren't."

Shorty gave a terse nod and turned his back on them. Before Marit or Lars had time to say another word, the two men crossed the meter and a half to the small gallery and reached for the door.

Isabelle processed Marit's words and the warning they implied. Two of Brinkerhoff's men were coming their way? She rushed toward the door to peek out, but she made it to only within a few meters before the door burst open. A man rushed in, and a second man took a guard-like stance in the doorway. The first, a light-haired man with broad shoulders, reached into his jacket. Isabelle caught the imprint of a shoulder holster. She hesitated a brief moment to remember which side the slit in her dress was on. Then she kicked out her leg, her heel spearing into the man's stomach.

His breath whooshed out, and his dark-haired partner pulled his weapon.

"Stay right there." His pistol now pointed in Isabelle's direction.

"Drop the gun," Cole said, now aiming his gun in the general direction of the dark-haired bodyguard. Unfortunately, Isabelle stood between them, blocking his ability to take a shot.

"Herr Brinkerhoff. Are you all right?" the upright bodyguard asked. His partner had yet to straighten after Isabelle's attack.

"These men seemed to have confused me with someone else." Brinkerhoff eyed Cole's gun before taking a step toward the door. "Let's get out of here."

Not call security or call the police, but get out of here. Any doubt Isabelle harbored that Brinkerhoff was involved with the bank robbers disappeared.

"Not so fast." Cole stepped into Brinkerhoff's path. Too bad he couldn't pull out credentials and arrest the man on the spot, but the CIA didn't work that way. They would need the local police to take him into custody. Cole's gun lifted a little higher. "Maybe we should have a nice chat at the police station."

Lars's voice carried from the open doorway. "Do you want me to call the police?"

What was Lars doing coming in here? Didn't he see that these men were armed? Isabelle's gaze swept the room. The bodyguard holding the gun was facing away from Lars. Cole's cousin had no idea he was walking into a potential gunfight.

Apprehension flashed on Cole's face. "Tell security to call them," Cole said, his voice calm despite his obvious concern. "Take your girlfriend with you."

Lars took a step back in the same moment the light-haired bodyguard reached for his gun.

Isabelle acted instantly. She pivoted on her heel and struck out with her hand to keep him from completing his intended move. He tried again, this time managing to draw his weapon. Isabelle used her hand to strike his wrist. The gun dropped from his grip and thudded against the carpet.

She ducked to give Cole a clear shot, her gaze darting to the doorway where Lars and Marit stood wide-eyed. "Go!"

Her single word broke them out of whatever trance they were in. Lars grabbed Marit's hand, and they disappeared down the hall.

"Don't do it." Cole kept his gun trained on the man.

The other guard moved toward his weapon, but Isabelle kicked it farther into the room.

"You have no idea who you're dealing with," Brinkerhoff said.

"I'd be thrilled if you would enlighten me," Cole countered.

Brinkerhoff exchanged a look with his dark-haired guard.

Isabelle read their intent. "Watch out!"

Her words were barely out of her mouth when Brinkerhoff rushed at Cole, using his shoulder to knock Cole off-balance.

The light-haired guard surged toward Isabelle. He wrapped a hand around her waist, the force knocking her off her pointy heels and onto the ground.

Across the room, Cole stumbled. His gun hand lowered for a brief moment, just long enough for Brinkerhoff to dart across the room.

The guns came up again, with Isabelle on the floor between Cole's trained gun and the armed bodyguard.

Brinkerhoff ducked behind the two bodyguards. "If they try to follow us, shoot them."

Cole held his ground, unable to do anything but keep his gun aimed at the bodyguard.

The three men disappeared out of the room.

"Not again." Isabelle's frustration rose. "We have to stop them."

"No." Cole shook his head. "We have to follow them."

CHAPTER 25

COLE WASN'T ABOUT TO RUSH after Brinkerhoff and his buddies until he was sure they weren't going to be walking into flying bullets. No need to push an escalation, not when what they really needed was information. Once they were clear of the palace, though, he planned on having another chat with the jeweler, but this time, he was determined to get different results.

Cole reached out and helped Isabelle to a stand. "Are you okay?"

"I'm fine, but they're getting away." Isabelle hurried to where she had kicked the bodyguard's gun. She grabbed it and checked the ammunition before starting for the door.

Cole holstered his weapon and followed. He looked down the hall in both directions, but Brinkerhoff wasn't anywhere in sight. "They must have headed for the exit."

He and Isabelle raced down the hall. When they reached the main foyer, Isabelle lowered her hand so the gun she held would be hidden within the folds of her dress.

Across the open space, Lars and Marit stood beside the security guard.

Cole rushed to them. "Where did they go?"

"They went out the front." Marit pointed at the tall doors a short distance away.

Cole jogged to the exit, bypassing the coat check, Isabelle matching him stride for stride. Even if the claim tickets for their coats weren't in Lars's pocket, he wasn't willing to let Brinkerhoff get too much of a lead on him.

When he pushed through the exit, cold air blasted him and snow swirled in the night sky. Isabelle shivered beside him.

"You should stay here. I'll be faster without you," he said to her.

"Look. That's them." Isabelle pointed at the three men standing at the curb as a limo approached.

A half dozen people stood nearby, a couple of valets and some late arrivals—six potential hostages. Not a situation Cole wanted in any circumstance.

"We'll need to wait until those civilians clear out," Isabelle said.

"I was thinking the same thing." He started down the stairs slowly to keep from drawing attention.

Isabelle shivered again.

"Here." Cole took off his tuxedo jacket and draped it around her shoulders.

"Thanks."

The two couples at the bottom of the stairs moved toward them. As soon as they passed, Cole and Isabelle increased their pace. They were nearly to the bottom when Isabelle lost her footing on the slick steps.

Cole reached out to steady her, his sense of urgency rising when Brinkerhoff and his guards stepped into the limo.

He couldn't wait for the valet to bring them Isabelle's car. They would have to fetch it themselves, or Brinkerhoff might disappear indefinitely.

Cole moved toward the valet stand.

"The car is this way." Isabelle tugged on his arm.

"We need the key."

"I have a spare." Isabelle held up a single key and headed for the parked cars a short distance away.

Where she hid a spare car key in that dress was beyond him, but he was quite certain it would be considered impolite to ask, so he just raced after her.

Her car came into view, with one on either side and another behind it. In front, another row of vehicles had been parked barely a car's length away. "We need the valet to move the car in front of yours."

"I'll be fine." Isabelle climbed in on the driver's side.

Resigned, Cole climbed into the passenger seat, a sick feeling settling into the pit of his stomach. They were going to lose Brinkerhoff and the chance to learn what he knew.

Isabelle started the car, pulled forward, and whipped the wheel to the right, her rear bumper angling toward the car beside them.

"Careful." Cole reached out and gripped the dashboard. "You're going to hit—"

Before he finished his sentence, Isabelle maneuvered out of the tiny parking space at an uncomfortably high speed, her bumper coming within centimeters of clipping the car beside her.

She pulled down the drive and followed the fading taillights of the limo.

Cole willed himself to relax, but he wasn't sure how much more of Isabelle's grand prix driving skills he wanted to experience firsthand.

Marit was unnaturally quiet. Lars didn't blame her. He'd seen Cole in action before, but watching Isabelle disarm a bodyguard with a few well-placed kicks took their recent experience in the small gallery to a whole new level of unreality. Even so, there was no escaping that it had actually happened. If Marit's pale complexion wasn't proof enough, the fact that they were now stranded at Schönbrunn Palace with no way to leave would do it.

Taking Marit's cold hand in his, he walked her back toward the ballroom.

"How are we going to get back to Cole's and Isabelle's flats?" Marit's voice was strained.

"Don't worry about it." Lars patted his pocket. "I have my phone. If Cole doesn't call me, I'll request an Uber."

She nodded.

"Hey." He stopped, drawing her into a small alcove near the great gallery's main doors. "It's going to be okay. I have no idea what Cole's up to, but I'm pretty sure he does."

She nodded again. "I'm sorry. After being held at gunpoint in the bank . . . and seeing weapons drawn again in the small gallery . . ." She shuddered.

He wrapped his arms around her, anger mounting at Cole's cavalier decision to withhold the fact that he was carrying a weapon. "When we see Cole again, he's going to have some serious explaining to do," he said. "But in the meantime, here's what we're going to do. First, we're going to go back into the ballroom and I'm going to dance with you again. Then we're going to try some of those weird cracker things that the waiters are carrying around."

Marit's lips curved upward. "You mean the canapés?"

"Sure."

She smothered a giggle. "Okay, then what?"

"If my knuckleheaded cousin still hasn't contacted me by then, I think maybe another dance." He pulled her closer. "I've decided I like waltzing with you rather a lot."

"Good," she said. "Because I like waltzing with you too."

The tension had left her shoulders, and her eyes were smiling again. His gaze moved to her lips. Behind them, the main doors opened, releasing a burst of laughter and music. Marit started, and Lars pulled back.

"Maybe we should go back into the ballroom," she said, a hint of pink in her cheeks.

Regret coursed through him, but he summoned a smile. "Good idea."

She tucked her arm through his, and they walked into the great gallery together. Lars guided her around the swaying, swirling couples to an empty spot on the right. Another couple approached. The gray-haired man eyed them curiously. It was such a common occurrence when he was with Marit that Lars disregarded it until the man spoke.

"I beg your pardon, but are you here with Isabelle Roberts? I thought I saw you come in together earlier."

"We did," Lars said, hoping he didn't need to qualify the answer further.

"Gerhart Wimmer," the man said, extending his hand. "I work with Isabelle at the bank. This is my wife, Lina, and my brother-in-law, Steven."

"Lars Hendriks. And this is Marit Jansen."

Marit smiled, seemingly oblivious to Lina's cool appraisal. "Your evening gown is beautiful, Lina. Is it a Simon Durand?"

Those, apparently, were magic words because in an instant, the banker's wife's entire countenance changed.

"It is," she said, swaying her hips to show the dress off to full effect. "I saw it in Paris earlier this year and couldn't resist."

"I think it's fair to say that you rarely resist when you see something you like," Steven said.

Lina shot him an irritated look. Steven ignored it.

"Your sister has excellent taste," Marit said. "And the lemon color suits her perfectly. Not many women can get away with that shade."

Lina's unnaturally black hair was echoed in the black piping on the yellow dress. Lars thought she looked remarkably like a banana, but what did he know?

Gerhart cleared his throat. Perhaps he thought it would also clear the air between the two siblings. "Is Isabelle nearby?" he asked. "I realize I shouldn't discuss work at these types of events, but I do have an item of business I was hoping to run past her."

"I believe she's stepped out for a little while," Lars said. "I don't suppose she'll be gone long."

"Ah well." Gerhart raised his arms in a shrug that showed off his mono-grammed gold cufflinks. "I daresay it will wait until Monday."

"Of course it will," Lina said. "Now, leave Lars and Marit be so they can dance the next waltz."

As if on cue, the music stopped.

"It was nice to meet you," Lars said. "As your wife said, I promised Marit the next dance, so if you'll excuse us, we're going to take our place on the floor."

Gerhart took a step back and gestured to the center of the room. Lars took Marit's hand and led her away.

She waited until there were several couples between them and the Wimmers before turning to offer Lars a puzzled look. "How much money do bankers make?" she asked.

He put his arm around her waist as the first strains of music began again.

"Isabelle would know better than me, but it probably depends on your position at the bank."

She pondered that while she glided across the floor.

"Why do you ask?" he said.

"I recognized Lina's dress because it was part of a show I did in Paris earlier this year. That means it's from this year's line."

"Okay."

She released a breath. "That also means it's expensive."

Lars got the impression he was missing something. "How expensive is expensive?"

"Over twenty thousand euros."

He tripped on his feet. "Are you serious?"

"Completely."

"That's almost as much as my car's worth."

"I know." She turned her head slightly to look back at where the Wimmers were standing. "Which makes me wonder what kind of car they drive."

CHAPTER 26

ISABELLE PULLED BEHIND A DELIVERY van to avoid having the limo driver and his passengers see them. The slushy mixture of melted snow and ice splashed onto her windshield, and she flipped her wipers on high.

They had been following Brinkerhoff through Vienna for more than fifteen minutes, but so far, the driver didn't seem to have a destination in mind. He also didn't seem the least concerned about the worsening weather conditions.

Beside her, Cole spoke with his guardian friend on his cell phone. After a series of brief phrases and one-word answers Isabelle couldn't decipher, he finally hung up.

"Any luck pulling up the cell phone signal for Brinkerhoff?" Isabelle asked.

"No. It's still showing that it's at his house," Cole said. "Either he left it at home or he has a second one he doesn't want anyone to know about."

"Since he brought two armed bodyguards with him to a ball, I have to think it's the latter." Isabelle pursed her lips. "Are you sure you don't want me to try to stop them?"

"I'd rather you not have to play chicken with a professional driver."

She spared him a glance. "Is that your way of saying I'm not a professional?"

"I wouldn't dare."

Isabelle doubted Cole meant his comment as a compliment, but she took it as one nonetheless. After another block behind the truck, she pulled out and passed him so she could keep the limo in sight.

"He has to be circling to make sure no one is following him," Cole said, stating the obvious.

"What are we planning to do when they get to where they're going?"

"Ghost is going to try to get to Vienna, but it won't be until morning," Cole said. "We may have a stakeout in our future."

Isabelle glanced down at the thin fabric of her gown before she reached out and turned up the heat. "Neither of us is dressed for a stakeout."

"You can drop me off and come back with warmer clothes for both of us."

"And leave you without a car? Not a good idea."

"Do you have a better plan?" Cole asked.

"Maybe. It depends on where we end up." Taxis, Uber, the U-bahn, a city bus. Any of them could give one of them transportation back to one of their apartments. She already felt bad that Lars and Marit would have to consider one of those options to get themselves home from the ball.

"If you think I'm going to have you hike to a train station wearing that gown and my tuxedo jacket, you have another thing coming," Cole said.

"I wasn't planning on being the one to make the hike."

The limo moved out of the left lane and made an immediate right. Isabelle debated briefly. Follow or try to circle to the next block and hope she could find him again?

"Follow him," Cole said.

She changed lanes and made the turn, her wheels skidding on the slick road. She controlled the car, but by the time she focused on the limo again, it had increased the distance between them.

"He knows we're here," Cole said.

The limo sped up. "It's not going to be much of a stakeout if they know we're following them."

"We may have to call in the local authorities," Cole said.

"And tell them what?" Isabelle asked. "That we held a prominent jeweler at gunpoint and he ran away?"

"No. We'll tell them that his bodyguards held us at gunpoint." Cole shot her an innocent look. "They did."

"You started it."

"Are we in kindergarten?" Cole angled one of the vents so the heat was blowing more fully on him.

"It doesn't matter what grade we're in; it's your word against theirs."

"Yeah, but getting them hauled in will buy us some time."

"And put us on the local police's radar."

"Some things can't be helped."

The limo made another quick turn. Again, Isabelle followed, but this time when she rounded the corner, her wheels locked up and her car spun out.

Headlights flashed in the windshield, heading straight toward them.

Cole gripped the dashboard. Isabelle gasped.

She pulled her foot from the brake and turned into the skid.

The other vehicle swerved, narrowly missing them.

Her heart racing, Isabelle hit the brakes, her car jerking to a stop. She blew out an unsteady breath. "Are you okay?"

"Yeah. You?"

She nodded, then turned her gaze to the street where the limo had been moments ago. "At least, I was. We lost Brinkerhoff."

"See if you can catch up to him."

Though her heart was still racing, she eased off the brake and pressed on the gas. After turning the car in the right direction, she headed down the road where they had last seen the limo. They circled the block, then widened their search, circling again.

"Nothing." Isabelle shook her head. "Sorry. They're gone."

Cole blew out a breath and tapped the screen on his phone.

"Are you calling Ghost?" Isabelle asked.

"No, Lars. Might as well go back and pick them up."

"I'm sure Marit will appreciate that, but you'd better prepare yourself for another interrogation."

"An interrogation for what?" Cole asked. "I don't need to ask Marit and Lars anything."

"No, but after seeing you pull a gun on Brinkerhoff, I guarantee they'll have plenty of questions for you."

"What did Cole say?" Marit asked as Lars disconnected the call and slipped his phone back into his pocket.

"They're on their way back to get us. Should be here in about ten minutes." He gave her an apologetic look. "Are you okay leaving a bit early?"

"Of course." The ball, with its accompanying socializing, continued behind them, but as much as she'd loved dancing with Lars, Marit was more than ready to bring the evening to a close. "Let's head down to the coat check. Do you still have my claim ticket?"

"Yes." He dug two small slips of paper out of his jacket's inside pocket. "In fact, I have Isabelle's too."

"Great. If we pick up her coat, Cole and Isabelle won't need to get out of the car."

"Sounds good."

They walked out of the great gallery and crossed the entrance hall to join the short line of people waiting to reclaim their outerwear at the coat check.

"It looks like we're not going to be the first ones to leave," Marit whispered.

"No. That would be Cole, Isabelle, and Brinkerhoff."

Marit heard the frustration in his voice. "At least they didn't leave us stranded," she said.

"True." He wrapped one arm around her waist and pressed a kiss to the top of her head. "And I got to dance with you more than Cole got to dance with Isabelle."

She laughed softly and then stepped aside as he moved up to the counter to claim her and Isabelle's coats.

"They should be pulling up any minute," Lars said once she had her coat on. "Shall we head outside?"

She nodded and slipped her hand into his.

With Isabelle's coat over Lars's other arm, they walked out into a world blanketed in sparkling white. Wispy flakes of snow were still falling, and the stone staircase was coated in a thin layer of slush. In the courtyard below, the valets' dark uniforms stood out in stark relief against the snowy backdrop as they hurried to and from the parking area. Four cars waited to approach the palace, their headlights spotlighting the swirling flakes and the three people standing near the valets.

"Is that the Wimmers?" Marit asked, pointing to the woman and two men waiting for the next car.

"It looks like her yellow dress from here."

"Come on." Marit lifted the lower edge of her gown with her free hand and tugged him down the stairs.

"What's the big hurry?"

"I want to see what kind of car they drive."

Icy water was seeping into her shoes by the time they rounded the bend in the staircase.

"The next car's pulling up," Lars said. "And it looks like the Wimmers are getting into it."

"Can you tell what it is from here?" They were almost to the courtyard.

"Hang on." Lars released her hand and loped down the last few steps. The crunch of his feet connecting with the gravel filled the night air as he took two more steps toward the idling vehicle. Seconds later, Marit reached him.

"A BMW i8 coupe," he said, staring at the Wimmers' car's rapidly moving taillights.

"What's that in a language I understand?"

She saw his teeth glint in the darkness. "A very new, very expensive vehicle."

Another car pulled up.

"Lars! Marit!"

They looked over to see Cole calling to them through Isabelle's half-lowered car window.

"Looks like we timed that just right," Lars said.

They crossed the short distance to the car as Cole got out.

"Where are you going?" Lars asked.

"To get Isabelle's key." Cole jogged to the valet stand.

Lars opened the back door for Marit and waited until she was in before running around to the other side of the vehicle. By the time he slid into the car, Cole had already reclaimed his seat in front.

"We saw you racing down the stairs," Cole said as Isabelle put the car in gear. "What was that about?"

"We wanted to see what kind of car Gerhart Wimmer drives," Marit said.

Isabelle took her eyes off the courtyard long enough to toss her a questioning look. "What did you find?"

"A BMW i8 coupe," Lars said.

Cole whistled through his teeth. "His paycheck must be bigger than yours, Isabelle."

"Yeah, well, with their loose change, Lina Wimmer buys designer dresses worth twenty thousand euros," Lars said.

"Her shoes and jewelry probably doubled that price tag," Marit added. "Not to mention the addition of Gerhart's designer suit, Italian shoes, and gold cufflinks."

Cole offered Isabelle a meaningful look. "Sounds like Gerhart Wimmer may have another source of income."

Isabelle kept her eyes on the road, but the dashboard lights illuminated her grim expression. "It looks that way."

"Maybe you could question him the same way you did Brinkerhoff." There was no mistaking the steely tone in Lars's voice. "Marit and I are still waiting to hear how that all turned out."

"Yes," Marit said, shifting her attention to Cole. "We weren't aware that embassy personnel were in the habit of carrying weapons to social functions in their host countries."

♦ ♦ ♦

Cole's gut clenched. He'd worked undercover for the CIA for the past seven years, and not once had he blown his cover.

He should have known better than to enlist Lars's help once he realized his cousin came as only one-half of a package deal. While Lars trusted easily and typically took things at face value, Marit's observational skills rivaled those of some of the best operatives in the intelligence community.

"Well?" Marit asked, clearly waiting for an answer. "Cole, who do you really work for?"

Isabelle shot him a warning glance. Even if Cole's cover was blown, Isabelle's wasn't. At least he hoped hers wasn't.

"It's been a long night," Cole finally said. "Can we talk about this once we get back to my place?"

"Why are we going back to your place?" Isabelle asked.

Cole could have kissed her for the way she jumped on the change of subject. The woman really was brilliant. Cole's gaze settled on her. And beautiful. "Between having the police follow you yesterday and the run-in with Brinkerhoff and that banker friend of yours today, I think we'll all be safer if we stay at my place tonight."

"Cole, I'll be fine," Isabelle insisted. "We never saw the cops outside my apartment last night or today. I think they've moved on to better suspects."

"Maybe, but that Wimmer guy knows you."

"It's not like I socialize with him. I doubt he knows where I live."

Cole started to debate that Wimmer could access the information through her personnel file. Then he remembered who he was talking to. Isabelle knew that. She was simply keeping the conversation going.

"Maybe it would be better for all of us to stick together tonight," Lars said.

"I think so too," Marit agreed. "Cole, you and Isabelle might be okay with having people pointing guns at you, but that's the kind of stuff that gives the rest of us nightmares."

"I do have two couches," Isabelle said.

"Fine, but we need to stop by my place. I want to pick up the laptops so I can work at your apartment," Cole said.

Isabelle changed lanes. She checked the rearview mirror, and her gaze lingered for a moment. When she made three unnecessary turns, Cole asked, "Everything okay?"

"Yeah. Just want to make sure we aren't being followed."

"There you go again," Marit said. "The two of you sound like you're straight out of a spy movie."

"Marit, as observant as you are, you would sound the same way if you were driving," Isabelle countered.

"She's got you there," Lars said.

"Maybe so, but I don't drive like Isabelle, and I certainly wouldn't survive fighting off some guy with a gun."

"That's not an experience I plan to go through again," Isabelle said. "Thank goodness for ten years of martial arts training and three older brothers who gave me plenty of opportunity to practice."

Cole chuckled. "How old were you when your brothers first realized they were outmatched?"

Isabelle's smile was instantaneous. "Eleven."

Marit leaned forward in the seat behind Cole. "Somehow, that doesn't surprise me."

CHAPTER 27

COLE RETRIEVED THE SAFE HIDDEN beneath some fallen clothes and unlocked it. If he was going to stay at Isabelle's tonight, possibly longer, he didn't want to have to keep coming back to his apartment. He retrieved an Austrian passport with his alias's name on it along with some extra cash and a spare magazine for his gun.

He secured everything in a leather duffel and added some more clothes and his new laptop.

When he returned to the living room, Lars already had his suitcase packed, the extra computer in his hand.

"Want me to put that in here?" Cole asked.

"Sure." Lars handed it over.

"I need to make a phone call, and I want to change before we leave. Would you mind letting Isabelle know I'll be out in a minute?"

"Is this the kind of phone call I can't hear?"

"Yeah. It's that kind of phone call."

"What do you really do for the embassy?" Lars asked.

"Give me a minute. We'll talk at Isabelle's."

Lars stared for a moment, as though debating whether to press. Finally, he nodded. "Okay. I'll be in the car."

As soon as Lars left, Cole retreated to his bedroom. No way he was going to chance Lars listening from the other side of the front door. Cole closed his bedroom door. After he changed out of his tux, he dialed Cas's number.

"I'm glad you called," Cas answered. "We had another bombing."

"Where?" Cole asked, his own concerns pushed to the back of his mind. "Casualties?"

"Florence. One dead, six injured," Cas said, her voice tight. "It happened at the main station right after a train arrived from Rome. The one casualty was an American tourist."

"That's rough." No matter how many incidents like this he had investigated, he could never quite distance himself from the truth that any time someone died, a family would have to bear the burden of that loss for years to come. "Same MO as Steven Powell?"

"Yes, except for one thing. The news came through Pulse, a social media site," Cas said. "With Powell, the headlines always broke on traditional news sites."

"I was talking to my cousin's girlfriend about Pulse. She said she'd never heard of it, which is odd since social media is a big part of her job."

"I'll touch base with Rogers and have him see if there's any connection between Pulse and Powell."

"Good idea." Cole picked up the tuxedo jacket he had discarded on his bed and hung it up. His mother would be so proud. "Any chance you can help me with a couple things?"

"Like?"

"First, I need a deep dive on Gerhart Wimmer. He's a banker who works with Isabelle." Cole hung up his pants.

"I can pawn that off on one of my associates. He'll email it to you as soon as he has anything."

"Great." Cole sat on the side of his bed to put on his shoes and socks. "Did you get anything back on Hans Koch yet?"

"A friend talked to him a few hours ago," Cas said.

Cole crossed to his bedroom door and peeked into the living room to make sure he was still alone in the apartment. "A friend or another guardian?"

"Same thing," Cas said. "Koch confirmed making the sale of the diamonds to Peter Brinkerhoff."

"How was the money transferred to him? And from where?"

"The phone call you saw Brinkerhoff make on the surveillance feed was him calling for the wire transfer for payment."

Cole paced the length of his room. "Did you track it?"

"It went back to some shell company. That's as far as we got so far."

"Send me the info. Maybe Isabelle will have better luck."

"I can do that," she said. "There's one more thing. Koch made a mistake in the sale he made to Brinkerhoff."

"What kind of mistake?"

"Brinkerhoff requested uncertified diamonds. One of the stones Koch sold him was registered."

"That makes a lot more sense," Cole said as much to himself as to Cas. "I never understood why they would use diamonds as currency but have one that was traceable."

"At least that part of the mystery is solved," Cas said. "What else did you need help with?"

Cole peered out the window. Lars stood on the sidewalk next to Isabelle's car. "I need clearance to tell my cousin and his girlfriend who I work for."

"That needs to go through agency channels."

"I know, but that's not something I'm willing to do right now," Cole said. "The last thing I want is to put Lars and Marit on the agency's radar when someone inside is leaking intel."

"How urgent is this request?"

"It's pretty obvious I'm blown," Cole admitted, swallowing the bitter pill of failure. "At this point, it's a matter of damage control."

"Did something happen?" Cas asked.

"We tried to question Peter Brinkerhoff tonight. It didn't go well." Cole relayed the night's events and his hunch that Brinkerhoff was involved in Rogers's kidnapping, or at least in the payment of it.

"As much as I hate to be the one to make the call, I don't know that you have much choice but to confide in your cousin," Cas said.

"That was my thought. Any chance you have some magical way to submit the paperwork for me to the agency to keep me from getting fired?"

"I'll make sure it's taken care of."

"I don't suppose you've heard from Jasmine, have you?"

"No, but I think she'd reach out to you before she'd call me."

"I'm not so sure." Cole liked to think Jasmine would trust him enough to contact him, but he also knew she wouldn't risk coming to him if their friendship might put either of them in danger.

"With Brinkerhoff in the wind, maybe it's time I dig deeper into what sent her into the dark in the first place," Cas said.

"I looked but didn't find anything. You're welcome to try."

"Can you send me what you've got?"

"Will do."

Cole ended the call and headed back into the living room. He stopped a few steps in, the odd sensation of someone else's presence tickling the back of his neck. His hand went to his gun, and he checked the apartment. Nothing. Cautiously, he opened the front door, half expecting Lars to be standing on the other side with his ear pressed against the door. Still nothing.

With a shake of his head, he returned to the coffee table, where he had left his duffel. On top of his leather duffel lay a hand-carved ornament in the shape of a bicycle. *Like riding a bicycle.* Jasmine said that every time anyone questioned her abilities.

Cole snatched up the ornament and rushed to the door again. He stopped and listened for footsteps going up or down the stairs but was only greeted by silence.

He looked down at the brightly painted carved wood. Could Lars have put this on his bag? Or was this a message from Jasmine? And why would she let him know she was okay but not take the time to tell him what was going on? With questions flooding his mind, he gathered his things. If Jasmine was in Vienna, he needed to find out why.

Lars set his suitcase at the end of one of Isabelle's sofas. Since he was scheduled to fly back to Amsterdam the next evening, he would've only had to put up with one more night on Cole's couch, but Isabelle's furniture looked considerably newer and more comfortable. No lumps at his back and Marit close by. Staying here tonight was a win-win.

The women had disappeared into the bedrooms to change out of their gowns. On the other side of the room, Cole set his duffel bag in the corner of the room before reaching for something in his pocket.

"Hey, Lars, did you leave this for me?"

Cole held out his hand, and Lars studied the small bicycle decoration lying on his cousin's palm.

"No. I've never seen that before. Where did you find it?"

"On my duffel bag."

"Weird."

"Yeah," Cole said, a thoughtful look on his face.

Lars dropped onto the sofa. "Chalk it up as one more unknown on your growing list." He raised his eyes to meet Cole's. "I'm ready to hear answers to some of those things."

"Me too," Marit said.

She walked into the room dressed in an oversized gray sweatshirt and a pair of blue pajama pants covered in tiny stars. She'd pulled the pins from her hair, and it now fell in a golden curtain halfway down her back. She took a seat beside him, and he put his arm around her; she inched a little closer.

At that moment, Isabelle appeared. Without saying a word, she crossed the room in her navy sweats and sat across from Lars and Marit.

Cole glanced at her before turning his attention to Lars. "I need your word that you will keep what I tell you confidential. You can't share this with anyone." Cole focused on Lars. "Not even Tess or Anna."

"You've got it," Lars said.

Marit shifted slightly. "I haven't known you as long as Lars has. Can you confirm that you're not doing anything illegal first?"

Something that looked remarkably like respect flickered in Cole's eyes. "I appreciate the question," he said. "And I think it's fair to say that I'm one of the good guys."

"Then you have my word too."

"Isabelle?" Cole said.

She nodded, her expression serious.

Cole took a deep breath. "My job at the US embassy is a cover for my assignment as a CIA agent."

In the complete silence that followed, Lars looked from Isabelle's grim countenance to Marit's stunned one before attempting to gather his wits. "Are you serious?" he said.

"One hundred percent."

"I don't claim to know a lot about these things," Isabelle said. Her voice sounded a little more brittle than usual. "But it seems to me that if you're undercover, telling us this has put your job on the line."

"It has." Cole ran his fingers through his hair. "And to be quite honest, if the information doesn't stay between the four of us, it also puts my life on the line."

Lars stared at him. Cole's confession shouldn't have come as a huge surprise. Between what he'd personally seen the man do in Amsterdam and here in Vienna, it was obvious that he had serious combat training. But a CIA operative? That took his skills—and his resources—to a whole new level. "If you're with the CIA, shouldn't you have had some leads on what happened to the Falcon Point jewelry and your diamonds by now?" Lars asked.

Cole's jaw tightened. "In theory, yes. But I believe there may be a leak in the agency. Until I figure out where it's coming from, I can't access the usual channels."

"Which also explains why encrypted computers magically appeared on your doorstep," Lars said.

Cole gave a brief nod.

"Thank you for telling us," Marit said. "I don't suppose you would have if it hadn't been absolutely necessary."

"No."

"Well then, what can we do to help?" Marit asked.

Lars had a pretty good idea of how much Cole and Brinkerhoff's altercation at the palace had shaken her, yet she was willing to put her trust in Cole regardless. If he hadn't already known that Marit was a keeper, he was assured of it now.

"Marit's right, Cole," he said. "We can dig through websites and read boring files as well as anyone. Put us to work."

Cole raised an eyebrow. "Now? It's getting late."

"If you think any of us are ready to go to sleep after the bombshell you just dropped," Lars said, "the CIA needs to take you in for a new intelligence test."

Cole chuckled, and a small amount of the tension in his shoulders eased.

"Fair enough." He opened his duffel and pulled out the computer Lars had been using. "Remember that social media website that was running the stories about the bombing at Centraal Station?"

"Pulse? Isn't that what it was called?" Marit said.

"Yeah." He offered Lars the computer. "We need to find out more about it. See what you can dig up on it. When it started. Who started it. How many subscribers it has. And most especially, how quickly it's posting news after the events happen."

"Has it featured reports from places other than the bombing in Amsterdam?" Marit asked.

"Yes. Over the last few days, there have also been bombings in Frankfurt, Berlin, and Florence. I want to know what Pulse reported about them and when."

"We can do that," Lars said.

"If we open an account, it would give us better access," Marit said.

"Good idea. But don't use your real IDs."

"What would you like me to do?" Isabelle asked.

Cole faced her, his expression unreadable. In fairness, Lars was pretty sure that if he'd just told Marit he was a CIA operative, he'd be feeling pretty anxious too.

"I was hoping you'd use your banking skills to trace Brinkerhoff's financials."

"I can do that," Isabelle said.

Marit looked over at him. "What about Wimmer?"

"Yeah," Cole said. "Wimmer too."

Isabelle rose to her feet. "There's a late-night market down the street that sells great hot chocolate. I think we could all use some. How about I pick some up for everyone first?"

"Good plan," Cole said. "I'll come with you."

CHAPTER 28

ISABELLE WALKED DOWN THE STAIRS, away from her apartment and the pantry that was fully stocked with hot chocolate mix and herbal teas. Her mind raced, replaying the conversation from moments ago.

She understood Cole's desire to confide in Lars and Marit, but to do so when she could be linked with his intelligence work put them both in danger and her cover at risk.

She exited her building, the snow still falling steadily. She glanced around to make sure they were alone before turning to Cole. "Are you crazy?"

"What?" Cole asked, dumbfounded. "You told me just yesterday that I should request clearance to tell Lars who I work for."

"Yeah, but I didn't expect you to circumvent procedure and tell him right after he witnessed the two of us working together."

"He thinks you were just helping me."

"Yeah, because you take all of your dates to interrogations," Isabelle said dryly.

"I'm sorry, but they've been as much part of this investigation as we have."

Isabelle couldn't deny that, but the truth didn't lessen her concern. She lowered her voice further. "That doesn't mean they should have access to my background. My own mother doesn't know who I work for."

An unspoken apology lit his face. "What do you want me to do? I can't untell them what I do for a living."

Isabelle's posture relaxed slightly. What did she want him to do? Even if he hadn't admitted he was CIA, Marit and Lars both already suspected as much.

She started down the sidewalk, each step leaving an imprint in the inch of snow already accumulated. "Come on. The late market is this way."

Cole fell in step beside her. "I'm sorry. I should have talked to you first before confessing everything to them."

The apology soothed but didn't take away the concern that still hummed inside her. "You didn't have a lot of opportunity to talk to me alone."

"Except when we were chasing Brinkerhoff."

"That was work."

"Are we working now?" Cole asked.

"I think an outing to the store qualifies as a break." She brushed a snowflake from her eyelash.

Cole's hand reached for hers, and he stopped walking. "I've missed you."

Isabelle's gaze lifted to his. The way he looked at her made her feel like she was the center of his whole world, and as the lingering ache in her heart eased, a seed of trust bloomed. Her voice wasn't quite steady when she spoke. "You've been with me nearly every waking moment for the past two days."

He leaned down until his breath mingled with hers. Her stomach jumped in anticipation, and her throat went dry. As much as she had promised herself she would keep Cole in her past, the last few days had proven that he had captured her heart those many months ago and she had never truly gotten it back.

No longer interested in denying her feelings, she pushed onto her toes as Cole leaned in. Their lips met, the kiss chasing away the chill in the air. Her arms encircled his neck, and Cole drew her closer as he deepened the kiss.

Every nerve ending went on alert, her senses heightened. Wheels of the cars passing by slushing through the snow-covered road, the scent of wood smoke lingering in the air, the faint hum of music filtering from a nearby apartment.

She surrendered herself to the attraction and friendship that kept Cole so firmly in her thoughts.

The moment stretched out until finally she drew away, her cheeks warm despite the falling snow.

Cole smiled and took her hand again. "It had been too long since our last break together."

Isabelle couldn't prevent her own smile from forming. "I think you're right."

They started down the street again.

"Are you really out of hot chocolate?" Cole asked.

"No, but I am out of whipped cream."

"We'd better buy hot chocolate too," Cole said. "Marit will notice if we don't."

"Yeah, she will. She sees everything."

"Maybe we should recruit her."

"I think we already have."

The sound of someone using the shower in the bathroom next door woke Marit the following morning. She opened her eyes to a bedroom filled with sunlight and the sight of her borrowed ball gown hanging from a hook on the door. Memories flooded back, bringing with them a full array of emotions. The joy of dancing with Lars, the stress of meeting Brinkerhoff, the fear associated with Cole and Isabelle's actions, and the shock of Cole's late-night revelation.

It had been the early hours of the morning when Cole had finally announced that they all needed to shut down their computers and go to bed. By then, a calm solidarity had descended upon the group and, with it, an unspoken determination to unravel the tangled web surrounding them.

The hiss of running water stopped. Marit slipped out from between the covers and crossed the small bedroom to her open suitcase. Grabbing her bathroom bag and some clean clothes, she opened the door a crack. No voices came from the living room or kitchen. If she was lucky, she might be able to claim the next shower.

The lock on the bathroom door clicked. Clutching her small bundle, Marit stepped into the short hall that connected Isabelle's room, the bathroom, and the guest room she was using. The bathroom door opened, and Lars stepped out.

"Good morning," he said.

He smiled, and a hundred butterflies took flight within her. He wore a pair of jeans and a black T-shirt that showcased his muscular shoulders all too well. His hair was damp, and she could smell his shampoo from where she stood.

"Hi," she said, horribly aware of her disheveled appearance. "I'm sorry. I just rolled out of bed, and I look—"

"Beautiful."

She shook her head. "Not even close."

He chuckled. "You could be covered in mud from head to toe and you'd be beautiful to me, Marit."

"Head-to-toe mud."

"Yeah."

He stepped closer and reached out to softly run his fingers through her hair. His devastating blue eyes held hers, and his fingers stilled. Awareness pulsed between them, and her breath caught in her throat. Surely he didn't mean to . . . She didn't have time to finish the thought before his arms circled her. Slowly, his head lowered, and his lips found hers. He pulled her closer, the smell of his newly washed skin assailing her as she lost herself in his kiss.

Sometime later, he drew back slightly.

"Marit." His breath danced across her lips.

"Hmm."

"Can we meet in the hall more often?"

She laughed softly. "Aren't you leaving today?"

"Yes." He did not sound happy about it.

She raised her head so she could see him better. He didn't look any happier than he sounded. "When's your flight?"

"Eight ten."

"KLM?"

He nodded. "What about you?"

"I don't have one yet," she said. He was still holding her. The look in his eyes was everything she'd hoped for, yet an unexpected shyness swept over her. "Originally, I wanted to see how things went between us before booking a return flight. Now I'm wondering if I should see if there's a seat available on KLM's eight ten flight tonight."

He smiled, a slow, warm smile that had the power to affect her knees. "I like that idea a lot."

"I'll check KLM's website right after I've taken a shower."

"Perfect. I'm heading out to get smoothies, but it shouldn't take me too long."

"Smoothies?"

He rolled his eyes. "I struck a deal with Cole. I got the shower first if I agreed to go pick up breakfast for everyone. Isabelle suggested smoothies."

"So, they're up already?" The flat was so quiet Marit had assumed the others were still asleep.

"Up and working on their computers," Lars said.

That explained the silent living room. "I had no idea I was the last one out of bed."

"They're still in their pajamas," he said. "Slip into the bathroom now and you'll have a head start on them."

She nodded. "Thanks."

"What flavor smoothie do you want? Isabelle requested mango, I'm getting strawberry-banana, and Cole asked for blueberry-spinach." He grimaced. "If he'd said kale, I'd have refused to pick it up."

Marit laughed. "Mango would be great."

"Mango it is." He pressed another brief kiss to her lips. "I'll see you in a bit."

Marit hurried into the bathroom to take the fastest shower ever. Fifteen minutes later, she was dressed in her jeans and her favorite pink sweater and was studying an account of the bombing in Florence on Lars's computer. Isabelle had taken her place in the bathroom.

Marit scrolled to the top of the CNN article and read it again, double-checking the times with the report she'd read last night on BBC's website. They matched. "Cole," she said.

"Yeah." He looked up from his computer.

"There's something really weird going on with the news reports out of Florence."

"What have you found?"

"According to CNN, BBC, and the Italian state-owned news station, Rai News, the bomb at the Piazza San Marco went off at ten thirty. The closest hospital is four and a half kilometers away. Even with no traffic holdups, it's hard to imagine an ambulance arriving less than five minutes after the blast."

"Agreed."

She chewed her bottom lip. "Pulse's first reports of the bombing came in at ten thirty exactly. By ten thirty-three, they had pictures of victims. By ten thirty-six, they'd posted video of emergency personnel leaving the hospital en route to the piazza."

"Like someone was waiting outside the hospital ready to film the ambulances heading out," Cole said grimly.

A pit formed in Marit's stomach.

"Unless the posted times are incorrect, it's the only thing that makes sense."

"What about Amsterdam?" Cole asked.

"As far as I can tell, the pictures of the destruction at Centraal Station were posted on Pulse almost ten minutes before any other news outlet reported the bombing."

Isabelle walked in. Like Marit, she was now dressed in jeans and a sweater. She reclaimed her spot on the sofa beside Cole, her gaze moving from his face to Marit's. "What's going on?" she asked.

"It looks like someone connected to Pulse is orchestrating the bombings," Cole said.

"Why would someone at a social media site bomb someone?" Marit asked.

"We had an incident a few months ago very similar to this," Cole said. "The man behind it paid to create newsworthy incidents, and then his news stations were the first to report them."

Just the thought of such arbitrary violence caused the pit in Marit's stomach to widen. "People do watch the news a lot more when something extreme happens."

"They do, and if we're right, the diamonds we're tracking are being used to pay off the bombers."

"I thought they were bank robbers or jewel thieves."

"The actual robbers were, but they were likely hired to reclaim the payment that had been lost," Cole said. "The Falcon Point jewels were a bonus."

Isabelle frowned. "What have you got so far on Pulse?"

"Not enough, unfortunately. Check the Frankfurt and Berlin news releases, Marit. Look for similar discrepancies in the timing. See if any patterns show up, and make note of who's posting about them on Pulse."

"Will do," Marit said, pulling up the BBC's original report on the Frankfurt bombing as he spoke.

"Do you want me to switch gears?" Isabelle asked.

Cole shook his head. "Not yet. Show me what you've found on the financials."

CHAPTER 29

ISABELLE LOGGED INTO THE BANK'S financial system using one of her coworkers' remote access, then pulled up the bank accounts for Gerhart and Lina Wimmer.

"I thought they suspended your access to the banking systems," Cole said.

"They did." Isabelle glanced over her shoulder to where Marit currently sat on the couch, her legs stretched out and the laptop resting on her thighs. Isabelle lowered her voice to a whisper. "One of my coworkers isn't the best about securing her passwords. With the encryption on this laptop, the bank won't be able to trace this back to me."

"Ah." Cole leaned closer. "See anything unusual?"

"The balances aren't out of line with what Gerhart's income would support, but I'll dig a little deeper."

"I'll see if I can track down where Pulse is headquartered. It looks like it uses servers in a half dozen different countries."

"We both have our work cut out for us." Isabelle clicked on Gerhart's main checking account and scanned through the transactions. The deposits were primarily from his biweekly paychecks, his expenses falling into the typical categories: mortgage, credit cards, car payment, utilities. Moving on, she searched his savings and money market accounts, then his brokerage account.

Cole glanced at the door. "I wonder what's taking Lars so long."

"The smoothie bar gets pretty long lines sometimes." Isabelle kept scanning the Wimmers' bank accounts. "I don't see anything out of the ordinary here."

Marit looked up from her laptop. "Did you figure out where the money came from for Lina's clothes?"

"No." Isabelle's eyebrows drew together, Marit's comment sparking a new possibility. "How much did you say her dress cost?"

"Twenty thousand euros, give or take."

"I'm not seeing any transactions in that range," Isabelle said.

"Her accessories would have been up there too," Marit said.

"I suppose if she put everything on a credit card, they could be paying it off slowly, but the amounts would only be enough to fulfill the minimum payments." Isabelle looked through the checking account again. Was this Wimmer's only account, or did he have more? "These expenses are all routine."

Cole looked up from his screen. "You think they have other accounts somewhere."

Leave it to Cole to read her thoughts. "Yeah, I do."

"I asked my friend to do a deep dive on the Wimmers. Maybe she'll come up with some other ideas."

"Tell her I already checked out their accounts at my bank," Isabelle said. "No need for her to do the same work twice."

"I'll text her."

"You might want to let your friend know that the payment for Lina's dress probably happened within the last six months," Marit said. "It was definitely from this year."

"Good idea." Cole sent the text.

"Any luck tracking the location of Pulse's headquarters?" Isabelle asked.

"Not yet," Cole said. "One of my associates is looking into it for me, but I haven't heard anything yet."

"Maybe you should make a call," Isabelle suggested. "If you and your associate compare notes, you might find the answer quicker."

"That's a good idea." Cole pulled his phone from his pocket.

"I'm going to get something to drink," Marit said. "Do either of you want anything?"

"Nothing for me, thanks," Isabelle said.

"A glass of water would be great," Cole said. "Thanks, Marit."

"Coming right up." Marit headed for the kitchen.

As soon as Marit left, Isabelle lowered her voice. "Who are you calling?"

"Rogers. Ghost has him trying to track down Powell's location." Cole hit the Call button. After he identified himself, he asked, "Any luck with finding Powell?"

He fell silent for a moment. "You're kidding."

More silence. "Let me know if you find him." Cole hung up.

"Rogers couldn't find Powell?" Isabelle asked.

"No, but guess who owns Pulse."

"Steven Powell."

"Got it on the first try." Cole leaned closer. "Not only that. Powell was one of the men Rogers saw right before he was kidnapped from Bratislava."

"Then our theories about all of this being connected are right. Rogers's kidnapping, the diamonds, the bombings, Pulse."

"Rogers saw a transaction he wasn't supposed to see, probably the payoff of diamonds for one of the bombings. The bank robbery was to either get the diamonds back or to recover the one that could be traced."

"And Pulse is building its site by being the first to report the news they're creating." Isabelle shook her head, disgusted.

"Exactly. Powell is rebuilding his news empire, only this time through social media."

"It's nice to have some answers, but it would be better to know where Steven Powell is hiding out."

"No joke." Cole pulled his laptop closer. "Now that we know Powell is behind all of this, I want to read through Jasmine's report again." He pulled the bicycle ornament from his pocket. "If this is from her, I have to think she left some clue as to why she went dark."

"You really think she was in your apartment?"

"She must have come in right after Lars went downstairs," Cole said. "I went into my room to change, and when I came out, this was on my bag."

"Why wouldn't she have just stayed and talked to you?"

"I don't know. Maybe she was afraid Lars would come back upstairs." Cole pulled up Jasmine's last report before she disappeared.

Isabelle leaned closer, reading the words on the screen. The contents didn't reveal anything significant.

Marit walked back in holding two glasses of water and handed one to Cole. "Here you go."

"Thanks."

"What are you working on now?" Marit asked. "Or can you tell me?"

"Just going over the report of the incident when we found the diamonds."

"I assume it says in there where you were keeping them." Marit shuddered, clearly fighting back the memory. "It's hard to believe that so many of your family jewels were stolen because the thieves were looking for a million euros in loose stones."

"A million euros." Cole's eyes lit up.

"What is it?" Isabelle asked.

Cole scrolled up to the spot in the report where Jasmine detailed the recovery of the diamonds and the description of them.

"Jasmine didn't know how much the diamonds were worth when she wrote this."

"So?" Isabelle said.

"So one of my coworkers mentioned the value when I spoke with her after they were stolen," Cole said. "I didn't tell her how much they were worth, so how did she know?"

"Who did you tell?" Isabelle asked.

"Only Jasmine."

"Am I allowed to know who Jasmine is?" Marit asked.

"She's a friend who disappeared the same day the diamonds did," Cole said.

"Disappeared? Like, kidnapped?"

"No. More like hiding out," Cole said. "I think she knows who the mole is, and she's trying to prove it."

"If your coworker knows how much the diamonds are worth, doesn't that prove it's her?" Marit asked.

"I hope so, but I need more than an offhand comment before I make any accusations," Cole said. "My boss was standing next to me when my coworker mentioned the value of the diamonds."

"That does make it more complicated," Isabelle said, feigning ignorance.

"Too complicated for me," Marit said. "I'm going back to the news reports."

As soon as Marit crossed to the couch, Cole opened up a new screen.

"What are you looking for now?" Isabelle asked.

Cole lowered his voice. "The call logs between the Vienna and Budapest offices."

"With the encryption on the phones, you aren't going to be able to tell whose desk the calls originated from."

"Sure I can," Cole said. "It's just a matter of decoding the encryption on the phone log."

"I didn't know decryption was one of your skills."

"Grandpa and Dad started teaching me when I was little." Cole pointed at the screen as he skimmed the calls. "The information must have been passed the morning Jasmine disappeared."

"She wasn't in the Budapest office for very long."

Cole checked his notes. "Forty-five minutes."

Isabelle read the time stamps on the log. "Six calls during that time."

"But only one between Budapest and Vienna," Cole said.

"If Zoe took the call . . ."

"We can prove who our mole is."

The smoothie shop was a popular place. Lars pulled his phone out of his pocket and glanced at the time. He'd been standing in line for over twenty minutes, and there were still a couple of customers ahead of him. It appeared that he and Isabelle were not on the same page when it came to fast breakfast foods.

"Looks like we chose the wrong time to come," the woman standing behind him said, offering him a rueful smile as he slid his phone back into his pocket.

"Yeah. It looks that way."

She pointed at the long list of offerings posted on the bright orange sign hanging behind the counter. "I haven't been here before. What do you recommend?"

"It's my first time too," he said. "But I'm picking some up for people who asked for the mango morning and the blueberry-spinach."

"Blueberry-spinach," the woman repeated, staring at the sign. "That sounds like it would be pretty good for you."

"Probably. As long as you can get past eating leaves for breakfast."

She chuckled. "That one's not for you, then."

"Nope. My cousin wanted that one. I'm more of a strawberry-banana guy."

"That's a good choice too."

One of the two young men behind the counter handed the man in front of Lars two cups, and he moved to the cash register.

"Next," the young man called.

Lars stepped up. Finally. "Two mango mornings, one strawberry-banana, and one blueberry-spinach," he said.

"Small, medium, or large?"

"Large. All of them." Lars thought it unlikely that Marit and Isabelle would want one that big, but after waiting this long for breakfast, he wasn't going to take a chance.

"Can I get a name for your order?"

"Lars."

"Thanks."

The young man scribbled Lars's name on a cardboard cup holder and turned away to start making the smoothies.

"Next." The second employee called up the lady standing behind Lars.

With a friendly nod, she joined him at the counter and placed an order for a large blueberry-spinach smoothie. It appeared that she was an I-eat-leaves-for-breakfast kind of person after all.

Lars's phone vibrated. It was probably Cole wondering what was taking him so long. He pulled his phone out of his pocket and glanced at the caller ID. Not Cole. Anna. He'd been half expecting—while simultaneously dreading—this call. She'd known he was headed to the bank in Vienna right after meeting her at Falcon Point, and she undoubtedly wanted to know how his inventory of the jewelry had gone.

His finger hovered over the screen one second longer, and then he hit Decline. He couldn't talk to her about the missing jewelry. Not in the middle of a smoothie shop. But when he got back to Isabelle's flat, he and Cole were going to have to come up with a legitimate plan to recover the jewelry, and then they'd need to draw straws to decide who would talk to Anna about it.

"Order for Lars."

Pocketing his phone again, Lars reached for the cup holder filled with four tall smoothies. "Thanks," he said and headed directly for the cash register at the other end of the counter.

Ten minutes later, Lars took a moment to catch his breath, gave a cursory knock on Isabelle's door, and walked into the flat. Cole, Isabelle, and Marit were all seated in the living room. They looked up from their respective computers as he entered.

"Hey," Cole said. "I was beginning to wonder if you got lost."

"Nope." Lars set the cup holder on the coffee table. "You have no idea all the things I've already crossed off my list of things to do this morning." He handed Marit and Isabelle their smoothies.

"Like what?"

"Practiced patience while waiting in line. Check. Conversed pleasantly with a total stranger. Check. Completed the worst stair-master exercise in Vienna. Check."

Cole was completely failing to contain his grin. "Nice."

"Yeah," Lars said. "Remind me to take my shower last next time."

Cole gave up the battle and started to laugh. Lars gave him a crusty look and lifted the blueberry-spinach smoothie free of the container.

"Oh man," he said. "They gave me the wrong one."

"It looks right to me," Cole said, reaching for the cup.

"The woman next to me ordered the same thing, so I guess it's okay." Lars handed him the smoothie. "It looks like they put her name on this one though."

Cole looked at the cup and all trace of humor evaporated. "Gwendolyn. It says Gwendolyn."

"Yeah, I know."

Cole set his cup down without tasting its contents. "Describe the woman who ordered this."

"Average height. Black hair. Dark skin." Lars shrugged. "Ready laugh. Eats leaves for breakfast."

"Jasmine," Cole said.

"Wait," Marit said. "You think Lars's order and your missing friend's order somehow got mixed up?"

"Not somehow," Cole said. "Jasmine did this on purpose."

"Gwendolyn," Marit repeated, her eyes on Cole. "What's the name of your boss, again?"

"Gwendolyn," he said.

Cole looked as though he'd been punched in the stomach.

"Would someone like to clue me in on what's going on?" Lars asked, his gaze moving from Cole to the two women, who both appeared similarly stunned.

"If the writing on Cole's cup is what he thinks it is," Marit said, "his boss has just been accused of being the one leaking information from his office."

"Whoa." Lars lowered himself onto the sofa next to Marit. "Sorry, Cole."

On the opposite sofa's armrest, Cole's phone began to vibrate. Releasing a tense breath, he picked it up and glanced at the screen. "It's Anna."

"Ignore it," Lars said. "She just tried calling me. I'll call her back." He paused. This was probably the worst possible time to broach the subject, but it had to be done. "We can't wait on the police any longer, Cole. If they haven't found the Falcon Point jewelry by now, it means the pieces are probably already out on the black market. The only chance we have to recover them is to access the dark web."

Cole didn't argue. "Pass me your computer."

Marit handed it to him. Cole entered something, waited for the screen to change, and then offered the computer back to Lars.

"You're in," he said. "You know exactly what we're looking for. If you can't find any of the pieces, drop a few fishing lines."

CHAPTER 30

COLE HAD HOPED LARS'S FISHING expedition would yield fast results, but so far, he hadn't received a single bite. Uneasiness and a growing wariness settled inside him.

Their makeshift team of four had spent all morning searching for clues of where Brinkerhoff had gone, what had happened to the Falcon Point jewels, if Wimmer was involved, and how Gwendolyn fit into the big picture.

If Jasmine was still in the dark, it had to be because she couldn't prove Gwendolyn's involvement. For whatever reason, Jazz was relying on Cole to find the missing pieces. He only wished she would have given him a hint on where to find them. He certainly didn't want to continue his search at the office.

The mere thought of going back to work on Monday set his teeth on edge. Pretending to be something he wasn't, he could manage. Facing a woman who had potentially put people in danger, he couldn't handle, especially when it had been people he cared about.

At the kitchen table beside him, Isabelle's phone buzzed with an incoming text message. She picked it up, and her eyebrows lifted.

"Looks like I've been cleared to go back to work on Monday."

"That's good," Marit said from across the room, where she sat with Lars on the couch.

"Yes, it is." Isabelle tilted her head. "Interesting that Gerhart called me when he said I couldn't go back to work after the robbery, but he's fine with simply sending a text to say I've been cleared."

"You've been cleared," Lars said. "That's the important thing."

"I'm surprised it happened so fast," Isabelle said. "Gerhart thought it would be at least a week before I would be back."

Cole furrowed his eyebrows. "Why were you cleared?"

"Excellent question," Isabelle said. "Lars, maybe you should call the police again to see if there are any updates in the case."

"I can do that." Lars pulled out his phone and made the call. After a brief hold and a three-minute conversation, he hung up. "Nothing yet on the recovery of anything stolen, and the officer I spoke to said he couldn't give me any information on their suspects yet."

"Did he say they had suspects?" Cole asked.

"Not specifically," Lars said. "He just said he couldn't give me information on them."

"They know something," Cole concluded. He pulled his phone free and dialed Cas's number. As soon as she answered, Cole said, "I need a favor."

"This is becoming a habit with you."

"Yep," Cole said unrepentantly. He had a puzzle to solve, and he was going to use whatever resources he had available. "I think the cops have suspects for the bank robbery. Any chance you can access the police report and send me a copy?"

"That's easy enough," Cas said. "I was about to forward you the sketches from the artist who worked with Rogers. You won't believe who he saw in Bratislava."

"Steven Powell," Cole said. "I talked to Rogers earlier. Not only that—I may have a lead on finding Powell."

"What's that?" Cas asked, her voice instantly alert.

"One of my friends was going through the social media site Pulse. Turns out you were right. All of the news reports coming out of there were hitting right as the events were unfolding. Someone at Pulse has to be involved. Since Rogers identified Steven Powell as the owner, it has to be him."

"We suspected as much, but so far, we haven't been able to track down where they're headquartered."

"If Rogers saw him in Bratislava, maybe narrowing down our search will yield some results."

"I'll pass that on to my computer experts," Cas said. "In the meantime, check your email in about ten minutes."

"Thanks." Cole ended the call. "My friend is going to send over the police report in a few minutes."

"You can get that?" Marit asked.

"If you know the right people, you can get just about anything," Cole said.

Lars set the borrowed laptop aside. "I'm afraid I struck out with the dark web. I guess whoever has the Falcon Point jewels isn't interested in selling."

"Not yet anyway." Cole fought back his impatience.

"While you're waiting for the police report," Isabelle said, "I'm going to package up my gown from last night."

Marit rose from her spot on the couch. "I should do the same thing. We need to get those returned before I fly out tonight."

"I guess I need to take care of my tux too." Lars shot a hopeful glance at Cole. "Unless my favorite cousin would be willing to take care of that for me."

"Nice try. We both know I'm only your favorite cousin when you want something."

"Yeah, well, Anna's a better cook."

"Does Anna cook?" Cole asked. "She's never cooked for me."

"I have no clue, but your idea of fixing dinner involves using a telephone. She can't be worse than you."

Lars had a point.

"Sidetracking me isn't going to work." Cole motioned toward the garment bag that housed Lars's tux. It was hanging over the edge of the couch. "You can take care of returning that yourself."

"Fine." Lars stretched out his legs in front of him. "Anna's my favorite again."

Marit and Isabelle both laughed as they disappeared into their respective bedrooms.

Cole opened his email, and an encrypted message popped up. He opened it along with the attached police file.

"Looks like they captured the men who robbed the bank."

Both Isabelle and Marit rushed back into the living room.

"Did they recover the stolen jewels?" Lars asked.

"No. They had the cash, but the diamonds and the Falcon Point jewels weren't there."

"Where did they find the men?" Isabelle asked.

"Berlin."

"Did the police report say anything else worthwhile?"

"Not really. They aren't talking, but our detectives are operating under the assumption that they were hired specifically to steal the diamonds."

"At least they're still following the right logic," Isabelle said.

Cole opened the other attachment Cas had sent and scrolled through the sketch artist's drawings. He made it only to the second one when he stopped.

"Isn't that interesting." Cole held up his laptop so they could all see the image.

Marit edged closer. "That looks just like Brinkerhoff."

"Yes, it does." Cole scrolled to the next photo, and Marit gasped. "What's wrong?" he asked.

"Steven." Marit pointed at the sketch. "We met him the night of the gala."

"Steven Powell is in Vienna?" Cole asked.

"If that man's last name is Powell, then yes. He is."

Marit followed Isabelle into her flat. A quick glance around the living room told her that in the time it had taken her and Isabelle to drive to Monique Martin's showroom and back, Lars had packed his case and Cole had yet to move from his position on the sofa.

"Hi." Cole looked up from his computer, his look of intense concentration softening when he saw Isabelle. "Did you have success?"

"Yes," Isabelle said. "Both gowns are returned, and I've made an enormous hole in my savings account to purchase the coat."

"No regrets," Marit said. "Consider it an investment. It's a classic cut with beautiful lines, and the fabric is gorgeous. You'll wear it and love it for years."

Isabelle gave her a quick hug. "Thanks, Marit."

"If I tell you how amazing you look in it, do I get a hug too?" Cole asked.

Isabelle laughed and moved to sit beside him. She glanced at his screen. "How's it going?"

"Slower than I'd like, but the process of elimination is part of moving forward, right?"

"I'm sorry Lars and I won't be here to help you this evening," Marit said.

"You've both done a lot already," Cole said. "I appreciate all of it."

Even though a ridiculous amount of Marit's free time in Vienna had been spent pouring over computer screens in Cole's or Isabelle's flats, she'd loved her time here and was genuinely sorry to be leaving.

"Make sure Lars brings you back again soon," Isabelle said as if she'd read Marit's thoughts. "Or come by yourself. You're always welcome to stay with me."

"Thank you. I'd love that."

A brief knock sounded, and the front door opened. Lars walked in. He paused just inside the threshold and took a ragged breath. "Man, those stairs get me every time."

"You have to pace yourself," Isabelle said, humor dancing in her eyes. "You can't start out too fast."

"Now she tells me." He walked over to Marit and put his arm around her. "I wasn't sure if you'd beat me back."

"We just got here. Did everything go okay at the tux shop?"

"Yep. Everything's been returned now except the jewelry." He turned to Isabelle. "Thanks for taking care of that for us."

"It's not a problem. I'll keep the earrings and necklace in my personal safe at the apartment until Monday. I have to return to work that day anyway. I can put the jewelry back in the safe-deposit box at the bank as soon as I get there."

"I appreciate it."

"Do you have everything?" Cole asked. "Passports, tickets, phones?"

"Yep. We checked in when Marit bought her ticket, so we should be good to go."

"You're sure you don't want me to drive you to the airport?" Isabelle asked.

"Absolutely. The U-bahn station's right on the corner, and the train goes directly there. Besides, you'll get stuck in rush-hour traffic at this time of day."

Isabelle conceded the point. "The trains will be busy too, but you'll probably get there faster that way."

Marit glanced at the clock on the wall. As reluctant as she was to accept the fact, it was time to leave. "I'll grab my stuff," she said.

Her suitcase was ready, so she had only to drag it into the living room and thread her purse strap over her shoulder.

"I'll trade you," Lars said. "I'll carry our suitcases down if you'll take my camera bag."

"Deal," Marit said.

"Remember to pace yourself," Isabelle warned.

Cole chuckled and rose to his feet. "Travel safely," he said. "It was great to see you again."

"You too," Lars said. "Keep him out of trouble, Isabelle."

"I'll do my best," she said, "but I can't promise you anything."

"Yeah. I know."

Marit glanced at Lars. There was no humor in his voice. Now that they knew what Cole really did for a living, the familiar phrase felt more meaningful than trite.

"Don't worry." Cole placed a reassuring hand on Lars's shoulder. "I'm sure you'll see me again before you're ready."

CHAPTER 31

EVEN IN THE FADING LIGHT of dusk, it was easy to spot the entrance to the U-bahn station. A large blue cube with a *U* printed on it hung above the arched access on the corner of the street, and the steady stream of people flowing in and out had yet to abate.

"It looks like it's still pretty busy," Lars said.

He reached for Marit's suitcase as they approached the stairs. Leaving Vienna with the Falcon Point jewelry still missing was difficult, but it would be infinitely harder if Marit weren't going with him.

She claimed his camera bag in exchange.

"If most of these people are commuters, maybe we'll be lucky with the ticket kiosks," she said. "I bet almost everyone has a transit pass."

"Let's hope you're right." If the train stopped at every station between here and the airport, they'd be pushing it to get through security in time.

In his pocket, Lars's phone pinged. An email. It was probably junk, but he'd been more conscientious about checking his inbox ever since he'd put out feelers for a couple of his great-grandmother's missing jewelry pieces on the dark web. He'd make a point to look at it before they boarded the train. Someone out there had to know where the jewelry was.

They made it to the bottom of the first flight of stairs and entered the cavernous tunnel that led to the platforms. A bank of ticket kiosks lined one side of the wall. Marit stepped up to the first vacant one and checked the map printed on the wall above.

"It looks like we need to go the Wien Mitte station first and change trains there for one to the airport."

"Sounds good," Lars said. "Go ahead and get your ticket first."

Marit began making selections on the electronic panel.

Lars waited beside the suitcases and took out his phone to pull up his email. One new message. He didn't recognize the sender's name, but the subject line caught his attention immediately. Emeralds. A quick glance at Marit told him she was still navigating the kiosk's infinite requests. He opened the email, and his breath caught. "Marit."

She must have heard the urgency in his voice because she stopped what she was doing to face him. "What is it?"

"You need to see this." He turned his phone so she could see the photo of the emerald earrings on the screen.

She gasped and stepped closer, reaching for his phone. "That's them," she said. "Look. They're still lying in the original box."

Lars studied the photo. Marit was right. The earrings were still in the faded box he'd handled at the bank. He scrolled down. There were no other photographs, just a terse message.

Jewelry auction. One-of-a-kind pieces. Neuer Markt 22, Wien. 6:00–7:00 p.m. Admittance by invitation only.

"Is this email the invitation?" Marit asked.

"It must be. There'd be no point in knowing about the auction if you couldn't get in."

She met his eyes. "It starts in forty minutes."

Lars read the message again. One-of-a-kind pieces. Did that mean they were auctioning off the entire contents of the Falcon Point safe-deposit box? He tightened his grip on the phone. He needed to call Cole. Now.

"Excuse me." A woman stepped up behind them. "Have you finished using the kiosk?"

Marit moved aside. "Sorry. Go ahead."

The woman nodded, eyeing Lars as he put the phone to his ear.

"I'm afraid you won't have much luck making a call down here," she said. "The reception underground is useless. You'll have to go back upstairs."

Lars's heart sank. "Thanks."

The woman's attention settled on the kiosk, and Marit grabbed his arm. She pointed to the U-bahn map she'd been consulting earlier. "Neuer Markt is only four stops from here," she said. "If we go now, we can get there in time."

"What about our flight?"

"We can leave on a later one."

If Lars were by himself, that was what he would do. No question. But could he really ask Marit to abandon the flight she'd only just purchased for what may end up being a wild goose chase? "You'd be out a lot of money," he said.

"Lars! I'm not even going to tell you how many frequent flier miles I have. Just believe me when I tell you that missing the eight ten flight tonight is not a big deal. A chance at reclaiming your family's jewelry, on the other hand, is huge."

She was right. And they were wasting time.

"Buy a ticket to the stop near Neuer Markt," he said, pointing to the kiosk the woman had just vacated. "I'll get one over there."

Dragging his suitcase behind him, he moved to the next available kiosk and pulled out his credit card. Two minutes later, they were racing through the tunnels to the U3 platform.

An overhead announcement broadcast the train's arrival as they were descending the last set of stairs. Lars heard the whoosh of the oncoming train seconds before the headlights broke through the tunnel. The people on the platform surged forward.

"Stay close," he said, weaving through the milling crowd.

Pulling her suitcase behind her, Marit followed him to the rear of the train, where the crowd was thinner. Lars boarded, holding the door open until she was inside.

"Let's stand by the door," she suggested. "That way we can be the first off."

"Good thinking." He studied the map painted on the inside of the train. "It looks like there's a short section of the track that's above ground between the second and third stops. I won't have time to place a call to Cole, but I could maybe forward the email before we go back underground."

Marit nodded. "Cole's smart enough to know what it means."

"I sure hope so."

Why had she been cleared? That question circled around Isabelle's brain, but she couldn't come up with a reasonable answer. If the police were still operating under the assumption that the bank robbers had been hired by someone else to go after the diamonds, logically, she should still be under scrutiny. Or maybe she never was.

No one had ever identified any issues with the policeman who had been following her the day she and Marit had gone to the dress shop, but it was possible the surveillance had been a routine part of their investigation. Although, to have the police department spend the resources to have a cop chase her through the city still felt like overkill.

Isabelle leaned back in her chair and glanced at Cole. "Do you think it's possible Gerhart made up the story about me being put on administrative leave?"

"I don't know. What would his reason be for that?" Cole asked.

"I'm not sure, unless he wanted to keep me out of the financial systems for some reason." Isabelle contemplated the new question.

"If that was the case, I'd have to think he was doing something he was afraid you would see."

"There's one way to find out." Isabelle logged into the banking system using remote access.

"What are you doing?"

"I'm going to run a report on all of the account changes that have occurred since the robbery."

"The robbery was three days ago. Won't there be a lot?"

"We're about to find out." Isabelle input her parameters for the customized report. Five hundred seventy-two results.

Cole leaned closer. "That will take forever to sort through."

"Let's see if we can narrow it down." Isabelle limited another search field, this time only including accounts over a hundred thousand euros. Forty-three results.

"Go up to a million. See what that gives you," Cole said.

Isabelle complied. "That's more like it. We're down to six."

"Anyone look familiar?"

She read the short list. "Brinkerhoff." Isabelle opened the recent transactions for his accounts. "He canceled all his safe-deposit boxes and closed out his accounts."

"Is there a reason stated?" Cole asked.

"Oh, this is good." Isabelle pointed at her screen. "He said after the robbery, he didn't feel he could trust the bank's security to keep his valuables safe."

"Yeah, that's rich." Cole put his hand on the back of her chair and scooted closer still. "Can you pull up the recent transactions?"

"That's my next move," Isabelle said. "Let's see if Brinkerhoff's real motivation for closing his accounts was to hide something."

She searched through Brinkerhoff's personal accounts but didn't see anything out of the ordinary. His corporate checking account came next.

Large deposits. Large withdrawals.

"That's a lot of money passing through," Cole said.

"Let's see where it's coming from." Isabelle deepened her search. "These regular deposits appear to be from daily sales."

"And the big ones?" Cole asked. "I'm sorry, but I'm not buying him having regular sales that push close to half a million euros a week."

"Me neither." Isabelle traced the transfer, disappointed when the origin appeared on her screen. "This money is coming from numbered accounts in Luxembourg."

"Any way to find out who owns them?"

"Not likely. Luxembourg is as intense as Switzerland when it comes to protecting the privacy of their account holders."

"What about the big withdrawals?" Cole asked.

"The same. All the big ones are going to Luxembourg or Switzerland."

"So all we have is more suspicions and no proof."

"There's got to be something here if Gerhart limited my access to keep me from seeing something," Isabelle said. "Maybe it was one of the other accounts."

"It's hard to believe it wouldn't be Brinkerhoff since he's the one who closed out his accounts."

"True." Isabelle let out a sigh. "Let's go through all of these. Maybe there's something hidden in one of these smaller transactions."

Cole slid his hand onto her shoulder and squeezed the tense muscles there. "We'll find it."

"I hope so." Isabelle opened one transaction after another, tracing the origins of the deposits as well as the recipients of the transfers and withdrawals.

Only a few minutes passed before a payment to a construction company popped up. "This might be something."

Cole slid back over to his computer and started typing. "The company is local."

Isabelle tagged the transaction and kept going. Less than a minute passed before she found another one. "Looks like the construction company is either a shell to hide money laundering or they're doing a significant amount of work for Brinkerhoff."

"They look legit," Cole said.

"Are you sure? If Wimmer really is involved, there has to be something he doesn't want me to find."

Cole opened another window, this time going to Brinkerhoff's website. He straightened. "Brinkerhoff is opening a new store."

"Does it say where?" Isabelle asked.

"No. Can you do your fancy tracking thing to find recent land transactions?"

"I can try." Isabelle did a search of recent mortgages. "Got it. Brinkerhoff bought a piece of property nine months ago. He must be either building a new store or retrofitting an existing building."

"Where is it?"

"Neuer Markt 22. Here in Vienna."

Cole pushed back from the table. "Let's go."

CHAPTER 32

It was dark by the time Marit and Lars emerged from the U-bahn station.

"Ten more minutes before the auction begins," Lars said. "Think we can make it?"

"Yes. It's not far." Marit studied the map she'd just pulled up on her phone before turning her attention to the surroundings. "This isn't what I was expecting."

Cars zipped by, their headlights illuminating the historic buildings housing the upscale boutiques and restaurants lining the busy road.

"Me neither," Lars said. "I was thinking we'd end up somewhere more like a warehouse or a dark alley."

"Well, this is an improvement over those alternatives."

"Yeah. But I'd feel better knowing Cole was on his way." He put his phone to his ear, and Marit could hear it ringing. When it rolled into Cole's voice mail, Lars started speaking. "Hey, Cole, this is Lars. Marit and I took a detour on our way to the airport. I've sent you an email with the location of a jewelry auction. It starts in the next few minutes, and it looks like they're going to try selling off Falcon Point jewelry. Call me back when you get this message."

Marit's stomach clenched. They'd been so consumed with reaching the auction's location in time, she hadn't given any thought to what they would do once they arrived. "Now what?"

Lars looked down the street. "Now we check out the auction."

Unlike the bistro occupying Neuer Markt 21, building number 22 was dark. As they drew closer, Marit strained to see past the light pouring onto the pavement from the bustling café's windows to study the shadowy entrance next door.

"Lars," she said. "There's a man standing in the doorway." She kept her voice low even though there could be no doubt the watchman had heard their approach. The clatter of suitcase wheels against the cobbles was impossible to miss.

"He probably wants to see the invitation," Lars said, pulling his phone out as he spoke.

It was the obvious reason for the man's presence, but it did little to assuage Marit's uneasiness. She'd seen far too many guns this week already.

Lars stepped up to the man. "We're here for the auction."

The man stayed in the shadows, his dark clothing and black-knit hat hiding all but his large physique.

"I need to see your invitation."

Lars turned his phone screen toward him.

The man grunted. "What's in the suitcases?"

"Clothes," Lars said. "We were on our way out of town when we received the email."

Lars didn't have a Viennese accent, but his German was good enough that not many people would guess he was Dutch. The less the guard knew about them, the better.

"You got the email," the guard said. "Not her. This is an exclusive sale."

"We work together. I do the bidding; she contacts our buyers."

Marit could feel the man's stare. She suppressed the urge to shudder.

"Open the cases."

"Here?" Lars asked. "Even if we do, you won't be able to see anything."

The guard opened the door and pointed to a spot just inside the doorway. "There."

Cole gripped the bright-yellow grab bar by the train exit, with Isabelle right beside him. He would have preferred to drive to Brinkerhoff's new jewelry store rather than take the U-bahn, but Isabelle had pointed out that at this time of day, public transportation would be faster than fighting their way through rush-hour traffic, especially with the freezing rain that was now falling. If only the train weren't so crowded. And so public.

Even though his questions about Wimmer were plentiful, he didn't dare ask them with so many people nearby. The orange plastic seats were barely visible beneath the commuters and winter coats currently occupying them.

"You okay?" Isabelle asked in German.

The use of the local language gave him a subtle reminder that they were supposed to blend in.

"*Gut*," Cole replied, offering a shorthanded answer in German to indicate everything was fine. He hoped everything was fine. Lars had tried calling him a minute ago, but either the interference from his train or the one Lars was on had prevented it from connecting when Cole had tried to answer.

Cole shook away his concern. Knowing Lars, he forgot something at the apartment and wanted Cole to mail it to him.

Isabelle glanced at her cell phone. "They should be to the airport by now," she said. "Once we get above ground, you can try your cousin again."

"Yeah." Cole didn't miss the way Isabelle avoided using Lars's and Marit's names. She was good at her job.

He reached out and put his hand on her back, a reminder to both of them of the changing dynamics of their relationship. Cole didn't know what it would look like once he had to start traveling again for work, but he wasn't going to make the same mistake twice. He only hoped Isabelle would be patient with him when he made new ones.

The sensation of being watched crept over him and pulled him out of his thoughts. He scanned the other train passengers. A couple dozen commuters, a tourist family, an older couple who appeared to be on their way to the opera, some teenagers chatting, two twenty-somethings with carryon suitcases beside them.

Cole caught a flash of movement behind the tourists, but he couldn't tell if it was the businessman juggling his messenger bag on his lap or something else.

He studied the compartment again before his gaze landed on the map on the wall. Two more stops and they would reach their destination.

Was the sensation of being watched his imagination, or was someone following them? And if so, who? After meeting Gerhart Wimmer at the ball, Cole seriously doubted he had the skills to blend into the crowd. Could Gwendolyn know he suspected her involvement in leaking information? He looked around again with a new purpose in mind. People could change their appearance but not their size.

Isabelle moved closer to him, her free hand sliding around his waist. "Everything okay?"

"I just thought my boss might take this train," Cole said.

Isabelle studied their fellow travelers. "I don't see her."

"I must have been mistaken." The train pulled to a stop, and Cole studied the passengers that remained. Still nothing. Either he was being paranoid, or whoever was following them was better at remaining hidden than Cole was at identifying suspicious characters.

They reached their station, and Isabelle led the way onto the platform. As soon as they were clear, Cole slowed his steps and withdrew his phone to call Lars back.

"He left a voice mail." Cole retrieved it and listened. His body tensed when he learned not only what his cousin had found but also what he intended to do about it. "Lars may have found the Falcon Point jewels."

"Where?"

Cole pulled up the email. The two seconds it took to load stretched into forever. Finally, it popped onto the screen. Cole skimmed down to the address, and his heart seized.

"It's here. The jewels are in Brinkerhoff's new store."

Isabelle whipped out her phone.

Cole started toward the soon-to-be jewelry store before she had the chance to dial.

She grabbed his sleeve and stopped him. "Cole, we should wait out here."

"I can't." Cole nodded at the store across the street. "Lars and Marit are in there."

Marit looked around the darkened space. It appeared to be a jeweler's show-room—although most of the cases were empty. Perhaps the owners were selling their merchandise because they were going out of business. Or maybe they were opening soon. The plush carpet smelled new, suggesting the latter. Display cases ran the length of the walls. Fluorescent bulbs glowed in the case closest to them, illuminating enough of the room to guide new arrivals from the front of the room to the back, where a chink of light shone beneath another door.

"That's far enough," the guard said. "Open them up."

Lars offered her an apologetic look before setting his case down and undoing the zipper. The man in black raised the lid and took Lars's sweatshirt off the top before running his hand around the inside. With a grunt, he turned to Marit's open case. She bit her lip, attempting to remain dispassionate as he pawed through her clothing.

When it became obvious that neither suitcase contained a weapon, the guard eyed Lars's camera bag.

"Now that one."

Lars opened the bag. "Camera, tripod, lenses, flash," he said. "And if this little exercise has caused us to miss bidding on the pieces we came for, your boss will hear about it."

The man scowled and pointed to the nearest display case. "Leave them all behind that," he said. "You can get them on the way out."

Lars's jaw tightened. Marit had a pretty good idea of how he felt about leaving his expensive photographic equipment in the care of crooks, but drawing attention to its worth was probably the worst possible tactic. Lars must have come to the same unfortunate conclusion because without another word, he set their cases and his bag behind the counter. "Satisfied?" he asked.

The guard pointed to the door at the other end of the room. "That way."

Lars placed his hand on Marit's back. Although his touch was reassuring, it did not fully remove her mounting apprehension. She released a tense breath.

"Once we've figured out what's happening, we'll leave," Lars said softly. "We just need enough information to get the authorities over here."

She nodded, and he reached for the door handle.

The small back room was well lit and crowded. A dozen or so chairs had been placed in two rows facing the other side of the room. Most of the seats were occupied, and a few more people stood against the walls. A low hum of conversation came from the three men standing together beside a long table at the front, but the rest of the occupants appeared to be guardedly and silently assessing each other.

Marit scanned the room, her gaze falling on a broad-shouldered man standing at the far end of the table. Her breath caught.

"Lars," she whispered. "One of Brinkerhoff's bodyguards is here."

"Where?"

"Right side of the table. He's watching the men who are talking."

One of the men at the front of the room shifted slightly, offering them their first view of the tall, white-haired man standing on the other side of the table.

"Brinkerhoff," Lars hissed.

"The moment he sees us, he'll recognize us."

"Yep," Lars said, taking a step back. "We've officially stayed long enough."

They turned to exit the room, and the door opened. A dark-haired woman wearing a deep-purple designer trouser suit stood framed in the doorway. Her calculating gaze brushed over Marit before settling on Lars.

"Well, well," Lina Wimmer said. "It looks like we may have some unwelcome guests at our auction."

CHAPTER 33

ISABELLE KEPT HER HAND ON Cole's arm. For a second, she thought he was going to charge straight through the front door without a care for his own safety. Thankfully, his training kicked in before he'd made it two steps.

With the rear of the store protected by gated access, their options were limited.

"I think taking out the guard at the front door is our quickest way in," Cole said.

"We'll draw less attention going in the front," Isabelle agreed. "But I don't think an altercation will bode well with the number of people around right now."

"I'm open to suggestions."

Isabelle held up her phone.

"Suggestions that don't include trusting the authorities to get them out alive," Cole said. "If Brinkerhoff is in there, he'll recognize both Lars and Marit. In a hostage situation, they'll be the first people he'll take out."

He was right. Hostage situations rarely ended well. At least one of them needed to get inside before they called the police.

Her hand tightened on her phone, and her gaze lowered to it. "Let me see that email from Lars again."

Cole pulled it up on his phone and handed it over, his brisk movements the only outward sign of his sense of urgency.

She skimmed the email, and the improbable presented itself. "We can get in the front door with this."

Awareness lit Cole's eyes. "Pretend we were sent the invitation?"

"Yes." Isabelle copied the invitation, reconfigured it into a new email and sent it to both Cole and herself. "I just resent it so it will look like it's an original rather than a forwarded email."

"That's brilliant." Cole took his phone from her and checked his email. "It looks like it came from them."

"What's the plan once we get inside?"

"Stay out of sight until we find Lars and Marit. As soon as we get them out of there, we come out and call the police."

"I'd feel better if we called the police before we go in," Isabelle said.

"If we call them now, they won't give us the extra time we need to find Lars and Marit." Cole debated a second. Then he pulled up a contact on his phone and hit the Call button.

"Who are you calling?"

"Ghost."

A moment later, a woman's voice came over the line. Isabelle strained to hear it but couldn't quite make out the words.

Cole explained their situation, gave her their location, and outlined their plan. After a brief conversation, he hung up.

"I'll keep Ghost up to date on what's going on. If she doesn't hear from me for more than five minutes, she'll call the police. Otherwise, she'll wait for our signal to make the call."

Isabelle squelched the sudden nerves that took flight inside her. She glanced at her watch. "Then we'd better get going."

Cole and Isabelle made their way to the crosswalk a short distance away and waited for a break in the traffic before they crossed the street together.

As they approached, the man standing at the jewelry story entrance tensed. He used his size to block the doorway. "Can I help you?"

"Yes." Cole didn't explain other than to pull up the email on his phone and show him the screen.

"That gets you in, but why are there two of you?"

"I have my own invitation." Isabelle showed her screen as well.

Apparently satisfied, he nodded. "Go inside there and wait. They'll get started shortly."

"Thanks." Isabelle followed Cole inside and walked into a room nearly void of light.

Lars met Lina Wimmer's cool appraisal without flinching, his initial shock at seeing her in the doorway quickly giving way to a wave of intense aversion.

"Frau Wimmer. I did not expect to see you here." He forced his lips into some semblance of a smile and reached for Marit's hand. "We were just leaving."

"Is that so?"

She did not move from the doorway.

"Yes." Lars took another step toward the exit. "If you would excuse us."

"Let me find you an escort."

Lars had a pretty good sense of what Lina's idea of being escorted out of the auction entailed.

"That won't be necessary," he said.

Lina ignored him. "Ivan!"

The burley bodyguard left his position by the table and moved quickly to join her.

"Take these visitors to the back room," she said. "Since he's here, Mr. Hendriks can give us the benefit of his expertise. After all, I believe he's already familiar with the items we have up for bid tonight."

Lars attempted to tamp down his anger at her blatant taunting, but frustration welled within him. They were trapped. Neither he nor Marit had a weapon. Ivan did. The bulge beneath the bodyguard's jacket was all too obvious. They were too far from the outside door to make a successful run for it. The guard was probably still standing there anyway.

"Over there," Ivan said, pointing to a door on the opposite wall.

Lars hazarded a glance at Marit. He recognized the fear in her eyes, but her head was high, her expression calm. Tightening his grip on her hand, he led her across the room. Ivan stayed within arms' length, and Lina followed close behind.

The door was ajar. Ivan pushed it open, waiting for Lars and Marit to precede him into a smaller room containing a large table and a couple of chairs. Jewelry boxes of various sizes and colors were lined up along the table, their lids open. And standing with his hands behind his back, perusing the valuable pieces with a calculating look, was Lina's brother, Steven.

Marit's gasp was barely audible. Lars steeled himself. He refused to give Lina the satisfaction of seeing him react to the sight of his stolen family heirlooms on display.

"Unfortunately, we've not had time to do more than a cursory appraisal of these treasures," Lina said, walking around the table. "As I'm sure you understand, time is of the essence when it comes to distributing such unique items." She offered him a mocking smile. "But now that you are here, you can help. Tell me, Lars, which piece do you consider most valuable?"

Lars set his jaw, saying nothing.

"My sister asked you a question," Steven said.

Lars ignored him. Steven's lip curled, and with a nod, he signaled the guard. Ivan drew his weapon.

Marit released Lars's hand, stepping closer to the table. "If we help you, do you promise to let us go?"

Lars's stomach dropped. What was Marit doing? Surely she realized that their chances of negotiating safe passage out of here was virtually nil.

"If you work with us, we will work with you," Lina said.

Marit turned to face him. "It's our only chance, Lars. Tell them about the gem-encrusted brooch."

Cole approached the door on the far side of the room with apprehension. He fought the urge to draw his gun before he entered, reminding himself that staying unnoticed was the preferred mode of operation today.

He opened the door and glanced at Isabelle. She nodded. She was ready. He hoped he was too. If anything happened to Lars and Marit, he'd never forgive himself. He should have known better than to involve civilians in his work.

Willing his heartbeat to steady, Cole stepped inside the brightly lit auction room and immediately stepped behind a man who was an inch or two over six feet. He wasn't about to give Brinkerhoff the chance to see him prematurely.

Cole peeked at the front of the room where a display table had been set up. One of Brinkerhoff's bodyguards stood at one end of it.

Brinkerhoff had taken his position at the center of the table.

"We have our first item up for sale." Brinkerhoff held up a dated jewelry case, the lid open to reveal an ornate sapphire-and-diamond necklace. "We will give you all a moment to take a closer look before we start the bidding."

Cole's stomach clenched. He had seen that necklace before, not only when he and his cousins had first looked through their ancestors' jewelry but also in his great-great-grandmother's portrait that currently hung in Falcon Point's residential wing.

Several people lined up in the aisle between the rows of chairs to examine the piece of jewelry that rightfully belonged to him and his family.

"That's my great-great-grandmother's," Cole whispered to Isabelle.

She squeezed his hand, a show of support as well as a reminder that the treasures of the past weren't as important as his family of today.

When the man in front of him fell in line, Cole moved to the center as well to remain out of sight. He looked around the room and whispered, "I don't see them."

"Me neither." She nodded toward the far corner. "We might have a better view from over there."

Keeping his face averted from the guard, Cole slid behind the back row of chairs and worked his way to the far side. Assuming Lars and Marit would be smart enough to not approach the front table, where Brinkerhoff would certainly see them, Cole scanned the few people who had opted to sit.

"Maybe they already left," Isabelle said.

"If everyone will take their seats," Brinkerhoff said, "we will start the bidding at thirty thousand euros."

The tall man Cole had used as a human shield a minute ago returned to his seat. Cole sat behind him, tugging on Isabelle's hand so she would do the same.

He leaned close and whispered in her ear, "As soon as they bring out the next piece, we'll slip out."

Isabelle nodded.

Brinkerhoff held up the necklace again and began the auction.

Cole pulled out his phone, turned down the volume, and opened his camera app. He turned on the video option and pushed Record so no one would hear the click of a photo being taken. Unobtrusively, he turned his phone to capture as many faces of the bidders as he could. He sent the video to Cas before starting a new video recording.

He held his cell in his hand as though searching something on his screen, the camera angled at the front of the room so he would have a recording of the highest bidder. No way the buyer was going to keep that necklace for long. Cole would make sure of it. For now though, he needed to figure out where Lars and Marit had disappeared to.

CHAPTER 34

MARIT WATCHED SHOCK FLIT ACROSS Lars's face. How quickly would he pick up on her ruse? The gem-encrusted brooch was dazzling, but it was also the newest piece in the collection and, therefore, of least value to an antique dealer. It contained a beautiful array of precious stones, but she knew that almost every other piece on the table was worth more. "To walk away is worth more than the brooch," she said.

He hesitated, watching her intently. "They'll find out about it soon enough."

Relief filled her. He was stalling, waiting for his next cue.

"But if you tell them how much you've been offered for it, they may put it up for auction first and . . . and let us go sooner."

The last part of Marit's reasoning had been an afterthought—and a weak one at that. But Lars was likely the only one in the room who would catch it. They both knew that being released was not an option at this point. But anything they could do that might buy Cole time to get here before Brinkerhoff sold off items of more value—both monetarily and sentimentally—was worth the effort.

Lina put on the pair of white gloves lying on the table and picked up one of the jewelry boxes. "Is this the one you're talking about?"

The hinges and clasp were shiny, and the black lacquer coating looked new. It made the boxes housing Lars's great-grandmother's favorite pieces seem shabby and neglected.

"Yes," Marit said.

Lina turned to Lars, her penciled eyebrows raised. "Talk."

For a brief moment, Lars's knowing eyes met Marit's. And then, feigning indecision, he looked from the glittering brooch to Lina's malicious expression.

"Now," Steven said, adding his demand to his sister's. "Mr. Brinkerhoff will be in to collect the next item up for bid any minute."

"The brooch was made by a renowned goldsmith in Milan, Italy," Lars lied. "It is one of a kind. The stones, alone, are worth hundreds of thousands of euros, but the setting is priceless."

Lina took the brooch out of the box and held it up to the light. Greed shone in her eyes. "Good to know."

The door swung open again, and Brinkerhoff walked in. His gaze landed on Lars, and his eyes narrowed. "What's going on in here?"

"I found these two leaving the auction room." She offered him a smug smile. "I decided to employ Mr. Hendriks's expertise to help us prioritize these pieces." She handed him the brooch. "This one should go up for bid next."

"Why?"

"Because it's so valuable."

Brinkerhoff snatched the black box from her hand and set the brooch back in it. "He's playing you for the fool that you are," he said. "Put this back on the table and hand me the diamond-and-emerald earrings."

Lina reclaimed the black box and seared Lars with a furious glare. "Ivan," she said. "Take their phones and lock them both in the storage room. We'll deal with our unwanted guests after everyone else is gone."

A ripple of unease skittered up Isabelle's spine. The man who won the auction for the necklace moved forward to settle his debt as Brinkerhoff appeared from the back room carrying a small box, likely housing a pair of earrings.

A man and woman followed him into the auction room.

Steven Powell and Lina Wimmer!

Isabelle slid lower in her chair. Cole tucked his chin against his chest, his eyes now on his cell phone.

"We have to get out of here," she whispered. "Now."

Cole gave a subtle nod toward the door. He pocketed his phone and tapped her knee before he stood, immediately turning his back to the front of the room. Isabelle followed suit.

She and Cole entered the darkened showroom and let the door close behind them. The guard standing by the door held a phone to his ear and nodded.

"Got it." He drew his weapon in a practiced move and aimed it at Cole and Isabelle. "Stop right there. Someone wants to talk to you."

Great. Only a few more meters and they would have made it. Isabelle's breath shuddered out. She held her hands out slightly to the side to indicate she wasn't a threat. Cole did the same. As expected, the guard focused on Cole as his primary target. Unfortunately, the move Cole would typically use to disarm the man would send the gun pointing right at her when it was most likely to discharge.

Hoping for a distraction, she forced a tremble into her voice as though she had never had a gun aimed at her before. "Please, don't shoot."

"We didn't do anything," Cole added, also offering a convincing demonstration of someone who was scared of rather than challenged by the weapon.

"Then you won't mind having a chat with my boss."

"I think your boss is a little busy with the auction right now." Cole took a half step to the side as though trying to get around the guard.

The man focused his attention on Cole again, and Isabelle took a half step forward.

"I said stay there." The gun swung toward Isabelle once more.

In her mind, she rehearsed her planned move. Grab the gun barrel with her left hand, duck out of the line of fire, karate chop the wrist with her free hand.

"Please . . ." Isabelle began. Then she sprang into motion. Her left hand shot out, and she forced the gun barrel away from Cole as she ducked toward him.

She stiffened her right hand as she struck the guard's wrist, but rather than releasing his weapon, he tightened his grip and countered her move by using his free hand to fight for control of the gun.

Isabelle used all her strength to aim the pistol away from her and toward the guard, but his strength threatened to overpower her. The gun turned back toward her. Another inch and it would be aimed right at her heart.

Beside her, Cole rushed forward, his hand fisted. He struck out, his fist connecting with the guard's jaw.

The man stumbled back a step, but his grip remained firm on the gun.

The door opened behind them, and an instant later, a gun barrel pressed into Isabelle's back.

A man's voice followed. "Let go."

Isabelle's breath whooshed out, and she forced herself to release the guard's weapon.

The guard jerked back two steps, his gun immediately swinging toward Cole. "Lina wants to see these two."

"I'll take care of it, but first, check them for weapons."

Isabelle recognized the voice behind her now from last night at the ball. He had been one of Brinkerhoff's bodyguards.

The guard checked Cole first, relieving him of his pistol and cell phone. Isabelle stiffened when the guard moved to her and patted down her legs and stomach. He pulled her cell phone from her pocket, she helpless to stop him.

"Now we're going to take a nice walk through the auction and to the back room." The pressure from the gun barrel eased slightly, but a hand clamped onto her shoulder. "Try anything with me and your girlfriend dies first."

Cole's eyes met hers before he trained his gaze on the man currently holding her captive. "I understand."

Lars heard the lock scrape back and whipped around to face the door. What now? As much as he wanted to get out of the confined storage room, he was willing to bet that nothing good would come of their captors opening the door again so soon. He stepped in front of Marit. If they wanted her, they'd have to get past him first.

The door flew open.

"Get in!" The brusque voice was Ivan's.

"All right. There's no need to shove."

Lars's eyes widened. Cole.

Behind him, Marit shifted, appearing at his side as Isabelle and Cole entered the confined space. Cole had barely cleared the doorway when Ivan yanked the door closed behind them and the sound of the bolt sliding into place echoed through the small room.

Cole glanced from Lars to Marit. "Great. We found you."

"Are you kidding?" Lars said. Maybe you had to be slightly mad to be a CIA operative. "You were supposed to be the cavalry. You know, the one who comes in to save the day." He gestured to the cramped room that contained nothing but empty shelves and a large safe. "If getting locked in here with us was part of your grand plan, it was a lousy one."

"You didn't give me much warning. I'm improvising as I go."

"In other words, you don't have a plan."

Cole studied the room. "I'm working on it."

"Brinkerhoff, Lina Wimmer, and Steven Powell have the Falcon Point jewelry," Marit said.

"Yeah, I saw that."

"And they're going to kill us when the people at the auction leave," Lars said.

"No, they won't."

New hope shot through Lars. "Did you send for reinforcements?"

"I placed a call, but I think we should proceed as though we're on our own."

That wasn't exactly what Lars wanted to hear. "Fine. Do you have your gun?"

"Nope. Ivan the Terrible took it."

"Did they take your phones too?" Marit asked.

"Yes," Isabelle said. She was running her hands along the empty shelves as though she expected to find something hidden there.

"Okay. Let me get this straight," Lars said. "We have no weapons and no phones. We're locked in a storage room surrounded by armed guards. And you think we're going to walk out of here."

"Or run," Cole said. "Not sure about our exit speed yet."

Isabelle had moved from her search of the empty shelves to an examination of the locked safe. "There's nothing here that we can use," she said. "It'll have to be the door hinges."

Cole grinned. "See. They may have taken our guns and phones, but we still have Isabelle."

Isabelle rolled her eyes. "I was hoping one of the construction workers might have left behind a tool we could use but no luck. We need something narrow enough to fit beneath the head of the hinge pin but strong enough to wiggle it loose." She looked from Cole to Lars to Marit. "What have you got?"

Lars dug his hands into his pockets and brought out a wallet filled with flimsy credit cards, the receipt for his U-bahn ticket, and a few coins. A quick glance at the objects in Cole's hand told him that his cousin had only upped him by a set of keys.

Marit was still rifling through her purse. "What about this?" She pulled out a metal nail file.

"That's perfect," Isabelle said. She took the nail file from Marit and handed it to Cole with a triumphant look. "You're better off than you thought. You've still got me *and* Marit."

CHAPTER 35

COLE USED MARIT'S NAIL FILE to work the last bolt free. Who knew having a model with him would be so useful?

Beside him, Lars stood with both hands on the door to keep it in place. Isabelle and Marit had alternated between helping Lars and taking the bolts from Cole as he freed them. He handed the last one to Marit, but he kept the nail file in his hand. It wasn't the best weapon, but it was better than nothing.

Voices carried from the back room, Lina's words distinguishable when Brinkerhoff asked for the next auction piece.

His voice low, Lars asked, "Now what?"

"Marit, come over here with Lars," Cole said. "When I say, Lars is going to pull the door open. If you both tuck yourselves in the corner behind the door, it will protect you in case anyone pulls a gun and bullets start flying."

"Do you know how crazy you sound right now?" Lars asked. "You're telling us to hide while you charge into a room where there are men with guns."

It was crazy, but Cole wasn't going to tell Lars that. If they waited for Brinkerhoff and his men to come back after the auction, they were all going to end up dead anyway.

"If you have a better idea, I'm listening," Cole whispered.

Lars fell silent.

"Well?" Cole asked.

"I'm thinking."

Marit stepped forward. "We could wait for the police to get here."

Cole debated whether to share the grim truth that if the cops arrived, they were dead anyway. No way Powell, Brinkerhoff, or Lina were going to leave witnesses to what they were doing, and a few dead people would give them the perfect distraction to get away. "I think it's riskier to wait," Cole said.

Lars's gaze met his, and understanding illuminated his face. Lars glanced at Marit briefly before he nodded. "I'm trusting you on this."

The weight of Lars's words pressed in on him. Lars was trusting him. So were Marit and Isabelle. If he messed this up, he could not only end up dead, but three people he cared deeply about could die right beside him.

Brinkerhoff spoke to Steven and one of his guards. At least four people were in the back room. If he could go in right after they took the next piece for auction, Cole would be certain the extra guard and either Lina or Brinkerhoff would be in the auction room. Isabelle put her hand on his shoulder and leaned close to whisper in his ear. "We go in together."

Cole swallowed and nodded. Isabelle's assessment of the situation must have matched his, or she would have offered another alternative, even if it was waiting for the police, as Marit had suggested. "Get ready."

Marit tucked herself back where the door would soon open, concern flashing in her eyes. "What about Isabelle?"

"I'll hide over here." Isabelle took position behind Cole on the now-unhinged side of the door.

Cole pressed his ear to the door. No one was speaking. Had Brinkerhoff already taken the next item into the auction? Go now, or wait until they were sure the number was manageable? A sense of urgency coursed through him. Go now, he decided. "On three," Cole whispered. He held up three fingers. He lowered one just as a new voice carried to him.

"Wait." Cole flashed a stop signal with his hand.

"What are you doing back here?" Brinkerhoff demanded.

"Sorry, sir," a man said. "She pushed past me."

"You couldn't stop her?" Derision colored Brinkerhoff's voice.

"I assure you, after you hear my offer, you won't have any reason to be mad at him," the woman said. Even though the words were spoken in German, Cole caught the familiar cadence in the voice. Jasmine?

"What's your offer?" Steven Powell demanded.

While Jasmine started speaking about the possibility of purchasing the remaining jewels for an impressive sum of money, Cole turned to Isabelle. "The woman in there. It's Jasmine."

"Describe her," Isabelle said.

"A younger, darker version of my grandmother but with a wicked right hook."

Isabelle's lips quirked up at the description. She put her hand on his back. Her silent cue that she was ready.

Voices raised on the other side of the door.

"I don't care who you say you are," Brinkerhoff said. "Search her for weapons."

"Boy, you had better keep your hands off me," Jasmine responded with her typical don't-mess-with-me attitude.

Cole held up three fingers again. He counted down quickly. The moment his last finger lowered, he curled his hand into a fist and tightened his grip on the nail file with the other.

Lars pulled the door open in a quick jerk of movement, and Cole rushed into the back room. Jasmine stood beside the guard, Lina behind her, with Brinkerhoff and Powell right in front of the storage room.

Brinkerhoff instantly turned toward Cole, and Cole swiped at him with the nail file. It cut across his cheek, and the man jumped back.

Isabelle rushed into the room, her fist connecting with Steven Powell's jaw and sending him stumbling.

Brinkerhoff's hand lifted to where Cole had drawn blood. "Ivan!" he shouted.

In a blur of movement, Jasmine struck Ivan before he could draw his gun.

The door to the auction burst open and knocked into Jasmine. A second guard rushed in, and his weapon appeared in his hand before Isabelle could reach him.

He lifted the pistol and aimed.

Cole's heart seized as a bullet exploded in the same instance Jasmine threw her shoulder against the guard to send the shot wide.

The bullet splintered into the door jamb leading to the storage room, and Cole prayed Lars and Marit would stay safely out of the line of fire.

Shards of wood dropped to the floor around her. Marit pressed herself farther into the corner. A man shouted, and through the gap between the hingeless door and the wall, she saw the guard raise his gun again. Isabelle swung her leg out and clipped his knee. He staggered back a few steps. Someone else jumped forward, blocking Marit's view of everything but the table covered in jewelry boxes.

Another gunshot pierced the door only inches above them.

Marit gasped. "Lars." She leaned closer. "We need to get out of here. We're sitting ducks."

He nodded, his expression grim. "After those gunshots, the people attending the auction are either going to scatter or they're going to take advantage of the chaos."

"I don't want to wait to find out which one."

"Me neither."

A third gunshot sounded, and the storage room door jerked back.

"Get down!" Lars grabbed her arm and pulled her to the floor.

There was another crash. It was followed by the sound of raining boxes.

"Was that the jewelry?"

"Yeah. The table's down." Lars's voice was overshadowed by the sound of another gunshot. "This room's a trap. We'd be safer out there." He rose to his feet. "If we can get to the table, we can shelter behind that. Give me a three-second head start. If no one notices what I'm doing, follow after me. If they come for me, stay here." He held her gaze. "No matter what."

It was a promise she wasn't willing to make. With her heart pounding uncomfortably in her chest, Marit released a tense breath. "Just be careful."

"You too."

He peered around the door. There was another resounding thud. A man shouted, and then Lars was gone. Marit rose to her feet and peeked into the other room. Lars had reached the table and dropped out of sight. Closer to the other door, Isabelle and Jasmine were working together to disarm Ivan and the other guard. Cole threw a punch at Brinkerhoff. Marit didn't wait to see it land. She darted around the door and sprinted across the room.

She reached the table and dropped down behind it as another thud and painful grunt sounded behind her.

Lars gave her an anxious look. "You okay?"

"Yeah. But there's no way we can reach the door from here."

"Not yet," Lars said, determination in his voice. "But we will. And when we do, we're taking the jewelry with us." He scooped up the jewelry boxes closest to him and started emptying them into his pockets.

Marit grabbed a couple of bracelets and a set of earrings, opened her purse, and dropped them in. She seized another set of earrings, and then she saw Lars's great-grandmother's wedding ring box.

Another gunshot. A bullet hit the wall above Lars's head. Simultaneously, Lars and Marit dropped lower. The sounds of violence continued behind them. Marit scooted sideways, stretching to claim the battered box containing the thin gold band. She dropped it into her purse. Movement at the other end of the table caught her attention.

"Lars! Brinkerhoff's taken the tiara."

The jeweler had one hand pressed against a bloody lip. In the other, he held the diamond headpiece. He swerved to avoid Isabelle's approach, heading directly for the door.

Like a sprinter from a starting block, Lars took off from his crouched position and tore across the room. Ivan swung around, aiming his gun at him. Lars launched himself at Brinkerhoff, tackling him to the ground. Ivan hesitated, his target now unclear.

And suddenly, Jasmine was there. She pressed her gun between Ivan's shoulder blades. "Drop the weapon."

Isabelle shook her hand, hoping the motion would stop the throbbing that had centered there from the last punch she had thrown. With Jasmine holding Ivan at gunpoint, she searched the man for additional weapons.

A second pistol at his ankle, a knife strapped to his calf. Zip ties in his shoulder holster along with an extra magazine of ammunition. The man was prepared. She'd give him that.

Cole released the other guard to Jasmine and moved to the doorway to help Lars contain Brinkerhoff.

Isabelle used one of the zip ties to secure Ivan's hands behind his back. She handed one to Jasmine and another to Cole. "Here."

"Thanks." Cole tied up his prisoner.

Isabelle moved to where Steven Powell lay crumpled at the side of the room. He had knocked himself unconscious when he'd hit his head against the wall after taking a punch to the jaw. He deserved much worse than that. Isabelle shook her hand again.

"Are you injured?" Marit asked Isabelle.

"I'll be fine," Isabelle said.

Marit scooped up more of the spilled jewelry. "What are we going to do about the people who were at the auction? At least a half dozen pieces were already sold, including the sapphire necklace."

"I took video of the people in there, including when the necklace was sold," Cole said. "Hopefully, the police can use facial recognition to ID who bought the other pieces."

"At least we got most of it back," Lars said, but his lips pressed into a firm line. "I can't believe they sold off our great-grandmother's necklace though. And the diamond-and-emerald earrings."

"I know, but give the police a chance to get it all back," Cole said.

"Where are the police anyway?" Isabelle asked. "I thought they would be here by now."

Marit looked around the room. "And where is Lina?"

"She was here a minute ago." Jasmine reached for the doorknob and yanked it open. The moment she looked through the doorway, she lifted her hands as though in surrender. "The police are here."

Two uniformed officers rushed in, their words spoken in clipped German. Everyone's hands went up, and the officers confiscated the weapons.

"She's getting away," Isabelle told the officer closest to her.

"All of them are," Marit added.

"No one is getting away," the officer said. "We have men outside. Everyone who goes outside is being taken into custody."

"I hope you don't plan to arrest us," Cole said. "We're the ones who called you."

"The call we received was from a woman."

"That was me," Isabelle lied. No way she was going to try to explain that a ghost had made the call. She wiggled her fingers to draw attention to her hand that was still raised over her head. "Can we put our hands down now? We've already secured your prisoners."

"She's with you?"

"Yes." Cole nodded. "They all are."

"The jewelry they were selling was stolen from our safe-deposit box in the bank robbery last week," Lars added.

"You can put your hands down," he said. "I'm Officer Binder. That's Officer Wolf. We'll need to confiscate all of this jewelry and enter it into evidence."

"Oh, no." Lars shook his head. "After what we went through to get it back, I'm not letting this out of my sight."

"Sir, I'm afraid I must insist," the officer said. "We have to process it all for fingerprints and catalog it for the file."

"I've already provided a detailed inventory and photos of what was taken," Lars said.

"And you aren't going to find any fingerprints," Isabelle added. "They never handled any of it unless they were wearing gloves."

"She's right." Cole retrieved his ID from his wallet and showed his embassy credentials to the officer. "Surely it won't be that big of a deal if my cousin rides with whoever is taking the jewelry back to the station for the inventory."

"Your cousin?"

"Yes," Cole said. "I'm asking a lot, but I'd appreciate the professional courtesy of letting us maintain possession of our family's treasures."

Officer Binder fell silent for a moment before he finally nodded. "We still have to follow procedure and photograph and log everything, but once that is done, I believe my captain will agree to let you take possession of your belongings."

"Thank you." Cole glanced at Lars. "Where's your camera? Maybe you can help speed things along."

"It's in the showroom," Lars said. "Is it safe to go out there?"

"I'll escort him," Officer Wolf said.

"Thanks." Officer Binder nodded his approval. "Now for the rest of you, can you tell me what happened?"

Isabelle took in the overturned furniture, the jewelry on the floor, the criminals now standing with their hands tied behind their backs, Steven Powell—the international terrorist—lying on the floor unconscious. What happened? Where should they even begin?

CHAPTER 36

LARS WAITED FOR THE LAST of the photographs he'd taken to upload onto Officer Wolf's computer.

"That's all of them," he said. "You should already have access to the inventory I gave Detective Meyer after the bank robbery."

"I do," Officer Wolf said. "Thank you. You've been most helpful."

Lars stood. Two hours at the police station on top of the grilling they'd already gone through at Brinkerhoff's empty jewelry shop was more than enough time to spend assisting the police.

"Great," he said. "Since the bank's safe-deposit box is long gone, can you find me something more substantial to put the jewelry in than the bag we used to bring it here?"

The police officer hesitated. "Under normal police procedure, those items—"

"Don't even go there," Lars warned. "I've already told you I'm not leaving the police station without every one of these pieces. They belong to my family. You know that as well as I do."

"I understand, but—"

Lars gritted his teeth. "No 'buts.' I'd like a box, but I'll take them in a bag if you don't have one."

Reluctantly, Officer Wolf rose from his position at the desk. "I'll see what I can find."

"Thanks." Lars crossed the waiting room to where Isabelle and Marit were sitting beside the two pieces of luggage. Marit offered him a sympathetic smile but uttered no word of complaint. He dropped onto the gray plastic seat beside her and put his arm around her. It felt so right to have her beside him, yet he could have lost her today. If one of those stray bullets had hit her . . . the very possibility made his blood run cold. He closed his eyes, attempting to block out the terrifying thought.

"Are you all right?" she whispered.

He opened his eyes to meet hers. "Yes. As long as you are."

She nodded and leaned her head against his shoulder. He pressed a kiss on the top of her head and caught Isabelle's gaze.

"How's the inventory going?" she asked.

"They have everything they need from me. As soon as Officer Wolf brings me the jewelry, we can go. Where are Cole and Jasmine?"

"Cole's still in with Officer Binder. He's the last one to be interviewed, but he should be out anytime. Jasmine's gone for her car. She's going to meet us around back."

Relief that he wouldn't have to carry a box full of invaluable gems on the U-bahn eased some of the tightness in his shoulders. "Sounds good. Are you holding up okay?"

"Yes," Isabelle said. "But I'm ready to get out of here."

"It looks like we won't have to wait much longer," Marit said, raising her head as Officer Wolf crossed the room to join them, a white cardboard box in his hands.

"You've been cleared to take the jewelry," he said, offering the box to Lars. "Everything's in here."

"Thanks. I appreciate it."

The door to the adjoining office opened, and Cole exited, followed by Officer Binder.

The policeman glanced at the box in Lars's hands. "Do you have everything you need, Wolf?"

"I believe so."

"We'll put the jewelry directly into a personal safe until it can be returned to the bank," Cole said. "But since we're leaving with it in a box, you'll understand if we choose to go through the back door."

Officer Binder nodded. "I'll walk you out."

They followed the policeman down a narrow hall lined with closed doors. Unlike the waiting room that was decorated with wanted posters and pictures of missing children, these walls were bare. A red fire alarm and black security cameras stood out against the antiseptic pale-green walls. Lars kept his focus on Officer Binder and tried to ignore the prickling feeling that they were being watched.

They reached a heavy metal door. The policeman scanned his ID, and the lock clicked. He pulled the door open. Cold air hit them, and the sounds of the city filtered in. A set of headlights approached in the darkness. Standing closest to the door, Cole waited, watching cautiously until the car came to a stop opposite them. His phone buzzed, and he checked the screen.

"We're clear," he said. "That's our ride."

"Then I'll wish you a good night," Officer Binder said, stepping back to let them pass.

Lars waited until Isabelle and Marit climbed into the back of the waiting vehicle before leaving the safety of the police station. Tightening his hold on the box, he crossed the short distance to the car.

Cole opened the passenger door. "Get in," Cole said. "There'll be more room for the box up front. I'll sit with Isabelle and Marit."

Lars slid in. Cole closed the door behind him. Seconds later, Cole was seated on the back seat and Jasmine was weaving through the parked cars lining the back road faster than Lars thought possible.

"So, Jasmine," he said, clutching the armrest with one hand even as he wrapped his other arm more firmly around the box. "Can I ask you two questions before we run into a lamppost?"

He caught the flash of her white teeth and hoped it was a smile rather than a grimace. "I'm listening."

"First, did you learn to drive at the same place as Isabelle?"

"Where did you learn to drive, Isabelle?" Jasmine asked.

"On the Washington Beltway."

Jasmine's teeth flashed white again. "Then it looks like we took the same real-life course." She whipped her vehicle past a bus and nipped into a space between two vehicles that was just a little bigger than a space for a motorbike.

"What's your second question?" she asked.

Lars let out a ragged breath. Was *Can I get out and walk?* an option? He guessed not.

"How was your blueberry-spinach smoothie?"

She chuckled. "It was all right. To be honest, I was kinda hoping for strawberry-banana. There's something weird about eating leaves for breakfast, you know?"

Lars smiled into the darkness and tugged on his seat belt to make sure it was secure. He had a feeling that if they made it back to Isabelle's flat alive, he and Jasmine were going to get along rather well.

Cole took a guard-like stance at Isabelle's front door as Lars did another inventory of the Falcon Point jewels. The adrenaline that had rushed through him since entering Brinkerhoff's store had yet to fully fade, and despite the knowledge that everyone he cared about was safe, the bone-jarring fear that someone could have been killed still hummed through him.

Jasmine picked up a diamond-and-ruby necklace from off the coffee table where Lars had spread everything out. "I can see why the guys at the bank grabbed these."

"I'm just glad we got them back," Lars said. "I was not looking forward to explaining what happened to the rest of the family."

"Me neither," Cole said. He checked the door behind him again. Despite the deadbolt and the additional electronic lock, he couldn't shake the feeling that someone was about to burst through any second.

He shook that thought aside. Everyone at the auction had been brought in for questioning. Everyone except Lina Wimmer. He had to think she was halfway to Switzerland by now.

"I still can't believe the police were able to recover everything," Marit said.

Lars looked up from the tiara in his hand, his gaze landing on Marit. "We were very lucky."

"In more ways than one," Cole said. The image of Lars and Marit scooping jewelry off the floor was just as surreal now as it had been when it was happening. "What were the two of you thinking, coming out of the closet?"

"We were thinking that people kept shooting at us in there."

"So you came out into the middle of a gunfight and decided to reclaim our family's jewelry?"

"It was there, and so were we." Lars shrugged.

"That just kind of happened," Marit added.

"I'm just glad you didn't get yourselves killed."

"Isabelle was already out there with you." Marit glanced at Isabelle, but there wasn't any accusation in the words. Rather, her tone was full of understanding.

"The police sure took their sweet time coming to the rescue," Jasmine said dryly.

"At least we had you," Cole said. "How did you even know we were there?"

"I'd been following Gwendolyn since I got to Vienna." Jasmine set the necklace back down on the table. "When I saw her with Lina Wimmer and Peter Brinkerhoff, I suspected they were involved. Once I figured out they were working as the money men for Steven Powell, I sent you the message about Gwendolyn."

"Why didn't you contact me directly?" Cole asked.

"Gwendolyn was watching."

"So you started watching me too," Cole said.

Jasmine nodded. "When you and Isabelle took off the way you did, I followed. It didn't take much to figure out what was going on."

"Any idea how Gwendolyn got mixed up in all this?" Isabelle asked.

"Best I can tell, she met Lina Wimmer at the opera a couple years ago. A vacation together in the Swiss Alps a few months later is the only other time I could prove they were together, but not long after that, Gwendolyn's work habits changed."

Cole debated whether he should wait to continue this conversation until after Lars and Marit were no longer in the room but dismissed the instinct. Jazz was a pro. She wouldn't share anything that went beyond what they were cleared to hear.

"What changed?" Cole asked.

"Coming in early before anyone else arrived. She also moved to a new apartment, one that is worth significantly more than what she pays in rent."

"She was receiving benefits."

"Yes. My guess is Lina saw Gwendolyn as an easy target after her divorce."

"I didn't know she was divorced," Cole said.

"Oh yeah. Her husband came from money and added a good amount to what he already had."

"You think she got used to having more, so she was willing to sell out her country to keep her lifestyle?" Marit asked, eyes wide.

Jasmine nodded. "I'm afraid so."

"How does Lina Wimmer play into all this?" Cole asked.

"I guess you never got as far as her maiden name," Jasmine said.

"It's Powell," Marit said.

Cole's eyes widened. "What?"

"She's right." Lars nodded. "Gerhart introduced Steven as his brother-in-law the night of the ball."

A flash of memory surfaced of when Cole had caught a glimpse of someone familiar. Had that been Steven Powell across the room, and he hadn't realized it? "You could have said something."

"Sorry." Lars shrugged. "I assumed you already knew."

Cole shook his head. "No."

"I thought it was her husband who was involved," Isabelle said. "The way I was put on administrative leave made me wonder if he made that up to keep me out of the office." Isabelle paused before she asked, "Was her husband involved?"

"Not that I can tell. My guess is either Ghost or someone with the CIA helped get you cleared with the local police," Jasmine said.

"It was probably Ghost since Gwendolyn wouldn't want her back at the bank too quickly," Cole said.

"I agree," Jasmine said. "Gerhart Wimmer's only mistake was marrying Steven Powell's sister."

Isabelle shook her head. "All this time, I was working with the brother-in-law of a wanted terrorist."

"I'm afraid so," Jasmine said. "And from what I can tell, she seems to share her brother's twisted need to make news and be the first to share it with the world. Narcissism at its finest."

"They must be completely depraved," Marit said.

"Agreed," Cole said.

Lars snapped a jewelry case closed. "Everything is here."

"I didn't think you'd dropped anything between the police station and here," Cole said.

"Can't be too careful." Lars loaded the jewelry back into the box Officer Wolf had given him at the station. "Isabelle, where is that safe of yours?"

"Right here." Isabelle leaned down and flipped up the edge of the area rug that covered the wood floor beneath the coffee table.

She pressed on two wooden planks at the same time. A click sounded, and she put pressure on the corner of one of the boards. A section of the flooring lifted, revealing a combination lock beneath. She quickly spun the dial and worked through the combination.

"You have a safe in the middle of your living room floor?" Lars asked.

Isabelle opened the safe and glanced over her shoulder. "Do me a favor and keep that to yourself, okay?"

"You keep these from being stolen again and I'll agree to just about anything." Lars glanced at Cole. "Even sleeping on Cole's lumpy couch."

Lars handed the box of jewels to Isabelle. She secured them inside the safe, closed the safe door, and spun the lock.

"All set. We can secure these at the bank on Monday, but until then, they're as safe as possible," she said.

"Thank goodness," Marit said. "Though, I'd feel a lot better if Lina Wimmer and that Gwendolyn person were already locked up."

"They will be soon enough," Jasmine said.

"That's right," Cole agreed. "It's only a matter of time."

CHAPTER 37

MARIT TRIED TO QUELL HER nagging uneasiness by drawing on Cole's and Jasmine's confidence. They were the professionals. If they believed Lina and Gwendolyn were nothing to worry about, surely they weren't.

Isabelle set the rug back in place and rose to her feet. "Is anyone hungry?"

"That's Isabelle's polite way of saying, 'Did anyone else hear Lars's stomach growling?'" Lars said.

Isabelle laughed. "In fairness, it has been a long time since we last ate."

"Yes, it has. And while we're on the subject of long-ago breakfasts, how about we ask, Who thinks going all day on a fruit smoothie is a good idea?"

Marit bit her lip to prevent a giggle from escaping. Most of her calorie-counting associates in the modeling world would consider a large fruit smoothie more than sufficient for one day. Lars's unabashed love of food was a refreshing change.

"Cole," Jasmine said, putting her hands on her hips. "Go get this poor boy some wiener schnitzel and french fries."

"Me? Why do I have to go?"

"Because you live here," Lars said with a grin.

"No, I don't. Isabelle does."

"In Vienna, you knucklehead. And don't tell me you haven't discovered the best place in the city to buy wiener schnitzel."

Cole rolled his eyes. "What's the weather like? I vote we find somewhere close by if the snow has started up again."

Marit got up from the sofa and moved to the window. Cars drove by on the road far below, their headlights picking up the shine on the asphalt.

"The roads are wet," she said. "I'm sure it's cold, but it's not raining or snowing right now."

"There's a place around the corner, if you like—"

The lights went out, cutting Isabelle off midsentence and plunging the flat into complete darkness.

"A power outage," Lars groaned. "Seriously?"

"Hang on, everyone." Isabelle already had her phone out with the light on. "I have a flashlight in the kitchen."

She crossed the living room, her phone lighting the way. Cole turned on the light on his phone and moved away from the door.

"Does this happen often, Isabelle?"

"Every once in a while," she said, her voice punctuated by the sound of drawers opening. "It doesn't usually last very long."

"Has it ever been your fuse box?"

"Once. When I had the oven, a space heater, and the hair drier on at the same time."

"I think it's the fuse box this time," Marit said. She had yet to move from the window to claim her phone, but she could see the outlines of everyone's faces as they turned to look at her. "From here, I can see the streetlights, the traffic lights, and the lights coming from all the neighboring flats and shops. Isabelle's flat is the only one out."

Isabelle used the light on her phone to search the drawers in the kitchen, her concern growing. Why would her fuse box trip? And why had she let her mother reorganize her kitchen when she'd visited last month? She hadn't been able to find anything since.

She opened the last of her junk drawers and rifled through it until she found what she was looking for. Finally.

She pulled the flashlight from the back of the drawer. A press of the button and a beam of light speared through the darkness.

"Do you have another one?" Cole asked from the doorway.

"Yeah. In my bedroom." She retrieved the small repair kit and some matches that she kept for just this type of electrical emergency. Marit's observation continued to circle through her mind. Why had the power gone out tonight? No one had been using any electricity beyond the lights. She hadn't even been charging her phone or laptop. She handed the flashlight to Cole. "Here. You can take this. I have a candle I can use."

Still using the flashlight on her phone to guide her, she moved to the built-in shelves that were dominated by plants and knickknacks. She retrieved a ceramic candleholder in the shape of a lantern, with a glass globe protecting the single taper candle inside. After she lit the candle, she replaced the globe and flipped off the light on her phone.

"Do you have any spare fuses?" Cole asked.

Isabelle picked up her repair kit. "Have you ever dealt with a fuse box?"

"No, but I'm sure I can figure it out."

"Maybe so, but I know I can." Isabelle crossed to him. "Like I said, this isn't the first time this has happened."

Cole whispered, "But it's the first time it's happened without a reason."

"Yes."

"We'll go together. You can fix the fuse, and I'll watch your back."

The concern in his voice enhanced Isabelle's unease. "What about everyone else?"

"They'll be fine," Cole said. "Jasmine will be with them."

Her defensive instincts heightened. She held her repair kit out. "Hold this. I have something else I need to get."

Cole took it from her, and Isabelle moved to the knife block on her kitchen counter. She glanced over her shoulder to make sure Cole was the only one in the kitchen before she tipped it on its side and pressed the third piece of wood on the bottom.

A hidden compartment popped open, and she pulled out the handgun she kept hidden there.

Cole's flashlight beam illuminated her efforts as she checked the safety and tucked the weapon into the front of her waistband.

"Ready?" Cole asked.

Her heartbeat quickened, but she nodded. "Yeah."

She followed Cole into the living room, where Lars was sitting on the couch with Marit, Marit's cell phone providing a wash of light over them. Jasmine had taken position by the front door, clearly preparing for a possible intruder.

"Isabelle and I are going to go fix the power." Cole handed the flashlight to Jasmine.

"Lars, if you want another flashlight, there's one in my bedside table," Isabelle said. "The one by the window."

"Thanks." Lars stood. "Be careful."

"We will."

Isabelle held the candle up to guide Cole to the door.

As soon as they reached Jasmine, Cole stopped. "Keep them safe."

"You got it, but make sure you let me know when you're coming back in," Jasmine whispered. "I don't want to hurt you."

Cole chuckled despite the gravity of what could be waiting for them outside. Keeping his back to Lars and Marit, he drew his pistol. Then he listened for a second before he pulled open the door.

A moment after he slipped into the hall, he whispered, "We're clear."

Isabelle followed him out of her apartment, the audible click of her lock snapping back into place sounding behind her.

She glanced at the dark wall sconce situated between her unit and the one next door. "The lights are out in the hall too."

"Seems a little too convenient to me."

"I agree. Let's find out what's really going on." Isabelle passed Cole and headed down the stairs.

Silently, they made their way through the dark stairwells to the basement. Isabelle entered the utility room in the far corner and flipped on the light switch. Nothing happened.

She caught the scent of something floral. Perfume maybe?

Her body tense, she opened the fuse box and held up her candle.

Her suspicions melted into surety. This wasn't an accident. "Cole. The wires have been cut."

CHAPTER 38

COLE AND ISABELLE HAD BEEN gone for several minutes. Lars and Marit had each returned to the sofa, but Jasmine had yet to move from the door.

"You're welcome to sit down, Jasmine," Lars said.

"Thanks," she said. But she didn't move.

Marit studied her through the faint glow of the flashlight on the table. "You're worried that the power outage is no accident."

"Something like that."

Lars expelled a tense breath. Hadn't they put this stuff behind them at the jewelry shop? The police already had all the auction participants in custody. Well, almost all. They didn't have Lina Wimmer.

A vision of the dark-haired woman fleeing the back room of the shop earlier this evening flooded his mind. Surely she'd continue her escape attempt by heading straight for one of Austria's border crossings.

His phone buzzed. He pulled it out of his pocket, noting that Jasmine was checking hers too. It was Cole.

Fuse box wires were cut.

Lars stiffened, turning his phone so that Marit could read the screen. "Did you get Cole's message?" he asked Jasmine.

"Yeah." The older woman's phone was already back in her pocket, and she was studying the room with fresh intensity. "We've got work to do, and we need to move fast."

"What kind of work?" Marit asked.

"Prevention of entry," she said. "Otherwise known as booby-trapping. Whoever's out there wants to get into Isabelle's apartment. We're going to do our best to stop them."

"The door's locked, and so are the windows," Lars pointed out.

"Yeah. That's a start, but it probably won't be enough."

Lars had noticed the electronic locks on Isabelle's door and windows. If Jasmine truly thought such state-of-the-art bolts weren't enough to thwart intruders, they were definitely in trouble. Then again, did the electronic locks work when the electricity was out?

His concern for Marit's safety ratcheted up a few more notches. She'd already been far too close to being injured—or worse—this evening. Not to mention everything else that had happened to her since she'd walked into the bank after their carriage ride. If it weren't for him and his family's jewelry, she'd be safely back in Amsterdam by now. He couldn't let anything more happen to her.

He came to his feet, now recognizing Jasmine's defensive stance at the door for what it was. A middle-aged woman might not be his first choice for a protection detail, but she obviously knew more about what to do in these kinds of situations than he did. "What do you have in mind?" he said. "And how can I help?"

Marit stood up beside him. "Set us to work, Jasmine."

Jasmine took a step toward them in the darkness. "We can't see well in here, but neither will an intruder, so we'll use the dim lighting to our advantage."

"What are the chances they'll have night-vision goggles?" Lars asked. It seemed to him that the bad guys in movies almost always had them when they were working in the dark.

"Coming here was a last-minute decision," Jasmine said. "It's unlikely they were that prepared, but if they're wearing them, shine your phone lights directly at their eyes. That'll slow them down." She pointed to the base of the door. "We need a tripwire here. If we can find enough extension cords or some other kind of wire or rope, we'll set others up around the flat."

"There's an extension cord in the guest bedroom," Marit said. "I'll get it."

Lars turned on his phone's light. "I'll check the power outlets for more."

Isabelle's flat was small enough that it didn't take long to make a fast check of all the walls. When Lars returned to the living room with two more extension cords, Jasmine was already attaching the end of the cord Marit had found to a chair leg, and Marit was dragging a heavy standard lamp across the living room floor.

"Let me get that," Lars said, exchanging his bundle of cords for the lamp. He carried it over to the door. "You want the other end of that cord attached to this, I'm assuming."

"Yeah," Jasmine said. "Make sure it's tied tight enough to hold if someone pushes against it."

"Got it."

"How many more cords do we have?"

"Two."

"Okay. One for the living room window and one in the hallway between the bedrooms." Jasmine turned to Marit. "While Lars and I are tying these, can you look through Isabelle's kitchen cupboards for something small, hard, and loose? Dried beans, rice, or something like that."

Marit hurried into the kitchen. Jasmine took one of the cords and disappeared into the hall. Lars finished cinching the standard lamp's cord, then crossed the room to the window. He dragged one of the sofas closer and lay on the floor to attach the cord to one of its legs.

From the kitchen, the sound of drawers and cupboards opening and banging closed in rapid succession filled the otherwise silent flat. Lars's sense of urgency increased, and he tugged on the cord. It held. Crawling over to the bookcase, he ran the line through his fingers, pulling it taut as he threaded it beneath the heavy pieces of furniture.

Rapid footsteps vibrated through the floor. Jasmine and Marit converged on the living room.

Lars came to his feet. "This wire's in place," he said.

"I found rice, macaroni noodles, and a big bag of hazelnuts," Marit said.

"Great," Jasmine said. "Those should do the trick. Give Lars the rice. I'll take the macaroni. We'll take care of the windows at the back of the flat and the kitchen if you'll do the front window. Take the hazelnuts and spread them along the windowsill and on the floor beneath the window. The goal is to make the landing unstable for anyone attempting to enter that way."

Lars accepted the bag of rice from Marit. He'd just set a tripwire by the window, and she wanted them to add something more. "We're on the fourth floor," he said. "Do you really think the windows are going to be an issue?"

"Believe me," Jasmine said grimly. "Windows are always an issue."

Cole moved through the darkness with only the flashlight on his phone to guide him as he checked the hall outside Isabelle's apartment. At least his phone was good for something right now. Right after he had sent a text to Lars and Jasmine, he had lost his signal.

He held up the light and searched the area around Isabelle's door. No sign of any explosives or booby traps. He turned and pointed the light down the hall one way and then the other. No sign of anyone lurking nearby either.

Satisfied that Lars, Marit, and Jasmine were safe for the moment, he lifted his phone with the intention of calling the police. Still no reception.

His eyes narrowed. If he was planning to breach an apartment building, knocking out the electricity and everyone's communications would be among the first things he would do.

He debated whether to check on Isabelle first or the people they had left in her apartment. Who was he kidding? Lars and Marit had Jasmine, and with Cole's luck, if he tried to knock on the door, Jasmine would take him out before he got the chance to announce himself. Besides, the last thing he wanted to do right now was create a distraction that might allow the intruders easier access.

Moving silently, Cole hurried back down the stairs toward the basement. Isabelle had insisted she had the tools and supplies needed to fix the damaged fuses, but Cole wasn't sure turning the lights back on would solve their problems. If anything, it would announce where they were.

His steps quickened when he reached the first floor, and he made the turn toward the basement. Isabelle was capable of taking care of herself, as was Jasmine, but he would prefer that they were all in the same place at the same time so they could face this newest threat together.

Who was out there? The faint scent of a woman's perfume in the utility room pointed at Lina Wimmer being the culprit behind the cut wires, but Cole seriously doubted the woman was here alone. Gwendolyn? Both Lina and Gwendolyn had the resources to find Isabelle's address. It would make sense that they would work together.

Cole reached the utility room. The candlelight flickered from where Isabelle had set the lantern on the floor.

Isabelle whirled when he entered.

"It's just me," he said.

"I'm glad you're here. I need you to shine some light on this before I connect the wire."

"As soon as you turn the electricity back on, whoever is out there will know where we are and that we know the power outage was deliberate." Cole turned off his flashlight app and slid his cell into his pocket.

"What do you suggest?" Isabelle lowered her hand, which was currently gripping a pair of pliers.

"I say we take another look around."

"Did you call the police?" Isabelle asked.

"Still no signal."

Isabelle checked her phone. "Me neither." She pocketed her cell and picked up the lantern. "Where do you want to start?"

"I already checked out the hall outside your apartment. I say we search the roof and the street outside your window."

"Which do you want?" Isabelle asked.

"Let's check the roof first." Cole moved into the hall.

"It would make more sense to split up."

It did make more sense, but Cole didn't like it. He debated how to broach the subject of sticking together without insulting her abilities.

The glow from the candle illuminated her face and went only as far as the nearby wall. His heart swelled with an unfamiliar sensation, a streak of panic shooting through him at the thought of Isabelle facing danger. Where had that come from? They had faced adversity together before. Why was this time any different?

"Cole?" Isabelle asked.

The flame in the lantern danced as though caught in a sudden breeze. Cole drew his weapon in the same moment a hulking figure rushed toward him, a second smaller figure standing behind him.

The man's hand connected with Cole's, knocking Cole's gun to the ground. In the faint light, the man's features came into view. The guard from the jewelry store. Apparently, the police didn't arrest everyone who had left the building.

A fist flew toward Cole. He blocked it and ducked as Isabelle drew her weapon.

A gunshot rang out, but it wasn't from Isabelle's direction. Rather, it came from somewhere down the hall.

Not willing to leave himself exposed to the guard's accomplice, Cole grabbed the man around the waist and threw his weight against him until the man's back smashed into the far wall. A punch followed by a second to the man's midsection left him gasping for air. Cole hooked him around the neck and used him as a shield.

Another shot fired, the bullet thudding into the wall near the utility room door.

The lantern in Isabelle's hands crashed to the ground, the flame diminishing to almost nothing. Had she dropped it intentionally to keep them from being visible to the shooter? Either way, the flame went out, leaving them in darkness.

The guard jammed his elbow into Cole's stomach, knocking the wind out of him. Cole's grip loosened.

He sensed movement behind him and struggled to keep the guard between him and the guard's accomplice.

Another gunshot sparked, but this time, it came from only a few meters from where he'd grappled with the guard. A woman grunted a short distance away. Cole prayed Isabelle wasn't on the losing end of her battle.

Cole's opponent tried to elbow him again, but Cole shifted to the side to prevent the contact. He hooked his arm more firmly around the man's neck and squeezed him in a choke hold. The man squirmed and grabbed at his hands, but after several seconds, his body went limp.

Cole lowered him to the ground. Something thudded against the floor. "Isabelle?"

"I'm fine." She turned on her flashlight app and shone the beam in his direction. "What about you?"

"Yeah." Cole retrieved a zip tie from his holster and secured the guard's hands. He glanced at the prone figure at Isabelle's feet. "Who is that?"

Isabelle illuminated the woman's face. "Lina Wimmer."

"If she and the guard were down here, we have to assume Gwendolyn is here too."

"That's not good. Gwendolyn isn't someone I'd want to meet in a dark anything." Isabelle motioned to Lina. "You tie her up. I'm going to get those lights back on. We need to make sure everyone upstairs sees her coming."

CHAPTER 39

MARIT SPRINKLED THE HAZELNUTS ALONG the windowsill. In the faint light coming from the street below, they looked like black spots against the white ledge. It was remarkable that the distant light from cars and businesses could reach Isabelle's fourth-floor window. It was even more astonishing that Jasmine believed someone could scale the building and reach the window without injury. It was the type of feat Marit associated with a superhero, not a very human criminal.

She backed up a few inches. Stepping over the wire Lars had stretched between the bookshelf and the corner of the sofa, she sprinkled a generous fistful of nuts across the floor. A few of them rolled out of sight beneath the sofa. With a frustrated murmur, Marit let them go. She crouched down to spread out the remaining nuts. Behind her, she heard Jasmine enter the kitchen from Isabelle's room. The rattle of macaroni noodles hitting the windowsill followed.

A shadow flitted across the floor, covering the nuts with another layer of darkness. The hairs on the back of Marit's neck rose. She raised her head and looked to the window. A soft thud sounded, and suddenly, there was someone standing on the outer window ledge.

Marit froze, barely believing what she was seeing. The outlined form produced a narrow object and slid it between the windows.

With a click, the window catch released, and Marit found her voice. "Jasmine!"

In one swift movement, the shadowy figure pushed the casement up and slid his legs inside.

"Move, Marit!"

Jasmine's voice penetrated Marit's shock, and Marit staggered around the sofa. Jasmine took another three steps toward the window and raised the gun in her hand.

The intruder's feet had reached the floor, but the nuts did their job. His black rubber-soled shoes slipped, and he swore.

Marit's breath caught. This Spider-Man was no man at all. It was a woman. Even if her small build had been an insufficient clue, her voice had given her away.

Righting herself, the intruder grasped the window frame with one hand and pulled herself into the room.

"That's far enough." Jasmine's command crackled through the air. "Put your hands up."

The woman swiveled. In a swift movement, she released the rope attached to her waist with one hand and launched the object she'd used to jimmy the window locks with the other. Jasmine ducked, and the woman bolted, running directly into Lars's tripwire as her knife penetrated the opposite wall with a sickening thud.

Catching herself before she fell, the woman rolled over the arm of the sofa. Marit saw her coming, grabbed one of the sofa cushions, and swung it as the woman came to her feet. The woman dropped but not fast enough. The pillow clipped her head. She grunted and rolled again, this time across the darkened floor.

Jasmine raced around the sofa. Marit stepped to the right to avoid her, and the back of her knees hit the coffee table. Marit's legs buckled. Out of the darkness, the woman's hands reached out and grabbed Marit's ankles. She yanked her further off-balance, and Marit went down, landing directly on her hands and knees.

Pain shot through Marit's kneecaps and palms. She blinked back tears and kicked her legs. One ankle came free of her captor's grip. Unable to make out the woman's outline clearly, she swung her free leg with no sure target in mind. Her foot connected with something firm, and the woman swore again.

"Enough," the woman growled, twisting Marit's trapped leg until she cried out in agony.

"The same goes for you," Jasmine said. She was standing immediately above them. "Let her go, Gwendolyn."

"I don't think so."

Gwendolyn. Marit's mind reeled, even as she fought to breathe through the pain in her leg. This was Cole's boss—a CIA operative.

Something hard jabbed into her rib cage. "Stand up, Miss Jansen."

Marit's leg was suddenly free. She crawled to the coffee table. The object pressed against her rib cage moved with her. Her legs trembled. She took an unsteady breath. If her legs wouldn't hold her, she'd come crashing down, but perhaps that would give Jasmine the opening she needed.

She pulled herself up. Her legs held. She managed a shaking step. And then the lights turned on.

Marit blinked. Gwendolyn stood beside her. Her gun was pressed against Marit's chest. Jasmine was a meter away, her gun aimed at Gwendolyn. There was no sign of Lars.

Isabelle sprinted up the stairs behind Cole, her heart pounding.

Cole hesitated briefly when they reached her floor. As soon as he saw that the hallway was clear, he gave her arm a squeeze. "Be careful."

"You too."

Cole continued up the stairs to the roof. Whether they actually did have another intruder, Isabelle didn't know. Would Gwendolyn really come here? And if so, for what purpose? The evidence against her and Lina went well beyond their witness statements. Surely, they wouldn't bother with revenge while the entire city's police department was looking for them.

Isabelle checked her phone in the hope she could call Jasmine, but she still didn't have a signal. She prayed the older CIA operative would look before shooting at her.

Isabelle keyed in her code to unlock her front door. The lock clicked open. She slowly turned the knob and quietly pushed it open. Voices sounded from inside. Female voices.

She opened her mouth to call out and identify herself as she entered, but the sound of Gwendolyn's voice stopped her. She *was* here. But why?

"Let her go, Gwendolyn," Jasmine said, her voice firm. "I'll put a bullet in you if you harm that girl."

"Put the gun away, or she dies right now," Gwendolyn countered. "No one has to get hurt. All I want is the jewelry."

"You can't be serious."

"Very. Because of you and your friends, I no longer have access to information worth selling. I need to pad my bank account before I leave here. Those jewels will accomplish that very nicely."

Jasmine shook her head. "You sold out your own country for money?"

"I didn't sell anyone out."

Isabelle slipped through the door. She pulled it most of the way closed, making sure she didn't make any sound.

"Telling your friend Lina her brother's diamonds were at the bank wasn't exactly upholding your secrecy agreement," Jasmine said.

"No one died."

"Luckily," Jasmine countered.

Fury welled up inside Isabelle as she thought of the two injured guards and the dozen terrified hostages during the robbery, not to mention the dead and injured from the terrorist bombings Steven Powell had been funding using the gems. She slipped behind the plant that separated her entryway from her living area and took in the scene before her.

Marit stood pale-faced in front of Gwendolyn, a gun aimed at her chest. Jasmine was a short distance away, her gun pointed at Gwendolyn.

"And what about me?" Jasmine continued. "Were you going to let me live if I came in from the cold?"

"You should know that getting in my way is never a good decision." Gwendolyn took a slight step to her side to put Marit more firmly between her and Jasmine. "What gave me away?"

"A million euros." Jasmine countered Gwendolyn's move, her gun still trained on her opponent. "When I talked to you on the phone, you mentioned the value of the diamonds, but the only people who had that information were me and Cole."

"That's weak. How could you be sure Cole didn't tell me?"

"Cole doesn't give information out without a reason. He'd already reported to me. There was no way he was going to share details with you unless you had a need-to-know, and even then, he would have asked my permission."

"None of that matters now. Where are the jewels?"

Isabelle lifted her gun, but with Marit between her and Gwendolyn, she couldn't do anything until one of them moved. Would Cole come rushing in and make things worse? She scanned the room again. And where was Lars?

This couldn't be happening. Lars pressed his back against the wall that separated him from the living room and attempted to think clearly. A rogue CIA operative was holding Marit at gunpoint. Jasmine, although armed, could currently do nothing to help her. And there was still no sign of Cole and Isabelle.

The lights were on. That had to mean Cole and Isabelle had repaired the fuses. But if that was the case, where were they? They must have encountered trouble of their own. And if they were dealing with their own crisis, Lars was going to have to come up with something to break the impasse in the living room before Gwendolyn snapped.

He needed a weapon, something that could be used as a distraction even if it didn't inflict a mortal wound.

Hardly daring to move in case the old floor creaked and alerted Gwendolyn to his presence, he tiptoed into the closest room. The bathroom was discouragingly free of clutter. It was possible that Isabelle had a hairdryer or a curling iron in one of the drawers, but opening them was too big a risk. He'd heard Marit opening the wooden kitchen drawers from across the apartment.

A basket filled with toilet paper sat beneath the sink, and next to the toilet, there was a toilet brush and a plunger. With mounting desperation, he zeroed in on the plunger. The wooden handle was sturdy enough, and if worse came to worst, he could use it as a short, rubber-tipped javelin.

Seizing the plunger, he slipped back into the hall. He inched along the wall until he reached the living room entrance. Jasmine and Gwendolyn were speaking, but he couldn't make out the women's words. It didn't matter. As long as they were still talking, Marit was safe.

Offering a silent prayer that no one was looking in his direction, he peeked around the edge of the wall. Gwendolyn had shifted slightly so that Marit was now more directly between her and Jasmine, and both guns were still in play.

Lars's gaze lingered on Marit's pale face. A draft of air lifted a few strands of her hair. Her hand started to lift, likely to brush them away, but when Gwendolyn's body tensed, Marit froze, then she slowly lowered her hand back to her side. Even from this distance, Lars caught the slight tremor in her fingers, and his own fingers tightened around the handle of the plunger. A breeze, no matter how small, would affect his throw. Where was the air coming from?

He turned his attention to the window. It was still open. No one had taken the time to close the curtains, and they were shifting in the breeze. Lars sharpened his gaze. The curtains weren't the only things shifting. Something was moving directly outside the window.

Switching his position so he could see the window better, he watched as a pair of feet landed on the outer windowsill. Moments later, fingers appeared around the top of the casement. Lars's heart picked up speed. Friend or foe? Whoever entered through that window would undoubtedly end Jasmine and Gwendolyn's standoff.

A blonde head ducked under the casement, and Lars tensed.

"Watch for the booby traps, Cole," he muttered.

As if he heard him, Cole looked up and met his eyes across the room. He held up three fingers. Lars nodded. He didn't know exactly what his cousin had planned, but whatever it was, he was ready.

Cole wasn't ready. He had expected to reach Isabelle's window to find Gwendolyn already in custody and had prepared himself to endure Jasmine's teasing about how he should trust her to take care of herself.

Jasmine was taking care of herself, but despite whatever preparations she had made, the presence of two civilians had thrown her off her game.

Marit stood stoically, the pawn in the current stalemate.

With the lights on, Cole couldn't miss the efforts at booby-trapping Isabelle's apartment, but seeing the scatter of nuts and macaroni on the floor wouldn't diminish their effectiveness. The minute his feet hit the ground, his balance would be compromised. He didn't want to become a victim any more than he wanted Marit to.

He used the rope Gwendolyn had left hanging from the roof to hold his weight as he pushed off the building and moved to the kitchen window to get a better view of Lars.

His cousin stood near the doorway, a weapon lifted over his head. Was that a plunger? Cole shook his head. The man really needed a lesson in makeshift weapons.

Gwendolyn's voice rose, her words carrying to him. "Show me the safe. Now."

Lars twitched, and for an instant, Cole was afraid he was going to rush to Marit's rescue and become victim number one.

With his cousin hyperfocused on the standoff in the other room, Cole moved back to the edge of the living room window. He used his hands to pull on the tail of the rope so he could gauge the length of slack he had. Six meters. Maybe seven.

It should be enough for what he had in mind.

Across the room, the leaves of the large potted plant by Isabelle's door rustled slightly. His eyes narrowed.

Fingers appeared between the leaves, palm out, fingers extended. After a brief moment, one finger lowered. A countdown. Isabelle was prepared to strike. Four against one, with Marit's life hanging in the balance.

Gwendolyn's voice rose again, the same demand repeating.

Another finger lowered. Three.

Cole's muscles bunched. He positioned his feet against the side of the building.

Two.

He bent his legs, and his fingers tightened on the rope.

One.

He pushed his feet against the building and swung himself back. His momentum carried him into the air above the sidewalk and then forward through Isabelle's open window.

Movement whirled in every direction. Gwendolyn turned as Cole landed a few meters from her. Lars charged out of the bedroom, wielding the plunger like a sword.

Isabelle straightened from her spot behind the plant. "Drop it!"

Jasmine bent one knee and swept out her leg, connecting with Gwendolyn's ankles in the same moment Marit ducked and Lars struck Gwendolyn's back with the plunger head.

Gwendolyn cried out and fell to the ground amid the scatter of hazelnuts and macaroni.

Gwendolyn's grip loosened on her gun, but it didn't fall.

Cole tried to gain his footing, but before he did, Marit reached out and grabbed the gun from Gwendolyn. Rather than point it at her former captor, she aimed it upward and looked helplessly at Cole and Jasmine. "Someone please take this."

With Isabelle now standing over Gwendolyn, her gun aimed at the criminal, Jasmine grabbed Gwendolyn by the arm and pulled her up.

"Lars, fetch me one of those extension cords," Jasmine said.

Cole kicked hazelnuts out of his way before stepping toward Marit and relieving her of the weapon. "Where did you learn how to do that?"

"I watched you do it a couple times." Marit's breath shuddered out. "I didn't like having a gun aimed at me."

Lars handed an extension cord to Jasmine. "I want to learn how to disarm bad guys." He looked at Gwendolyn. "Or girls."

"Maybe we should teach you both some self-defense."

"Only if this is a situation where if we learn, we'll never have to use it," Marit said.

"We can hope," Isabelle said.

Jasmine tied Gwendolyn's hands behind her back, their soon-to-be-former boss glaring at all of them.

Ignoring her, Cole spoke to Jasmine. "Just like riding a bike?"

Jasmine's rich laughter rang out. "Sorry. I had a flat tire."

"That's okay. With this group, we always manage to find a spare."

"Now what?" Marit asked, her body still shaking.

"Yeah." Lars stepped beside his girlfriend and wrapped a hand around her waist. "What now?"

"There's a signal jammer on the roof," Cole said. "I'll go disable it so we can call the police and the FBI."

"The FBI?"

"Yeah. Gwendolyn here is going to have a lot of explaining to do."

"And us?" Marit asked. "Will they need to talk to us too?"

"The police will take your statement, but they should be able to do that here," Cole said.

"I know it's hard after an invasion, but if you're okay with it, you're all welcome to stay here until you leave town." Isabelle's gaze met Cole's briefly before she focused on Marit again. "After all we've been through, I think we can convince the police department to assign an officer to keep watch outside my apartment."

"That would make me feel a lot better," Marit admitted.

"Me too," Lars said.

"Jasmine and I will probably have to go into the embassy to file statements with the FBI," Cole said.

Isabelle's eyes met his. "Don't be gone too long."

Cole leaned forward and kissed her cheek. "I won't."

CHAPTER 40

ISABELLE'S BREATH PLUMED OUT IN front of her as she walked from the U-bahn station toward the bank. A light dusting of snow shimmered beneath the sunlight and crunched beneath her boots. Despite the winter wonderland before her, a sense of loss pooled in her chest. Not a single word from Cole since he'd left with the police on Saturday night. Not to her, not even to Lars.

She should have known. The moment they'd resolved the current crisis, he had disappeared without a trace.

She could understand his need to make sure Gwendolyn was turned over to the proper authorities. After all, with Gwendolyn's knowledge of US intelligence operations, the CIA could hardly have the former station chief sitting in a jail cell in Austria when she should be in FBI custody. That detail could have been handled in a phone call. But no. Cole saw a problem, and he had to fix it.

At least Marit and Lars had opted to stay at her apartment so she had some company after Cole left. What would it be like once they flew home tonight?

A sigh escaped her. She was going to miss them, almost as much as she would miss the future she had started to envision once again with Cole.

Her stomach clenched, and she fought for calm. She couldn't think about him today or the way her text messages had gone unanswered all day yesterday. She lifted her chin and walked into the bank.

She was barely inside when the bank president approached. "Isabelle. It's so good to have you back."

"Thank you, Herr Fischer. It's good to be back."

"Do you have a minute? I have some things we need to discuss."

"Yes, of course." Isabelle walked with him to the elevator, her curiosity heightened. Though she wanted to press for information, she forced herself to wait. Herr Fischer tended to be rather meticulous and always operated at his own pace no matter what was going on around him.

He led her into his office and closed the door. "Please sit down."

Isabelle chose the chair closest to the door, and Herr Fischer settled behind his desk.

"I have spent the past several days working with our security team to determine both what happened during the robbery last Wednesday and what could have been done differently."

"And?" Isabelle asked.

"First, your conduct was beyond exemplary. Not many people in your situation are able to keep their wits about them, and having the instinct to fight back is nearly unheard of."

"I didn't do much."

"I beg to differ. I thought the use of your shoe as a weapon was quite ingenious." Herr Fischer reached below his desk and straightened, holding a thin box wrapped in silver paper. "This is a small token of my appreciation."

"That isn't necessary."

"I believe it is." He handed it to her. "Go on. Open it."

She peeled back the paper to uncover a long jewelry case. She flipped open the lid to reveal a diamond bracelet. "This is stunning."

"As you were responsible for protecting so many of our customer's valuables, it is well-deserved."

"I don't know what to say." She looked up and opted for simplicity. "Thank you."

"You are most welcome." Herr Fischer settled back in his seat. "There is one other issue I would like to address."

Isabelle closed the jewelry case and settled it on her lap.

"As you are well aware, Gerhart Wimmer's wife was arrested on Saturday night."

"Yes."

"Due to Gerhart's involvement in the robbery and his wife's attack on you, he has been dismissed."

"I didn't think Gerhart knew anything about his wife's illegal activity."

"He didn't, but his lack of security at home allowed Lina access to information that made it possible for her hired accomplices to breach the bank's security system."

"She was using his remote access?"

"Yes. He had written down his passwords in his office at home. It didn't take much for her to figure out his username."

Sympathy welled up in Isabelle. "That was poor judgment certainly, but is firing him really the answer?"

"Technically, he will be taking an early retirement. That will allow him to maintain some dignity as he tries to move past the harm his wife has caused us all."

"I'm relieved to hear that."

"His departure, nevertheless, creates an opening in upper management," Herr Fischer said. "I would like you to fill it."

"Me?" Isabelle's eyes widened.

"Yes, you. What do you say?"

Isabelle swallowed her surprise and let her smile bloom. "I'm honored. Thank you."

"You've earned it. I left another small token for you in your office." Herr Fischer pushed back from his desk and shook her hand. "I suggest you make your first order of the day packing up your office. I will have someone move everything for you this afternoon."

"Thank you again." Isabelle left his office, her mind still reeling. A promotion at the bank, increased access for her intelligence work. Today was a good day. If only her heart could heal from Cole's latest disappearing act.

She caught the scent of roses three steps before she reached her office. When she passed through the doorway, she stopped and stared. Yellow roses in a glass vase, sprigs of baby's breath intermixed among the two dozen blooms.

"Cole." His name escaped her lips on a whisper. She crossed the room and breathed in the fragrance. Her quick search didn't reveal a card. Her eyebrows drew together. Were these from Cole? Or were they the other thank-you gift Herr Fischer had mentioned?

Hope warred with the hurt from the past. Surely Herr Fischer wouldn't think to send her yellow roses, would he?

She did a quick search of her desk for any sign of another gift, but the desktop was bare, except for her computer and the flowers. Maybe Herr Fischer did send them.

Isabelle dropped into her chair. At least her professional life was going in the right direction even if her personal one was once again in shambles.

She tried to muster the energy to go to the copy room in search of boxes but couldn't quite manage it. A knock sounded on her open door.

She pasted on a professional smile and greeted the woman standing in her doorway. "Hi, Amelia. What can I do for you?"

"Herr Fischer asked me to bring this to you." She handed Isabelle an envelope.

"What's this?" Isabelle opened it and slid out the contents. Four tickets to the opera for tomorrow night.

"I was supposed to have those in your office before you finished your meeting with Herr Fischer, but the armored vehicle carrying the stolen jewelry arrived a minute ago, and I had to sign for the delivery."

Isabelle held up the tickets. "This is the gift Herr Fischer mentioned?"

"It is."

Isabelle motioned to the flowers. "Then where did these come from?"

"They were delivered as we were opening this morning."

Hope rose again.

Marit appeared behind Amelia. "I'm sorry. I didn't mean to interrupt."

"Oh, you're not." Amelia stepped back and offered Isabelle a smile. "Let me know if you need any help packing today."

"I will. Thanks."

"Packing?" Marit asked.

"I just got a promotion."

"That's great!" Marit took another step forward. "Any chance you can spare an hour or two this morning? I know you're just getting back to work, but Lars and I wanted to thank you for everything."

"That isn't necessary. You've already thanked me."

"At least come outside for a minute so you can say goodbye to Lars."

"I thought he was escorting the Falcon Point jewelry back to its safe-deposit box."

"He already finished with that. Now he's outside with his camera."

"I suppose I can spare a minute." Isabelle made it as far as the elevator before she asked, "Have either of you heard from Cole?"

"Lars has."

"Oh." A new dagger pierced her. So much for things being different this time.

Her steps slowed as she followed Marit outside into the crisp winter air.

A white horse-drawn carriage stood at the curb, and Cole stood beside it, a single yellow rose in his hand.

"Cole?" Her gait quickened as he moved toward her. "What are you doing here?"

"I told you I wasn't going to make the same mistakes again."

"You didn't call or text."

"I know." He lowered his voice. "I found a tracker on my phone. I won't get my replacement until this afternoon."

"How did you manage all this, then?"

"Jasmine helped." He motioned to where Marit and Lars now stood beside the fiaker. "Can I take you for a ride?"

Pack up her office or spend time with Cole? The decision took less than a second. "I'd love that."

Cole handed her the rose. "You can add this to the others in your office."

"Those were from you? Why didn't you include a card?"

"I didn't think I'd need to." His eyebrows drew together. "Do you have other men sending you gifts?"

"Today, yes." She laughed when his eyes narrowed. "I promise you're the only person sending me gifts who matters."

"I'd better be." He leaned down for a brief kiss. "I think I may be the jealous type."

She smiled. "Good to know."

Cole spread the carriage blanket over his and Isabelle's legs, and Isabelle scooted a little closer to him. Marit watched, a small smile playing across her lips. What a difference a week made.

She was happy for Isabelle. And for Cole. It was heartwarming to see two people she cared about come together despite what had once seemed like insurmountable obstacles in their way. Was it too much to hope that she and Lars could do the same? They'd drawn closer than ever during this time in Vienna, yet real life awaited when they left this evening. Real life with real jobs and real distances.

She glanced at the man sitting beside her in the carriage. His attention was on a small group of children playing football in the park they were passing. Their brightly colored coats and hats were in stark contrast to the frosted tree limbs and grass, and Marit guessed he was viewing the scene through a photographer's lens.

"It would make a great picture," she said.

"Yeah." He turned to face her and smiled. "I love that you recognize it too."

"I'm sorry you don't have your camera with you."

"Don't be. I'd rather focus on other things right now."

A new emotion flickered in his deep-blue eyes, and his arm circled her, pulling her close.

"This is it," Cole said, his voice severing her indiscernible connection with Lars.

Marit blinked. Pushing past her feeling of loss, she looked around. The park was gone, and they were entering the cobbled square in front of a magnificent white-stone building. The fiaker came to a halt beside an enormous equestrian statue.

"Why are we stopping?" Marit asked.

"This is the Austrian National Library," Lars said.

"I know. I recognize it from when Isabelle pointed it out last time."

Lars slipped the blanket off her lap and set it on the seat. "You said you wanted to visit it before we left."

Marit stared at him. "You remembered that?"

"Of course."

Her stunned gaze moved from Lars to the impressive building in front of them. She swallowed. This carriage ride hadn't been simply for Cole and Isabelle's benefit after all. Lars had planned this detour for her.

"Marit?" His voice was suddenly uncertain. "Do you still want to go in?"

"Yes," she said in a rush. "Very much."

A smile stole over his face that set her stomach fluttering.

"Come on, then." He stepped out of the carriage and reached for her hand to help her out. "The driver will wait here until we're ready to go, but I can't guarantee how long Cole will last. It is a library, after all. I'm hoping Isabelle's presence will help."

Isabelle climbed out after them and waited for Cole to join her on the cobbled courtyard. "Don't worry," Isabelle said, slipping her arm through Cole's. "I've got this."

Cole rolled his eyes. "If I can endure a twelve-hour stakeout, I can handle visiting an old library."

"Well, that pretty much explains how Cole feels about libraries," Lars said, leading Marit to the main doors. "Good luck, Isabelle."

Marit laughed. "Thanks for coming with us, Cole."

"It'll be good for me," Cole said. "At least, that's what Isabelle just told me."

It was Lars's turn to laugh. "True. But not nearly as good as Isabelle is for you."

"Yeah." Cole had the grace to concede the point. "I think you might be right about that."

They entered the building together. Posters advertising various exhibits hung on the wall of the tiled foyer. Marit and Isabelle studied them with interest as Lars and Cole purchased tickets for the library's state hall.

"Ready?" Lars asked, offering Marit a ticket.

"So ready."

He chuckled. "Let's go see what all the fuss is about."

Following the arrows, they climbed the grand staircase to the security desk. Marit spared Cole an anxious glance. He wouldn't bring his gun on a carriage ride and a visit to the library, would he? Not daring to ask, she opened her purse for inspection. Beside her, Isabelle did the same. They moved forward to stand beside a sign listing all the library's rules. Moments later, with no alarm raised, both men joined them, and Marit breathed a quiet sigh of relief.

"That's quite the list," Cole said, pointing to the sign.

"It's what happens when priceless books are stored in a historic building," Isabelle said. "It's worth keeping the rules to see this place. I promise."

They moved through a small gallery before entering a vast rotunda with cathedral-like ceilings and multipaned arched windows.

"Wow," Lars breathed.

Marit gripped his hand tighter as she stood, spellbound by the sight before her. From the intricately patterned marble-tile floor to the mural-covered vaulted ceilings, every inch of the room was a work of art.

A highly polished wooden balcony ran along the circumference of the room, separating the rows of wooden bookshelves below from the rows above. Pillars— some made of polished wood with gold-leaf detail and some white marble— supported the balcony and broke the hall into sections. A large statue of one of Austria's former kings stood in the center of the room, bordered by smaller statues and enormous globes. Gold filigree decorated the ceiling, pillars, and furniture. All around the room, wheeled ladders hung from the bookshelves.

"For the record," Cole said. "This doesn't look anything like the library in my hometown."

Isabelle gave him an I-told-you-so look. "Let me show you the eighteenth century astronomical globe," she said.

She led Cole across the rotunda, but Lars made no move to follow. Marit gave him a questioning look. He shook his head slightly.

"I came here for you, Marit. Whenever you're ready, we'll wander around. Until then, take all the time you need."

It was hard to speak past the lump in her throat. How had he known that she craved a few quiet minutes to soak in the majesty of this place? "Thank you," she managed. His gentle smile was nearly her undoing. She kept ahold of his hand and tipped her head back, gazing at the detailed painting above. "It feels like we're in a cathedral," she said.

"With rows and rows of books instead of pews."

"Yes." There was no hiding her enthusiasm. "And lots of nooks and crannies to explore."

He chuckled. "Which one first?"

She pointed to the right. "Let's see what's over there."

They wandered past a couple of statues and a grouping of antique chairs. The docent standing beside an ancient globe acknowledged them with a brief inclination of his head, and a handful of tourists walked by, their voices low.

"I think I've found my favorite spot in the library," Lars said as they circled around a row of pillars and entered a small alcove filled with leather-bound books.

"It is lovely," Marit said.

"Yes." He reached out and brushed a piece of hair back from her face, the touch of his fingers leaving a tingling trail across her cheek. "Completely lovely."

His eyes met hers, and the hushed sounds of the library faded.

"Marit," he said softly. "I know that once we leave Vienna and return to our respective jobs, our lives will become more complicated, but spending this week with you has been the most incredible, wonderful . . ." He took an unsteady breath.

"Terrifying, thrilling, perfect time ever," she finished for him.

"Yes." He released her hand and slipped his arm around her waist. "And I don't want it to end when we get off the plane in Amsterdam."

Tears of joy sprang to Marit's eyes. "Neither do I."

"Then there's only one more thing we have to overcome."

"What's that?"

His smile set her heart racing. "The library rules."

"The library rules?"

"Did you read the ones on that sign when we first came in?"

"Not all of them," Marit admitted. "I remember no food, no drink, no running, and no flash photography."

"Anything about no kissing?"

With new understanding, Marit slipped her arms around his neck. "Not that I saw, but there's probably an unwritten rule for that sort of thing."

His blue eyes sparkled. "There's a docent out there, and even though I don't want to be caught breaking any rules—especially if it means we end up in front of Officers Binder or Wolf again—I think this time it might be worth the risk."

"You do, do you?"

He lowered his head. "Absolutely."

"Good," she whispered, her lips a breath away from his. "I do too."

OTHER BOOKS AND AUDIOBOOKS
BY TRACI HUNTER ABRAMSON

UNDERCURRENTS SERIES
Undercurrents
Ripple Effect
The Deep End

SAINT SQUAD SERIES
Freefall
Lockdown
Crossfire
Backlash
Smoke Screen
Code Word
Lock and Key
Drop Zone
Spotlight
Tripwire
Redemption

ROYAL SERIES
Royal Target
Royal Secrets
Royal Brides
Royal Heir

GUARDIAN SERIES
Failsafe
Safe House
Sanctuary
On the Run
In Harm's Way
Not Dead Yet

DREAM'S EDGE SERIES
*Dancing to Freedom**
An Unlikely Pair
*Broken Dreams**
Dreams of Gold
*The Best Mistake**
(Coming December 2022)
Worlds Collide
(Coming February 2023)

FALCON POINT SERIES
Heirs of Falcon Point
The Danger with Diamonds

STAND-ALONES
Obsession
Deep Cover
Chances Are
Chance for Home
Kept Secrets
*Twisted Fate**
Proximity
*Entangled**
Mistaken Reality
A Change of Fortune
*Sinister Secrets**

* Novella

ABOUT TRACI HUNTER ABRAMSON

Traci Hunter Abramson was born in Arizona, where she lived until moving to Venezuela for a study abroad program. After graduating from Brigham Young University, she worked for the Central Intelligence Agency, eventually resigning in order to raise her family. She credits the CIA with giving her a wealth of ideas as well as the skills needed to survive her children's teenage years. She loves to travel and enjoys coaching her local high school swim team. She has written more than thirty best-selling novels and is a seven-time Whitney Award winner, including 2017 and 2019 Best Novel of the Year.

She also loves hearing from her readers. If you would like to contact her, she can be reached through the following:

www.traciabramson.com

Facebook group: Traci's Friends

bookbub.com/authors/traci-hunter-abramson

twitter@traciabramson

facebook.com/tracihabramson

instagram.com/traciabramson.com

OTHER BOOKS AND AUDIOBOOKS
BY SIAN ANN BESSEY

GEORGIAN GENTLEMEN SERIES
The Noble Smuggler
An Uncommon Earl
An Alleged Rogue
An Unfamiliar Duke

CONTEMPORARY
Forgotten Notes
Cover of Darkness
Deception
You Came for Me
The Insider
The Gem Thief

HISTORICAL
Within the Dark Hills
One Last Spring
To Win a Lady's Heart
For Castle and Crown
The Heart of the Rebellion
The Call of the Sea
(Coming November 2022)

FALCON POINT SERIES
Heirs of Falcon Point
The Danger with Diamonds

KIDS ON A MISSION SERIES
Escape from Germany
Uprising in Samoa
Ambushed in Africa

CHILDREN'S
A Family is Forever
Teddy Bear, Blankie, and a Prayer

ANTHOLOGIES AND BOOKLETS
The Perfect Gift
A Hopeful Christmas
No Strangers at Christmas

ABOUT SIAN ANN BESSEY

SIAN ANN BESSEY WAS BORN in Cambridge, England, and grew up on the island of Anglesey off the coast of North Wales. She left her homeland to attend Brigham Young University, where she earned a bachelor's degree in communications, with a minor in English.

She began her writing career as a student, publishing several articles in magazines while still in college. Since then, she has published historical romance and romantic suspense novels, along with a variety of children's books. She is a *USA Today* best-selling author, a Foreword Reviews Book of the Year finalist, and a Whitney Award finalist.

Sian and her husband, Kent, are the parents of five children and the grandparents of three beautiful girls and two handsome boys. They currently live in Southeast, Idaho, and although Sian doesn't have the opportunity to speak Welsh very often anymore, Llanfairpwllgwyngyllgogerychwyrndrobwllllantysiliogogogoch still rolls off her tongue.

Traveling, reading, cooking, and being with her grandchildren are some of Sian's favorite activities. She also loves hearing from her readers. If you would like to contact her, she can be reached her through her website at www.sianannbessey.com, her Facebook group, Author Sian Ann Bessey's Corner, or Instagram @sian_bessey.